Rick Raphael was born in 1919. He has worked as a journalist and in politics (for American Senator Frank Church). His first science fiction story was published in *Astounding Science Fiction* magazine in 1959.

'Raphael's picture of the future is the most original and well-rounded since Heinlein' *Books and Bookmen*.

By the same author

The Thirst Quenchers

IMPRIMÉ EN FRANCE

RICK RAPHAEL

Code Three

PANTHER
Granada Publishing

Panther Books
Granada Publishing Ltd
8 Grafton Street, London W1X 3LA

Published by Panther Books 1968
Reprinted 1985

First published in Great Britain by
Victor Gollancz Ltd 1966

Parts of this novel appeared, in slightly different form,
in *Analog Science Fiction – Science Fact*

ISBN 0-586-02570-7

Made and printed for
William Collins Sons & Co. Ltd, Glasgow

Set in Times

The late-afternoon sun hid behind gray banks of snow clouds and a cold wind whipped loose leaves across the drill field in front of the Philadelphia Barracks of the North American Continental Thruway Patrol. There was the feel of snow in the air but the thermometer hovered just at the freezing mark and the clouds could turn either into icy rain or snow.

Patrol Sergeant Ben Martin stepped out of the door of the barracks and shivered as a blast of wind hit him. He pulled up the zipper on his loose blue uniform coveralls and paused to gauge the storm clouds building up to the west.

The broad planes of his sunburned face turned into the driving cold wind for a moment and then he looked back down at the weather report secured to the top of a stack of papers on his clipboard.

Behind him, the door of the barracks was shouldered open by his junior officer, Patrol Trooper Clay Ferguson. The tall, young Canadian officer's arms were loaded with paper sacks and his patrol work helmet dangled by its strap from the crook of his arm.

Clay turned and moved from the doorway into the wind. A sudden gust swept around the corner of the building and a small sack, perched atop one of the larger bags in his arms, blew to the ground and began tumbling toward the drill field.

'Ben,' he yelled, 'grab the bag.'

The sergeant lunged as the sack bounced by and made the retrieve. He walked back to Ferguson and eyed the load of bags in the blond-haired officer's arms.

'Just what in hell is all this?' he inquired.

'Groceries,' the young man said with a grin. 'Or to be more exact, a few gourmet items for our moments of gracious living.'

Ferguson turned into the walk leading to the motor pool, and Martin swung into step beside him. 'Want me to carry some of that junk?'

'Junk,' Clay cried indignantly. 'You keep your grimy paws off these delicacies, peasant. You'll get yours in due time and perhaps it will help Kelly and me to make a more polished product of you than the cold-like cop you are today.'

Martin chuckled. This patrol would mark the start of the second year that he, Clay Ferguson and Medical-Surgical Officer Kelly Lightfoot had been teamed together. After twenty-two patrols, cooped up in a semi-armored vehicle with a man for ten days at a time, you got to know him pretty well. And you either liked him or you hated his guts.

As senior officer, Martin had the right to reject or keep his partner after their first eleven-month duty tour. Martin had elected to retain the lanky Canadian. As soon as they had pulled into New York Barracks at the end of their last patrol, he had made his decision. After eleven months and twenty-two patrols on the Continental Thruways, each team had a thirty-day furlough coming.

Martin and Ferguson had headed for the city the minute they put their signatures on the last of the stack of reports needed at the end of a tour. Then, for five days and nights, they tied one on. MSO Kelly Lightfoot had made a beeline for a Columbia Medical School seminar on tissue regeneration. On the sixth day, Clay staggered out of bed, swigged down a handful of anti-reaction pills, showered, shaved and dressed and then waved good-bye. Twenty minutes later he was aboard a jet, heading for his parents' home in Edmonton, Alberta. Martin soloed around the city for another week, then rented a car and raced up to his sister's home in Burlington, Vermont, to play Uncle Bountiful to Carol's three kids and to lap up as much as possible of his sister's real cooking.

While the troopers and their med officer relaxed, a service crew moved their car down to the Philadelphia motor pool for a full overhaul and refitting for the next tortuous eleven-month tour of duty.

The two patrol troopers had reported into the Philadelphia Barracks five days ago – Martin several pounds heavier, courtesy of his sister's cooking; Ferguson several pounds lighter courtesy of three assorted, starry-eyed, uniform-struck and willing Alberta maidens.

They turned into the gate of the motor pool and nodded to the sentry at the gate. To their left, the vast shop buildings echoed to the sound of body-banging equipment and roaring jet engines. The darkening sky made the brilliant lights of the shop seem even brighter and the hulls of a dozen patrol cars cast deep shadows around the work crews.

The troopers turned into the dispatcher's office and Clay carefully placed the bags on a table beside the counter. Martin peered into one of the bags. 'Seriously, kid, what do you have in that grab bag?'

'Oh, just a few essentials,' Clay replied. '*Pâté de foie gras*, sharp cheese, a smidgen of cooking wine, a handful of spices. You know, essentials.'

'Essentials,' Martin snorted. 'You give your brains to one of those Alberta chicks for a souvenir?'

7

'Look, Ben,' Ferguson said earnestly, 'I suffered for eleven months in that tin mausoleum on tracks because of what you fondly like to think is edible food. You've got as much culinary imagination as Beulah. I take that back. Even Beulah turns out some better smells when she's riding on high jet than you'll ever get out of her galley in the next hundred years. This tour, I intend to eat like a human being. And I'll even teach you how to boil water without burning it.'

'Why you ungrateful young . . .' Martin began.

The patrol dispatcher, who had been listening with amused tolerance, leaned across the counter.

'If Oscar Waldorf is through with his culinary lecture, gentlemen,' he said, 'perhaps you two could be persuaded to take a little pleasure ride. It's a lovely night for a drive and it's twenty-six hundred miles to the next service station. If you two aren't cooking anything at the moment, I know that NorCon would simply adore having the services of two such distinguished Continental Commandos.'

Ferguson flushed and Martin scowled at the dispatcher. 'Very funny, clown. I'll recommend you for trooper status one of these days.'

'Not me,' the dispatcher protested. 'I'm a married man. You'll never get me out on the road in one of those blood-and-guts factories.'

'So quit sounding off to us heroes,' Martin said, 'and give us the clearances.'

The dispatcher shrugged, then opened a loose-leaf reference book on the counter and punched the first of a series of buttons on a panel. Behind him, the wall lighted with a map of the eastern United States to the Mississippi River. Ferguson and Martin had pencils out and poised over their clipboards.

The dispatcher glanced at the order board across the room where patrol-car numbers and team names were displayed on an illuminated board. 'Car 56–Martin–Ferguson–Lightfoot' glowed with an amber light. In the column to the right was the number '26-W.' The dispatcher punched another button. A broad belt of multi-colored lines representing the eastern segment of North American Thruway 26 flashed onto the map in a band extending from Philadelphia to St Louis. The thruway went on to Los Angeles in its western segment, not shown on the map. Ten bands of color – each five separated by a narrow clear strip, detailed the thruway. Martin and Ferguson were concerned with the northern five bands; NAT 26 – Westbound. Other unlighted lines radiated in spokes to the north and south along the length of the multicolored belt of NAT 26.

This was just one small segment of the Continental Thruway System that spanned North America from coast to coast and criss-crossed north and south under the Three Nation Road Compact from the southern tip of Mexico through Canada and into Alaska.

Each arterial cut a 5-mile-wide path across the continent and from one end to the other. The only structures along the roadways were the turret-like NorCon Patrol check-and-relay stations – looming up at 100-mile intervals like the fire-control islands of earlier-day aircraft carriers.

Car 56, with Patrol Sergeant Ben Martin, Trooper Clay Ferguson and Medical-Surgical Officer Kelly Lightfoot, would take their first 10-day patrol on NAT 26-West. Barring major disaster, they would eat, sleep and work the entire time from their car; out of sight of most cities until they had reached Los Angeles at the end of the Patrol. Then a five-day resupply, repairs and briefing period and back onto another thruway.

During the coming patrol they would cross ten state lines as if they didn't exist. As far as thruway traffic control and authority was concerned, state and national boundaries didn't exist. With the growth of the old Interstate highway system and the Alaska Highway it became increasingly evident that variations in motor vehicle laws from state to state and country to country were creating impossible situations toward uniform safety control.

With the establishment of the Continental Thruway System, two decades later, came the birth of a supracop – the North American Continental Thruway Patrol, known as NorCon. Within the 5-mile-wide bans of the thruways – all federally owned land by each of the three nations – the blue-coveralled 'Continental Commandos' of NorCon were the sole law-enforcement agency and authority. Violators of thruway law were cited into NorCon district traffic courts located in the city nearest to each access port along every thruway.

There was no challenge to the authority of NorCon. Public demand for faster and more powerful vehicles had forced the automotive industry to put more and more power under the touch of the ever-growing millions of drivers crowding the continent's roads. Piston drive gave way to turbojet; turbojet was boosted by a modification of ramjet, and air-cushion drive was added. In the last two years, the first of the nuclear-reaction-mass engines had hit the roads. Even as the hot Ferraris and Jags of the 60's would have been suicide vehicles on the Model-T roads of the 20's, so would today's vehicles be on the Interstates of the 60's. But building roads capable of handling 300- to 400-mile-an-hour speeds was beyond the financial and engineering capabilities of individual states and nations. Thus grew the continental thruways with their four speed lanes in each direction, each a half-mile wide, separated east and west and north and south by a half-mile-wide landscaped divider. Under the Three Nation Compact, the thruways now wove a net across the entire North American continent.

On the big wall map, NAT 26-West showed as four colored lines; blue and yellow as the high- and ultra-high-speed lanes; green and white for the intermediate and slow lanes. Between the blue-and-yellow and the white-and-green was a red band. This was the police emergency lane, never used by other than official vehicles and crossed by the traveling public shifting from one speed lane to another only at sweeping crossovers.

The dispatcher picked up an electric pointer and aimed the light beam at the map. Referring to his notes, he began to recite.

'Resurfacing crews working on 26-W blue at milestone marker 185 to marker 187, estimated clearance 0300 hours Tuesday.' He looked up at them. 'That's tomorrow morning.'

The two officers, writing the information down on their trip-analysis sheets, nodded.

'Ohio State is playing Cal under the lights at Columbus tonight, so you can expect a traffic surge sometime shortly after 2300 hours, but most of it will stay in the green and white. Watch out for the drunks, though. They might filter out onto the blue or yellow.

'The crossover for NAT 163 has painting crews working. Might watch out for any crud on the roadway. And they've got the entrance blocked there so that all 163 exchange traffic is being rerouted to 164 west of Chillicothe.'

The dispatcher thumbed through his reference sheets. 'That seems to be about all. No, wait a minute,' he added. 'This is on your trick. The Army's got a priority missile convoy moving out of the Aberdeen Proving Ground bound for the West Coast tonight at 1800 hours. It will be moving at green-lane speeds, so you might watch out for it. They'll have thirty-four units in the convoy. And that is all. Oh, yes. Kelly's already aboard. I guess you know about the weather.'

Martin nodded. 'Yup. We should be hitting light snows by 2300 hours tonight in this area and it could be anything from snow to icy rain after that.' He grinned at his young partner. 'The vacation is over, sonny. Tonight we make a man out of you.'

Ferguson grinned back. 'I've got character witnesses back in Edmonton who'll give you glowing testimonials about my manhood.'

'Testimonials aren't legal unless they're given by adults,' Martin retorted. 'Come on, lover boy. Duty calls.'

Clay carefully picked up his grocery sacks and the two officers turned to leave. The dispatcher leaned across the counter.

'Oh, Ferguson, one thing I forgot. There's some light corrugations in red lane just east of St Louis. You might be careful with your soufflés in that area. Wouldn't want them to fall, you know.'

Clay paused and started to turn back. The grinning dispatcher ducked into the back office and slammed the door.

The wind had decreased by the time the troopers entered the brilliantly lighted parking area. The air seemed warmer, with the lessening winds, but in actuality the mercury was dropping. The snow clouds to the west were much nearer and the overcast was getting darker.

But under the great overhead light tubes, the parking area was brighter than day. A dozen huge patrol vehicles were parked on the front 'hot' line. Scores more were lined out in ranks to the back of the parking zone. Martin and Ferguson walked down the line of blue military cars. Number 56 was fifth on the line. Service mechs were just rehousing fueling lines into a ground panel as the troopers walked up. The technician corporal walked up to meet them. 'All set, sarge,' he said. 'We had to change an induction jet at the last minute and I had the port engine running up to reline the flow. Thought I'd better top 'er off for you, though, before you pull out. She sounds like a purring kitten.'

He tossed the pair a waving salute and then moved out to his service dolly, where three other mechs were waiting.

The officers paused and looked up at the bulk of the huge patrol car.

'Beulah looks like she's been to the beauty shop and had the works,' Martin said. He reached out and slapped the maglurium plates. 'Welcome home, sweetheart. I see you've kept a candle in the window for your wandering son.' Ferguson looked up at the lighted cab, 16 feet above the pavement.

Car 56 – 'Beulah' to her team – was a standard NorCon Patrol vehicle. She was 60 feet long, 12 feet wide and 12 feet high; topped by a 4-foot-high bubble canopy over her cab. All the way across her nose was a 3-foot-wide luminescent strip. This was the variable beam headlight that could cut a day-bright swath of light through night, fog, rain or snow and could be varied in intensity, width and elevation. Immediately above the headlight strip were two red-black plastic panels which, when lighted, sent out a flashing red emergency signal that could be seen for miles. Similar emergency lights and back-up white light strips adorned Beulah's stern. Her bow rounded down like an old-time tank and blended into the track assembly of her dual propulsion system. With the exception of the cabin bubble and a two-foot stepdown on the last 15 feet of her hull, Beulah was as free of external protrusions as a baby's behind. Racked into a flush-decked recess on one side of the hull was a crane arm with a 200-ton lift capacity. Several round hatches covered other extensible gear and periscopes used in the scores of multiple operations the NorCon cars were called upon to accomplish on routine road patrols.

Beulah resembled a gigantic offspring of a military tank, sans heavy armament. But even a small stinger was part of the patrol-car equipment. Beulah had light weapons to meet every conceivable skirmish in the deadly battle to keep continental thruways fast-moving and safe. Her own 250-ton bulk could reach speeds of close to 600 miles an hour utilizing one or both of her two independent propulsion systems.

At ultra-high speeds Beulah never touched the ground – floating on an impeller air cushion and driven forward by a pair of 150,000-pound thrust jets and ramjets. At intermediate high speeds, both her air cushion and the 4-foot-wide tracks on each side of the car pushed her along at 200-mile-an-hour-plus speeds. Synchromechanisms reduced the air cushion as the speeds dropped to afford more surface traction for the tracks. For slow speeds and heavy duty, the tracks carried the burden.

Martin thumbed open the portside ground-level cabin door.

'I'll start the outside check,' he told Clay. 'You stow that garbage of yours in the galley and start on the dispensary. I'll help you after I finish out here.'

As the younger officer entered the car and headed up the short flight of steps to the working deck, the sergeant unclipped a checklist from the inside of the door and turned toward the stern of the big vehicle.

Clay mounted to the work deck and turned back to the little galley just aft of the cab. As compact as a spaceship kitchen – as a matter of fact, designed almost identically from models on the moon run – the galley had but 3 feet of open counter space. Everything else, sink, range, oven and freezer, were built-ins with pull-downs for use as needed. He set his bags on the small counter, to put away after the prestart check. Aft of the galley and on the same side of the passageway were the double-decked bunks for the patrol troopers. Across the passageway was a small enclosure for latrine and shower. Clay tossed his helmet on the lower bunk as he went down the passageway. At the bulkhead to the rear, he pressed a wall panel, and a thick, insulated door slid back to admit him to the engine compartment. The service crews had shut down the big power plants and turned off the air exchangers and already the heat from the massive engines made the compartment uncomfortably warm.

He hurried through into a small machine shop. In an emergency, the troopers could turn out small parts for disabled vehicles or for other uses. It also stocked a good supply of the most common failure parts. Racked against the ceiling were banks of cutting torches, a grim reminder that death and injury occurred on the thruways with increasing frequency.

In the tank storage space between the ceiling and the top of the hull were the chemical fire-fighting liquids and foam that could be applied by nozzles, hoses and towers now telescoped into recesses in the hull. Along both sides and beneath the galley, bunks, engine and machine shop compartments, and between the walls, deck and hull, were Beulah's fuel-storage tanks.

The last after-compartment was a complete dispensary, one that would have made the emergency room or even the light-surgery rooms of earlier-day hospitals proud.

Clay tapped on the door and went through. Medical-Surgical Officer Kelly Lightfoot was sitting on the deck, stowing sterile bandage packs into a lower locker. She looked up at Clay and smiled. 'Well, well, you *did* manage to tear yourself away from your adoring bevies,' she said. She flicked back a wisp of golden-red hair from her forehead and stood up. The patrol-blue uniform coverall with its belted waist didn't do much to hide a lovely, properly curved figure. She walked over to the tall Canadian trooper and reached up and grabbed his ear. She pulled his head down, examined one side critically and then quickly snatched at his other ear and repeated the scrutiny. She let go of his ear and stepped back. 'Damned if you didn't get all the lipstick marks off, too.'

Clay flushed. 'Cut it out, Kelly,' he said. 'Sometimes you act just like my mother.'

The olive-skinned redhead grinned at him and turned back to her stack of boxes on the deck. She bent over and lifted one of the boxes to the operating table. Clay eyed her trim figure. 'You might act like my mother sometimes,' he said, 'but you sure as hell don't look like her.'

It was the Irish-Cherokee Indian girl's turn to blush. She became very busy with the contents of the box. 'Where's Ben?' she said over her shoulder.

'Making outside check. You about finished in here?'

Kelly turned and slowly scanned the confines of the dispensary. With the exception of the boxes on the table and floor, everything was behind secured locker doors. In one corner the compact diagnostican – capable of analyzing many known human bodily ailments and every possible violent injury to the body – was locked in its riding clamps. Surgical trays and instrument racks were all hidden behind locker doors along with medical and surgical supplies. On either side of the emergency ramp door at the stern of the vehicle, three collapsible auto-litters hung from clamps. Six hospital bunks in two tiers of three each lined another wall. On patrol, Kelly utilized one of the hospital bunks for her own use except when they might all be occupied with accident or other kinds of patients. And this would never be for more than a short period, just long enough to transfer them to a regular ambulance or hospital vehicle. Her meager supply of personal items needed for the ten-day patrol were stowed in a small locker. She shared the latrine with the male members of the team.

Kelly completed her scan, glanced down at the check-list in her hand. 'I'll have these boxes stowed in five minutes. Everything else is secure.' She raised her hand to her forehead in a mock salute. 'Medical-Surgical Officer Lightfoot reports dispensary ready for patrol, sir.'

Clay smiled and made a checkmark on his clipboard. 'How was the seminar, Kelly?' he asked.

Kelly hiked herself onto the edge of the operating table. 'Wonderful, Clay, just wonderful. I never saw so many good-looking, young, rich and eligible doctors together in one place in all my life.'

She sighed and smiled vacantly into space.

Clay snorted. 'I thought you were supposed to be learning something new about tissue regeneration,' he said.

'Generation, regeneration, who cares?' Kelly laughed. 'It all begins the same way the first time.'

Clay started to say something, got flustered and wheeled around to leave – and bounced right off Ben Martin's chest. Ferguson mumbled something and pushed past the older officer.

Ben looked after him and then turned back to Car 56's combination doctor, surgeon and nurse. 'Glad to see the hostess aboard for this cruise. I hope you make the passengers more comfortable than you've just made the first mate. What did you do to Clay, Kelly?'

'Hi, Ben,' Kelly said, 'Oh, don't worry about Junior. He just gets all fluttery when a girl takes away his masculine prerogative to make cleverly lewd witticisms. He'll be all right. Have a happy holiday, Ben? You look positively fat.'

Ben patted his stomach, 'Carol's good cooking. Had a nice restful time. And how about you? That couldn't have been all work. You've got a marvelous tan.'

'Don't worry,' Kelly laughed, 'I had no intention of letting it be all study. I spent just about as much time under the sun dome at the pool as I did in class. I learned a lot, though.'

Ben nodded and headed back to the front of the car. 'Tell me more after we're on the road,' he said from the doorway. 'We'll be rolling in ten minutes.'

When he reached the cab, Clay was already in the right-hand control seat and was running down the instrument-panel check. The sergeant lifted the hatch door between the two control seats and punched on a light to illuminate the stark compartment below them at the lower front end of the car. A steel grille with a dogged handle on the upper side covered the opening under the hatch cover. The front hull door was without an inside handle. Two swing-down bunks were racked up against the walls on either side. This was the patrol car brig, used for bringing in unwilling violators or other violent or criminal subjects who might crop up in the course of a patrol tour. Satisfied with the appearance of the brig, Ben closed the hatch cover and slid into his own control seat on the left of the cab. Both control seats were molded and plastiform padded to the contours of the troopers. The armrests on both were studded with buttons and a series of small, finger-operated knobs. All drive, communication and fire-fighting controls for the massive vehicle were controlled by the knobs and buttons on the seat arms, while acceleration and braking controls were duplicated in two footrest pedals.

Ben settled into his seat and glanced down to make sure his work helmet was racked beside him. He reached over and flipped a bank of switches on the instrument panel. 'All communications to "on",' he said. Clay made a checkmark on his list.

'All pre-engine start check complete,' Clay replied.

'In that case,' the senior trooper said, 'let's give Beulah some exercise. Start engines.'

Clay's fingers danced across the array of buttons on his seat arms and flicked lightly at the throttle knobs. From deep within the engine compartment came the muted, shrill whine of the starter engines, followed a split second later by the full-throated roar of the jets as they caught fire. Clay eased the throttles back and the engine noise softened to a muffled roar.

Martin fingered a press-panel on the right arm of his seat.

'Car Five Six to Philly Control,' Ben called.

The speakers mounted around the cab came to life. 'Go ahead, Five Six.'

'Five Six fired up and ready to roll,' Martin said.

'Affirmative, Five Six,' came the reply, 'you're clear to roll. Philly Check estimates white density 300; green, 840; blue, 400; yellow, 75.'

Both troopers made mental note of the traffic densities in their first 100-mile patrol segment; an estimated 300 vehicles for each 10 miles of thruway in the white, or 50-to-100-mile-an-hour, slow lane; 840 vehicles in the 100–150-mile-an-hour green; 400 in the 150–200-mile-an-hour blue and 75 vehicles per mile in the 200–500-mile-an-hour fastest lane. More than 16,000 westbound vehicles on the thruway in the first 100 miles; nearly 5,000 of them traveling at speeds between 150 and 300 miles an hour.

Over the always-hot intercom throughout the big car Ben called out, 'All set, Kelly?'

'I'm making coffee,' Kelly answered from the galley. 'Let 'er roll, Ben.'

Martin started to kick off the brakes, then stopped. 'Oops,' he exclaimed, 'almost forgot.' His finger touched another button and a blaring bull horn reverberated through the vehicle.

In the galley, Kelly hurled herself into a corner. Her body activated a pressure plant and a pair of mummy-like plastifoam plates slid curvingly out of the wall and locked her in a soft cocoon. A dozen similar safety clamps were located throughout the car at every working and relax- ation station.

In the same instant, both Ben and Clay touched another plate on their control seats. From kiosk-type columns behind each seat, pairs of body-molded crash pads snapped into place to encase both troopers in their seats, their bodies cushioned and locked into place. Only their fingers were loose beneath the spongy substance to work arm controls. The half-molds included headforms with a padded band that locked across their foreheads to hold their heads rigidly against the backs of their reinforced seats. The instant all three crew members were locked into their safety gear, the bull horn ceased.

'All tight,' Ben called out as he wiggled and tried to free himself from the cocoon. Kelly and Clay tested their harnesses.

Satisfied that the safety cocoons were operating properly, Ben released them, and the molds slid back into their recesses. The cocoons were triggered automatically in any emergency run or chase at speeds in excess of 200 miles an hour.

Again he kicked off the brakes, pressed down on the foot feed and Car 56 – Beulah – rolled out of the Philadelphia motor pool on the start of its ten-day patrol.

The motor-pool exit opened into a quarter-mile-wide tunnel sloping gently down into the bowels of the great city. Car 56 glided down the slight incline at a steady 50 miles an hour. A mile from the mouth of the tunnel the roadway leveled off and Ben kicked Beulah up another 25 miles an hour. Ahead, the main tunnel ended in a series of smaller portal ways, each emblazoned with a huge illuminated number designating a continental thruway.

Ben throttled back and began edging to the left lanes. Other patrol cars were heading down the main passageway, bound for their assigned thruways. As Ben eased down to a slow 30, another patrol vehicle slid alongside. The two troopers in the cab moved. Clay flicked on the car-to-car transmit.

The senior trooper in Car 104 looked over at Martin and Ferguson. 'If it isn't the gruesome twosome,' he called. 'Where have you two been? We thought the front office had finally found out that neither of you could read or write and had canned you.'

'We can't read,' Ben quipped back. 'That's why we're still on the job. The front office would never hire anyone who would embarrass you two by being smarter than either of you. Where're you headed, Eddie?'

'Got 154-North,' the other officer said.

'Hey,' Clay called out, 'I've got a real hot doll in Toronto and I'll gladly sell her phone number for a proper price.'

'Wouldn't want to hurt you, Clay,' the other officer replied. 'If I called her up and took her out, she'd throw rocks at you the next time you drew the run. It's all for your own good.'

'Oh, go get lost in a cloverleaf,' Clay retorted.

The other car broke the connection and with a wave veered off to the right. The thruway entrances were just ahead. Martin aimed Beulah at the lighted orifice topped by the number 26-W. The patrol car slid into the narrower tunnel, glided along for another mile and then turned its bow upward. Three minutes later they emerged from the tunnel into the red patrol lane of Continental Thruway 26-West. The late-afternoon sky was a covering of gray wool and a drop or two of moisture struck the front face of the cab canopy. For a mile on either side of the police lane streams of cars sped westward. Ben eyed the sky, the traffic and then peered at the outer-hull thermometer. It read 32 degrees. He made a mental bet with himself that the weather bureau was off on its snow estimates by six hours. His Vermont upbringing told him it would be flurrying within the hour.

He increased speed to a steady 100 and the car sped silently and easily along the police lane. Across the cab,

Clay peered pensively at the steady stream of cars and cargo carriers racing by in the green and blue lanes – all of them moving faster than the patrol car.

The young officer turned in his seat and looked at his partner.

'You know, Ben,' he said gravely, 'I sometimes wonder if those old-time cowboys got as tired of looking at the south end of northbound cows as I get looking at tail pipes.'

The intercom speaker exploded into laughter. From the dispensary Kelly said, 'From your crack a while ago, I thought you drew considerable pleasure from the contemplation of rear ends.'

Ben guffawed and even Clay chuckled.

The radio came to life. 'Philly Control to Car Five Six.'

Clay touched his transmit plate. 'This is Five Six. Go ahead.'

'You've got a bad one at marker eight two,' Control said. 'A sideswipe in the white.'

'Couldn't be too bad in the white,' Ben broke in, thinking of the 100-mile-an-hour limit in the slow lane.

'That's not the problem,' Control came back. 'One of the sideswiped vehicles was flipped around and bounced into the green. That's where the real mess is. Make it Code Three.'

'Five Six acknowledged,' Ben said, 'On the way.'

He slammed forward on the throttles. The bull horn blared and a second later, with MSO Kelly Lightfoot snugged in her dispensary cocoon and both troopers in body cushions, Car 56 lifted a foot from the roadway and leaped forward on a turbulent pad of air. It accelerated from 100 to 250 miles an hour.

The great red emergency lights on the bow and stern began to blink. From the special transmitter in the hull a radio siren wail raced ahead of the car, to be picked up by the emergency receptor antennas required on all vehicles.

The working part of the patrol had begun.

Conversation died in the speeding car, partly because of the concentration required by the troopers, partly because all transmissions, whether intercom or radio, on a Code Two or Three run, were taped and monitored by Control. In the center of the instrument panel an oversized radiodometer was clicking off the mileage marks as the car passed each milestone. The milestone posts beamed a coded signal across all five lanes and as each vehicle passed the marker the radiodometer clicked up another number.

Car 56 had been at MM 23 when the call came. Now, at better than 4 miles a minute, Beulah whipped past MM 45 with ten minutes yet to go to reach the scene of the accident. Light flurries of wet snow splashed off the canopy, leaving thin, fast-drying trails of moisture. Although it was still a few minutes short of 1700 hours, the last of the winter afternoon light was dimming behind the heavy snow clouds overhead. Ben turned on the patrol car's dazzling headlight. To the left and right Clay could see streaks of white lights from the traffic on the blue and green lanes on either side of the quarter-mile-wide emergency lane.

The radio filled them in on the movement of other patrol emergency vehicles being routed to the accident site. Car 82, also assigned to NAT 26-West, was more than 150 miles ahead of Beulah. Pittsburgh Control ordered 82 to hold fast to cover anything else that might come up while 56 was handling the current crisis. Eastbound Car 119 was ordered to cut across to the scene to assist Beulah's crew and another eastbound patrol vehicle was held in place to cover for 119.

At mile marker 80, yellow caution lights were flashing on all westbound lanes, triggered by Philadelphia Control the instant the word of the crash had been received. Traffic was slowing down and piling up despite the half-mile-wide lanes.

'Philly Control, this is Car Five Six.'

'Go ahead, Five Six.'

'It's piling up in the green and white,' Ben said. 'Let's divert to blue on slowdown and seal the yellow.'

'Philly Control acknowledged,' came the reply.

The flashing amber caution lights on all lanes switched to red. As Ben began deceleration, diagonal red flashing barriers rose out of the roadway on the green and white lanes at the 75-mile marker and lane crossing. This channeled all traffic from both lanes to the left and into the blue lane, where the flashing reds now prohibited speeds in excess of 50 miles an hour around the emergency situation. At the same time, all crossovers on the ultra-high yellow lane were sealed by barriers to prevent changing of lanes into the congested area.

As Car 56's speed dropped back below the 200-mile-an-hour mark the cocoon automatically slid open. Freed from her safety restraints, Kelly jumped for the rear entrance of the dispensary and cleared the racking clamps from the six auto-litters. That done, she opened another locker and reached for the mobile first-aid kit. She slid it to the door entrance on its retractable casters. She slipped on her work helmet with the built-in transmitter and then sat down on the seat by the rear door to wait until the car stopped.

Car 56 was now less than two miles from the scene of the crash and traffic in the green lane was at a standstill. A half mile farther westward, lights were still moving slowly along the white lane. Ahead, the troopers could see a faint wisp of smoke rising from the heaviest congregation of headlights. Both officers had their work helmets on and Clay had left his seat and descended to the side door, ready to jump out the minute the car stopped.

Martin saw a clear area in the green lane and swung the car over the dividing curbing. The big tracks floated the patrol car over the 2-foot-high rounded abutment that

24

divided each speed lane. Snow was falling faster as the headlight picked out a tangled mass of wreckage smoldering 100 feet inside the median separating the green and white lanes. A crumpled body lay on the pavement 20 feet from the biggest clump of smashed metal, and other fragments of vehicles were scattered down the roadway for 50 feet. There was no movement.

NorCon Thruway laws were strict and none was more rigidly enforced than the regulation that no one other than a member of the patrol could set foot outside his vehicle while on a thruway. This meant not giving any assistance whatsoever to accident victims. The ruling had been called inhuman, monstrous, unthinkable, and law-makers in the three nations of the compact had forced NorCon to revoke the rule in the early days of the thruways. After speeding cars and cargo carriers had cut down twice as many do-gooders as the accidents themselves caused, the law was reinstated. The lives of the many were more vital than the lives of a few.

Martin halted the patrol vehicle a few feet from the wreckage and Beulah was still rocking gently on her tracks when Ferguson and Kelly hit the pavement on the run.

In the cab Martin called in on the radio. 'Car Five Six is on scene. Release blue at marker nine five and resume speeds all lanes at marker nine five in . . .' he paused and looked back at the halted traffic piled up before the lane had been closed . . . 'seven minutes.' He jumped for the steps and sprinted out of the patrol car in the wake of Ferguson and Kelly.

The team's surgeon was kneeling beside the inert body on the road. After putting an ear to the victim's chest, Kelly opened her field-kit bag and slapped an electrode to his temple. The needle on the encephalic meter in the lid of the kit never flickered. Kelly shut the bag and hurried with it over to the mass of wreckage. A thin column of black, oily smoke rose from near the bottom of the heap.

It was almost impossible to identify at a glance whether the mangled metal was the remains of one or more cars. Only the absence of track equipment made it certain that they even had been passenger vehicles.

Clay was carefully climbing up the side of the piled-up wrecks to a window that gaped near the top.

'Work fast, kid,' Martin called up. 'Something's burning down there and this whole thing may go up. I'll get this traffic moving.'

He turned to face the halted mass of cars and cargo carriers east of the wreck. He flipped a switch that cut his helmet transmitter into the remote standard vehicular radio circuit aboard the patrol car.

'Attention, please, all cars in green lane. All cars in the left line move out now, the next line fall in behind. You are directed to clear the area immediately. Maintain fifty miles an hour for the next mile. You may resume desired speeds and change lanes at mile marker nine five. I repeat, all cars in green lane . . .' he went over the instructions once more, relayed through Beulah's transmitter to the standard receivers on all cars. He was still talking when the traffic began to move.

By the time he turned back to help his teammates, cars were moving in a steady stream past the huge, red-flashing bulk of the patrol car.

Both Clay and Kelly were lying flat across the smashed, upturned side of the uppermost car in the pile. Kelly had her field bag open on the ground and was reaching down through the smashed window.

'What is it, Clay?' Martin asked through the intercom.

The younger officer looked down over his shoulder. 'We've got a woman alive down here, but she's wedged in tight. She's hurt pretty badly and Kelly's trying to slip a hypo into her now. Get the arm out, Ben.'

Martin ran back to the patrol car and flipped up a panel on the hull. He pulled back on one of the several levers recessed into the hull and the big wrecking crane swung smoothly out of its cradle and over the wreckage. The end of the crane arm was directly over Ferguson. 'Lemme have the spreaders,' Clay called. The arm dipped, and from either side of the tip a pair of flanges shot out like tusks on an elephant. 'Put 'er in neutral,' Clay directed. Martin pressed another lever and the crane now could be moved in any direction by fingertip pulls at its extremity. Ferguson carefully guided the crane with its projecting tusks into the smashed car window. 'OK, Ben, spread it.'

The crane locked into position and the entire arm split open in a 'V' from its base. Martin pressed steadily on the two levers controlling each side of the divided arm and the tusks dug into the sides of the window frame. There was a steady screeching of tearing and ripping metal as the crane tore the frame apart. 'Hold it,' Ferguson yelled, then eased himself into the widened hole.

'Ben,' Kelly called from her perch atop the wreckage, 'litter.'

Martin raced to the rear of the patrol car where the sloping ramp stood open to the lighted dispensary. He snatched at one of the auto-litters and triggered its tiny drive motor. A homing beacon in his helmet guided the litter as it rolled down the ramp, turned by itself and rolled across the pavement a foot behind him. It stopped when he stopped. He touched another switch, cutting the homing beacon.

Clay's head appeared out of the hole. 'Get it up here, Ben. I can get her out. And I think there's another one alive still farther down.'

Martin raised the crane and its ripper bars retracted. The split arm spewed a pair of cables terminating in magnalocks. The cables dangled over the ends of the auto-litter, caught the lift plates on the litter and a second later the cart was swinging beside the smashed window as Clay and Kelly eased the torn body of a woman out of the wreckage and onto the litter. As Ben brought the litter back to the pavement, the column of smoke thickened. He disconnected the cables and homed the stretcher back to the patrol car. The hospital cart, with its unconscious victim, rolled smoothly back to the car, up the ramp and into the dispensary, where it halted beside the surgical table.

Martin climbed up the wreckage beside Kelly. Inside the twisted interior of the car the thick smoke all but obscured the bent back of the younger trooper and his powerful hand-light barely penetrated the gloom. Blood was smeared over almost every surface, and the stink of leaking jet fuel was virtually overpowering. From the depths of the twisted metal came a tortured scream. Kelly reached into a coverall pocket and produced another sedation hypo. She squirmed around and started to slip down into the wreckage by Ferguson. Martin grabbed her arm. 'No, Kelly, this thing's ready to blow. Come on, Clay, get out of there! Now!'

Ferguson continued to pry at the twisted plates below him.

'I said "get out of there," Ferguson,' the senior officer rasped, 'and that's an order.'

Clay straightened up and put his hands on the edge of the window to boost himself out. 'Ben, there's a guy alive down there. We just can't leave him.'

'Get down from here, Kelly,' Martin ordered. 'I know a man's down there. But we won't be helping him one damn bit if we get blown to hell with him. Now get out and maybe we can pull this thing apart and get to him before it does blow.'

The lanky Canadian eased out of the window and the two troopers moved back to the patrol car. Kelly was already in her dispensary, working on the injured woman.

Martin slid into his control seat. 'Shut your ramp,

Kelly,' he called over the intercom, 'I'm going to move around to the other side.'

The radio broke in. 'Car One One Nine to Car Five Six, we're just turning into the divider. Be there in a minute.'

'Snap it up,' Ben replied. 'We need you in a hurry.'

As he maneuvered Beulah around the wreckage he snapped orders to Ferguson. 'Get the foam nozzles up, just in case, and then stand by on the crane.'

A mile away, they saw the flashing emergency lights of Car 119 as it raced diagonally across the yellow and blue lanes, whipping with ponderous ease through the moving traffic.

'Take the south side, One One Nine,' Martin called out. 'We'll try and pull this mess apart.'

'Affirmative,' came the reply. Even before the other patrol vehicle came to a halt, its crane was swinging out from the side and the ganged magnalocks were dangling from their cables.

'OK, kid,' Ben ordered, 'hook it.'

At the interior crane controls, Clay swung Beulah's crane and cable mags toward the wreckage. The magnalocks slammed into the metallic mess with a bang almost at the same instant the locks hit the other side from Car 119.

Clay eased up the cable slack. 'Good,' Ben called to both Clay and the operating trooper in the other car, 'now let's pull it . . . *look out! Foam . . . foam . . . foam!*' he yelled.

The ugly, deep red fireball from the exploding wreckage was still growing as Clay slammed down on the fire-control panel. A curtain of thick chemical foam burst from the poised nozzles atop Beulah's hull. A split second later another stream of foam erupted from the other patrol car. The dense, oxygen-absorbing retardant blanket snuffed the fire out in three seconds. The cranes were still secured to the foam-covered heap of metal.

'Never mind the caution,' Ben called out, 'get it apart. Fast.'

Both crane operators slammed their controls into reverse, and with an ear-splitting screech the twisted frames of the two vehicles ripped apart into tumbled heaps of broken metal and plastics. Martin and Ferguson jumped down the hatch steps and into ankle-deep foam and oil. They waded and slipped around the front of the car to join the troopers from the other car.

Ferguson was pawing at the scum-covered foam near the mangled section of one of the cars. 'He should be right about . . .' Clay paused and bent over . . . 'here.' He straightened up as the others gathered around the scorched and ripped body of a man, half-submerged in the thick foam. 'Kelly,' he called over the helmet transmitter, 'open your door. We'll need a couple of sacks.'

He trudged to the rear of the patrol car and met the girl standing in the door with a pair of folded plastic morgue bags in her hands. Behind her,Clay could see the body of the woman on the surgical table, an array of tubes and probes leading to plasma drip bottles and other equipment racked out over the table.

'How is she?'

'Not good,' Kelly replied. 'Skull fracture, ruptured spleen, broken ribs and double leg fractures. I've already called for an ambulance.'

Ferguson nodded, took the bags from her and waded back through the foam.

The four troopers worked in the silence of the deserted traffic lane. A hundred yards away, traffic was moving steadily in the slow white lane. Three quarters of a mile to the south, fast and ultra-high traffic sped at its normal pace in the blue and yellow lanes. Westbound green was still being rerouted into the slower white lane, around the scene of the accident. It was now 26 minutes since Car 56 had received the accident call. The light snow flurries had turned to a steady fall of thick wet flakes, melting as they hit on the warm pavement but beginning to coat the pitiful flotsam of the accident. The troopers finished the gruesome task of getting the bodies into the morgue sacks and laid beside the dispensary ramp for the ambulance to pick up with the surviving victim. Car 119's MSO had joined Kelly in Beulah's dispensary to give what help she might. The four patrol troopers began the grim task of probing the scattered wreckage for other victims, personal possessions and identification. They were stacking a small pile of hand luggage when the long, low bulk of the ambulance swung out of the police lane and rolled to a stop. Longer than the patrol cars but without the nonmedical emergency facilities, the ambulance was in reality a mobile hospital. A full, scrubbed-up surgical team was waiting in the main operating room even as the ramps opened and the techs headed for Car 56. The team had been briefed by radio on the condition of the patient; had read the full recordings of the diagnostican; were watching transmitted pulse and respiration graphs on their own screens while the transfer was being made.

The two women MSO's had unlocked the surgical table in Beulah's dispensary and a plastic tent covered not only the table and the patient but also the plasma and Regen racks overhead. The entire table and rig slid down the ramp onto a motor-driven dolly from the ambulance. Without delay, it wheeled across the open few feet of pavement into the ambulance and to the surgery room. The techs locked the table into place in the other vehicle and left the surgery. From a storage compartment they wheeled out a fresh patrol dispensary table and rack and placed it in Kelly's miniature surgery. The dead went into the chill box aboard the ambulance, the ramp closed and the ambulance swung around and headed across the traffic lanes to eastbound NAT 26 and Philadelphia.

Outside, the four troopers had completed the task of

collecting what little information they could from the smashed vehicles.

They returned to their cars and 119's medical-surgical officer headed back to her own cubbyhole.

The other patrol car swung into position, almost touching Beulah's left flank. With Ben at the control seat both cars, on command, extended broad bulldozer blades from their bows. 'Let's go,' Ben ordered. The two patrol vehicles moved slowly down the roadway, pushing all of the scattered scraps and parts into a single great heap. They backed off, shifted direction toward the center police lane and began shoving the debris, foam and snow out of the green lane. At the edge of the police lane, both cars unshipped cranes and magnalifted the junk over the divider barrier onto the 100-foot-wide service strip bordering the police lane. A slow cargo wrecker was already on the way from Philadelphia barracks to pick up the wreckage and haul it away. When the last of the metallic debris had been deposited off the traffic lane, Martin called Control.

'Car Five Six is clear. NAT Twenty-six-west green is clear.'

Philly Control acknowledged. Seven miles to the east, the amber warning lights went dark and the detour barrier at crossover 75 sank back into the roadway. Three minutes later traffic was again flashing by in the green lane past the two halted patrol cars.

'Philly Control, this is Car One One Nine clear of accident,' the other car reported.

'Car One One Nine resume eastbound patrol,' came the reply.

The other patrol car pulled away. The two troopers waved at Martin and Ferguson in Beulah. 'See you later and thanks,' Ben called out. He switched to intercom. 'Kelly. Any ID on that woman?'

'Not a thing, Ben,' she replied. 'About forty years old,

and she had a wedding band. She never was conscious, so I can't help you.'

Ben nodded and looked over at his partner. 'Go get into some dry clothes, kid,' he said, 'while I finish the report. Then you can take it for a while.'

Clay nodded and headed back to the crew quarters.

Ben racked his helmet beside his seat and fished out a cigarette. He reached for an accident report form from the work rack behind his seat and began writing, glancing up from time to time to gaze thoughtfully at the scene of the accident. When he had finished, he thumbed the radio transmitter and called Philly Control. Somewhere in the bloody, oil-and-foam-covered pile of wreckage were the registration plates for the two vehicles involved. When the wrecker collected the debris, it would be machine-sifted and the plates fed to records and then relayed to Philadelphia, where the identifications could be added to Ben's report. When he had finished reading his report he asked, 'How's the woman?'

'Still alive, but just barely,' Philly Control answered. 'Ben, did you say there were just two vehicles involved?'

'That's all we found,' Martin replied.

'And were they both in the green?'

'Yes, why?'

'That's funny,' Philly controller replied, 'we got the calls as a sideswipe in white that put one of the cars over into the green. There should have been a third vehicle around somewhere.'

'By God, that's right,' Ben exclaimed. 'We were so busy trying to get that woman out and then making the try for the man I never even thought to look for another car. You suppose that son-of-a-bitch took off?

'It's possible,' the controller said. 'I'm calling for a gate filter until we know for sure. I've got the car number on the driver who reported the accident. I'll get hold of him and see if he can give us a lead on the third car. You go ahead with your patrol and I'll let you know what I find out.'

'Affirmative,' Ben replied. He eased the patrol car onto the police lane and turned west once again. Clay reappeared in the cab, dressed in fresh coveralls. 'I'll take it, Ben. You go and clean up now. Kelly's got a pot of fresh coffee in the galley.' Ferguson slid into his control seat and took over the driving duties as Ben headed back to change clothes.

A light skiff of snow covered the service strip and the dividers as Car 56 swung back westward in the red lane. Snow was falling steadily but melting as it touched the warm ferrophalt pavement in all lanes. The wet roadways glistened with the lights of hundreds of vehicles. The chronometer read 1840 hours. Clay pushed the car up to a steady 75, just a little faster than the slowest traffic in the white lane. To the south, densities were much lighter in the blue and yellow lanes, and even the green had thinned out. It would stay moderately light now for another hour until the dinner stops were over and the night travelers again rolled onto the thruways.

Kelly was putting frozen steaks into the infra-oven when Ben walked through to crew quarters. Her coverall sleeves were rolled to the elbows as she worked. A vagrant strand of copper hair curled over her forehead. As Martin passed by, he caught a faint whisper of perfume and he smiled appreciatively.

In the tiny crew quarters, he shut the door to the galley and stripped off his wet coveralls and boots. He eyed the shower stall across the passageway.

'Hey, mother,' he yelled to Kelly, 'have I got time for a shower before dinner?'

'Yes, but make it a quickie,' she called back.

Five minutes later he stepped into the galley, his dark, crew-cut hair still damp. Kelly was setting disposable plastic dishes on the little swing-down table that doubled as a food bar and work desk. Ben peered into a simmering pot and sniffed. 'Smells good. What's for dinner, Hiawatha?'

'Nothing fancy. Steak, potatoes, green beans, hot apple pie and coffee.'

Ben's mouth watered. 'You know, sometimes I wonder whether one of your ancestors didn't come out of New England. Your menus always seem to coincide with my ideas of a perfect meal.' He noted the two places set at the table. Ben glanced out the galley port into the headlight-striped darkness. Traffic was still light. In the distance the night sky glowed with the lights of Chambersburg, north of the thruway.

'We might as well pull up for dinner,' he said. 'It's pretty slow out there.'

Kelly shoved dishes over and began laying out a third setting. About half the time on patrol the crew ate in shifts on the go, with one of the patrol troopers in the cab at all times. When traffic permitted, they pulled off to the service strip and ate together. With the communications system always in service, control stations could reach them anywhere in the big vehicle.

The sergeant stepped into the cab and tapped Ferguson on the shoulder. 'Dinnertime, Clay. Pull her over and we'll try some of your gracious living.'

'Light the candles and pour the wine,' Clay quipped. 'I'll be with you in a second.'

Car 56 swung out to the edge of the police lane and slowed down. Clay eased the car onto the strip and stopped. He checked the radiodometer and called in. 'Pitt Control, this is Car Five Six at marker 158. Dinner is being served in the dining car to the rear. Please do not disturb.'

'Affirmative, Car Five Six,' Pittsburgh Control responded. 'Eat heartily, it may be going out of style.' Clay grinned and flipped the radio to 'remote' and headed for the galley.

Seated around the little table, the trio cut into their steaks. Parked at the north edge of the police lane, the patrol car was just a few feet from the green lane divider strip, and cars and cargo carriers flashed by as they ate.

Clay chewed on a sliver of steak and looked at Kelly. 'I'd marry you, Pocahontas, if you'd ever learn to cook steaks like beef instead of curing them like your ancestral buffalo robes. When are you going to learn that good beef has to be bloody to be edible?'

The girl glared at him. 'If that's what it takes to make it edible, you're going to be an Epicurean delight in just about one second if I hear another word about my cooking. And that's also the second crack about my noble ancestors in the past five minutes. I've always wondered about the surgical technique my ancestors used when they lifted a paleface's scalp. One more word, Clay Ferguson, and I'll have yours flying from Beulah's antenna like a coontail on a kid's scooter.'

Ben nearly choked. 'Hey, kid,' he spluttered at Clay, 'ever notice how the wrong one of her ancestors keeps coming to the surface? That was the Irish.'

Clay polished off the last of his steak and reached for the individual frozen pies Kelly had put in the oven with the steaks. 'Now that's another point,' he said, waving his fork at Kelly. 'The Irish lived so long on potatoes and prayers that when they get a piece of meat, they don't know how to do anything but boil it.'

'That tears it,' the girl exploded. She pushed back from the table and stood up. 'I've cooked the last damned meal this big, dumb Canuck will ever get from me. I hope you get chronic indigestion and then come crawling to me for help. I've got something back there I've been wanting to dose you with for a long time.'

She stormed out of the galley and slammed the door behind her. Ben grinned at the stunned look on Clay's face. 'Now what got her on the warpath?' Clay asked.

Before Ben could answer, the radio speaker in the ceiling came to life.

'Car Five Six, this is Pitt Control.'

Martin reached for the transmit switch beside the galley table. 'This is Five Six, go ahead.'

'Relay from Philly Control,' the speaker blared. 'Reference the accident at marker eight-two at 1648 hours this date; Philly Control reports a third vehicle definitely involved.'

Ben pulled out a pencil and Clay shoved a message pad across the table.

'James J. Newhall, address 3409 Glen Cove Drive, New York City, license number BHT 4591 dash 747 dash 1609, was witness to the initial impact. He reports that a white over green, late model Travelaire, with two men in it sideswiped one of the two vehicles involved in the fatal accident. The Travelaire did not stop but accelerated after the impact. Newhall was unable to get the full license number, but the first six units were QABR dash 46 . . . rest of numerals unknown.'

Ben cut in. 'Have we got identification on our fatalities yet?'

'Affirmative, Five Six,' the radio replied. 'The driver of the car struck by the hit-and-run vehicle was a Herman Lawrence Hanover, age 42, of 13460 One Hundred and Eighty-First Street South, Camden, New Jersey, license number LFM 4151 dash 603 dash 2738. With him was his wife, Clara, age 41, same address. Driver of the green lane car was George R. Hamilton, age 35, address Box 493, Route 12, Tucumcari, New Mexico.'

Ben broke in once more. 'You indicate all three are fatalities. Is this correct, Pitt Control? The woman was alive when she was transferred to the ambulance.'

'Stand by, Five Six, and I'll check.'

A moment later Pitt Control was back. 'That is affirmative, Five Six. The woman died at 1745 hours.

Here is additional information. A vehicle answering to the general description of the hit-and-run vehicle is believed to have been involved in an armed robbery and multiple murder earlier this date at Wilmington, Delaware. Philly Control is now checking for additional details. Gate filters have been established on NAT 26-West from Marker-Exit 100 to Marker-Exit 700. Also, filters on all interchangers. Pitt Control out.'

Kelly Lightfoot, her not-too-serious peeve forgotten, had come back into the galley to listen to the radio exchange. The men got up from the table and Clay gathered the disposable dishware and tossed them into the waste receiver.

'We'd better get rolling,' Ben said. 'Those clowns could still be on the thruway, although God knows they've had time enough to get off before the filters went up.'

They moved to the cab and took their places. The big engines roared into action as Ben rolled Car 56 back onto the policeway. Kelly finished straightening up in the galley and then came forward to sit on the jump seat between the two troopers. The snow had stopped again but the roadways were still slick and glistening under the headlights. Beulah rolled steadily along on her broad tracks, now cruising at 100 miles an hour. The steady whine of the cold night wind penetrated faintly into the sound-proofed and insulated cabin canopy. Clay cut out the cabin lights, leaving only the instrument panel glowing faintly along with the phosphorescent buttons and knobs on the arms of the control seats.

A heavy express cargo carrier flashed by a quarter of a mile away in the blue lane, its big bulk lit up like a Christmas tree with running and warning lights. To their right, Clay caught the first glimpse of a set of flashing amber warning lights coming up from behind in the green lane. A minute later, a huge cargo carrier came abreast of the patrol car and then pulled ahead. On its side was a glowing star of the U.S. Army. A minute later, another Army carrier rolled by.

'That's the missile convoy out of Aberdeen,' Clay told Kelly. 'I wish our hit-runner had tackled one of those babies. We'd have scraped him up instead of those other people.'

The convoy rolled on past at a steady 125 miles an hour. Car 56 flashed under a crossover and into a long, gentle curve. The chronometer clicked up to 2100 hours and the radio sang out. 'Cars Two Oh Seven, Five Six and Eight Two, this is Pitt Control. 2100 hours density report follows . . .'

Pittsburgh Control read off the figures for the three cars. Car 82 was 150 miles ahead of Beulah, Car 207 about the same distance to the rear. The density report ended and a new voice came on the air.

'Attention all cars and all stations, this is Washington Criminal Control.' The new voice paused, and across the continent, troopers on every thruway, control station, checkpoint and relay block reached for clipboard and pen.

'Washington Criminal Control continuing, all cars and all stations, special attention to all units east of the Mississippi. At 1510 hours this date, two men held up the First National Bank of Wilmington, Delaware, and escaped with an estimated $175,000. A bank guard and two tellers, together with five bank customers were killed by these subjects, who used automatic-weapon fire to make good their escape. They were observed leaving the scene in a late-model, white-over-green Travelaire sedan, license unknown. A car of the same make, model and color was stolen from Annapolis, Maryland, a short time prior to the holdup. The stolen vehicle, now believed to be the getaway car, bears USN license number QABR dash 468 dash 1113 . . .'

'That's our baby,' Ben murmured as he and Clay scribbled on their message forms.

. . .otor number ZB 1069432,' Washington Criminal Control continued. 'This car is also now believed to have been involved in a hit-and-run fatal accident on NAT twenty-six-West at marker eight-two at approximately 1648 hours this date.

'Subject Number One is described as WMA, 30 to 35 years, 5 feet 11 inches tall, medium complexion, dark hair and eyes, wearing a dark gray sports jacket and dark pants, and wearing a gray sports cap. He was wearing a ring with a large red stone on his left hand.

'Subject Number Two is described as WMA, 20 to 25 years, six feet, light, ruddy complexion and reddish brown hair, light-colored eyes. Has scar on back left side of neck. Wearing light brown suit, green shirt and dark tie, no hat.

'These subjects are believed to be armed and psychotically dangerous. If observed, approach with extreme caution and inform nearest control of contact. Both subjects now under multiple federal warrants charging bank robbery, homicide and vehicular homicide. All cars and stations acknowledge. Washington Criminal Control out.'

The air chattered as the cars checked into their nearest controls with 'acknowledged.'

'This looks like it could be a long night,' Kelly said, rising to her feet. 'I'm going to sack out. Call me if you need me.'

'Goodnight, Princess,' Ben called.

'Hey, Hiawatha,' Clay called out as Kelly paused in the galley door. 'I didn't mean what I said about your steaks. Your ancestors would have gone around with their bare scalps hanging out if they'd had to use buffalo hide cured like that steak was cooked.'

He reached back at the same instant and slammed the cabin door just as Kelly came charging back. She slammed into the door, then stormed back to the dispensary while Clay doubled over with laughter.

Ben smiled at his junior partner. 'Boy, you're gonna regret that. Don't say I didn't warn you.'

Martin turned control over to the younger trooper and relaxed in his seat to go over the APB from Washington. Car 56 bored steadily through the night. The thruway climbed easily up the slight grade cut through the hills north of Wheeling, West Virginia, and once more snow began falling.

Clay reached over and flipped on the video scanners. Four small screens, one for each of the westbound lanes, glowed with a soft red light. The monitors were synchronized with the radiodometer and changed view at every 10-mile marker. Viewing cameras mounted on towers between lanes lined the thruway, aimed eastward at the oncoming traffic back to the next bank of cameras 10 miles away. Infrared circuits took over from standard scan at dark. A selector system in the cars gave the troopers the option of viewing either the block they were currently patrolling, the one ahead of the next 10-mile block, or the one they had just passed. As a rule, the selection was based on the speed of the car. Beamed signals from each block automatically switched the view as the patrol car went past the towers. Clay put the slower lane screens on the block they were in, turned the blue and yellow lanes to the block ahead.

They rolled past the interchange with NAT 114-South out of Cleveland, and the traffic densities picked up in all lanes as many of the southbound vehicles turned west onto NAT 26. The screens flicked and Clay came alert. Some 15 miles ahead in the 150-to-200-mile-an-hour blue lane, a glowing dot remained motionless in the middle of the lane. The other racing lights of the blue-lane traffic were sheering around it like a racing river current parting around a boulder. 'Trouble,' he said to Martin, as he shoved forward on the throttle. A stalled car in the middle of the high-speed lane was an invitation to disaster. The

41

bull horn blared as Beulah leaped past the 200-mile-an-hour mark and safety cocoons slid into place. Aft in the dispensary Kelly was sealed into her bunk by a cocoon rolling out of the wall and encasing the hospital bed. Car 56 slanted across the police lane with red lights flashing and edged into the traffic flow in the blue lane. The great, red winking lights and the emergency radio siren signal began clearing a path for the troopers. Vehicles began edging to both sides of the lane to shift to crossovers to the yellow or green lanes. Clay aimed Beulah at the motionless dot on the screen and eased back from the four-mile-a-minute speed. The patrol car slowed and the headlight picked up the stalled vehicle a mile ahead. The cocoons opened and Ben slipped on his work helmet and droped down the steps to the side hatch. Clay brought Beulah to a halt a dozen yards directly to the rear of the stalled car, the great bulk of the patrol vehicle with its warning lights serving as a shield against any possible fuzzy-headed speeders who might not be watching the road.

As Martin reached for the door, the WANTED bulletin flashed through his head. 'What make of car is that, Clay?'

'Old jalopy Tritan with some souped-up rigs. Probably kids,' the junior officer replied. 'It looks OK.'

Ben nodded and swung down out of the patrol car. He walked quickly to the other car, flashing his handlight on the side of the vehicle as he went up to the driver. The interior lights were on and inside two obviously frightened young couples smiled with relief at the sight of the uniform coveralls. A freckle-faced teenager in a dinner jacket was in the driver's seat and had the blister window open. He grinned up at Martin. 'Boy, am I glad to see you, officer,' he said.

'What's the problem?' Ben asked.

'I guess she blew an impeller,' the youth answered. 'We

42

were heading for a school dance at Cincinnati and she was boiling along like she was in orbit when "blooey" she just quit.'

Ben surveyed the old jet sedan. 'What year is this clunker?' he asked. The boy told him. 'You kids have been told not to use this lane for any vehicle that old.' He waved his hand in protest as the youngster started to tell him how many modifications he had made on the car. 'It doesn't make one bit of difference whether you've put a first-stage Moon booster on this wreck. It's not supposed to be in the blue or yellow. And this thing probably shouldn't have been allowed out of the white – or even on the thruway.'

The youngster flushed and bit his lip in embarrassment at the giggles from the two girls in the car.

'Well, let's get you out of here.' Ben touched his throat mike. 'Drop a light, Clay, and then let's haul this junk pile away.'

In the patrol car, Ferguson reached down beside his seat and tugged at a lever. From a recess in Beulah's stern, a big portable red warning light dropped to the pavement. As it touched the surface it automatically flashed to life, sending out a bright, flashing red warning signal into the face of approaching traffic. Clay eased the patrol car around the stalled vehicle and then backed slowly into position, guided by Martin's radioed instructions. A tow-bar extruded from the back of the police vehicle and a magnaclamp locked onto the front end of the teenagers' car. The older officer walked back to the portable warning light and rolled it on its four wheels to the rear plate of the jalopy where another magnalock secured it to the car. Beulah's two big rear warning lights still shone above the low silhouette of the passenger car, along with the mobile lamp on the jalopy. Martin walked back to the patrol car and climbed in.

He slid into his seat and nodded at Clay. The patrol car,

with the disabled vehicle in tow, moved forward and slanted toward the police lane. Martin noted the mileage marker on the radiodometer and fingered the transmitter. 'Chillicothe Control, this is Car Five Six.'

'This is Chillicothe. Go ahead, Five Six.'

'We picked up some kids in a stalled heap on the blue at marker 382 and we've got them in tow now,' Ben said. 'Have a wrecker meet us and take them off our hands.'

'Affirmative, Five Six. Wrecker will pick you up at marker 412.'

Clay headed the patrol car and its trailed load into an emergency entrance to the middle police lane and slowly rolled westward. The senior trooper reached into his records rack and pulled out a citation book.

'You going to nail these kids?' Clay asked.

'You're damn right I am,' Martin replied, beginning to fill in the violation report. 'I'd rather have this kid hurting in the pocketbook than dead. If we turn him loose, he'll think he got away with it this time and try it again. The next time he might not be so lucky.'

'I suppose you're right,' Clay said, 'but it does seem a little rough.'

Ben swung around in his seat and surveyed his junior officer. 'Sometimes I think you spent four years in the patrol academy with your head up your jet pipes,' he said. He fished out a cigarette and took a deep drag.

'You've had four solid years of law; three years of electronics and jet and air-drive engine mechanics and engineering; pre-med, psychology, math, English, Spanish and a smattering of Portuguese, to say nothing of dozens of other subjects. You graduated in the upper tenth of your class with a B.S. in both Transportation and Criminology, which is why you're riding patrol and not punching a computer or tinkering with an engine. You'd think with all that education that somewhere along the line you'd have learned to think with your head instead of your emotions.'

44

Clay kept a studied watch on the roadway. The minute Ben had turned and swung his legs over the side of the seat and pulled out a cigarette, Clay knew that it was school time in Car 56. Instructor Sergeant Ben Martin was in a lecturing mood. It was time for all good pupils to keep their big, fat mouths shut.

'Remember San Francisco de Borja?' Ben queried. Clay nodded. 'And you still think I'm too rough on them?' Ben pressed.

Ferguson's memory went back to last year's fifth patrol. He and Ben, with Kelly riding hospital, had been assigned to NAT 200-North, running out of Villahermosa near the Guatemalan border of Mexico to Edmonton Barracks in Canada. It was the second night of the patrol. Some 750 miles north of Mexico City, near the town of San Francisco de Borja, a gang of teenage Mexican youngsters had gone roaring up the yellow at speeds touching on 400 miles an hour. Their car, a beat-up, 15-year-old veteran of less speedy and much rockier local mountain roads, had been gimmicked by the kids so that it bore no resemblance to its original manufacture.

From a junk yard they had obtained a battered airlift, smashed almost beyond use in the crackup of a $10,000 sports cruiser. The kids pried, pounded and bent the twisted impeller lift blades back into some semblance of alignment.

From another wreck of a cargo carrier came a pair of 4,000-pound-thrust engines. They had jury-rigged the entire mess so that it stuck together on the old heap. Then they hit the thruway – nine of them packed into the jalopy – the oldest one just 17 years old. They were doing 350 when they flashed past the patrol car and Ben had roared off in pursuit. The senior officer whipped the big patrol car across the crowded highspeed blue lane, jockeyed into the ultra-high yellow and then turned on the power. By this time the kids realized they had been spotted and they

45

cranked their makeshift power plant up to the last notch. The most they could get out of it was 400 and it was doing just that as Car 56, clocking better than 500, pulled in behind them. The patrol car was still 300 yards astern when one of the bent and rebent impeller blades let go. The out-of-balance fan, turning at close to 35,000 rpm's, flew to pieces and the air cushion vanished. At 400 miles an hour the body of the old jalopy fell the 12 inches to the pavement and both front wheels caved under. There was a momentary shower of sparks, then the entire vehicle snapped cart-wheeling more than 80 feet into the air and exploded. Pieces of car and bodies were scattered for a mile down the thruway. The only identifiable human bodies were those of the three youngsters thrown out and sent hurtling to their deaths more than 200 feet away.

Clay's mind snapped back to the present.

'Write 'em up,' he said quietly to Martin. The senior officer gave a satisfied nod and turned back to his citation pad.

At marker 412, which was also the Columbus turnoff, a big patrol wrecker was parked on the side strip, engines idling, service and warning lights blinking. Clay pulled the patrol car alongside and stopped. He disconnected the tow bar and the two officers climbed out into the cold night air. They walked back to the teenagers' car. Clay went to the rear of the disabled car and unhooked the warning light while Martin went to the driver's window. He had his citation book in hand. The youngster in the driver's seat went white at the sight of the violation pad. 'May I see your license, please?' Ben asked. The boy fumbled in a back pocket and then produced a thin metallic tab with his name, age, address and license number etched into the indestructible and unalterable metal.

'Also your car registration,' Ben added. The youth unclipped another similar metal strip from the dashboard.

The trooper took the two tabs and walked to the rear of the patrol car. He slid back a panel to reveal two thin slots in the hull. Martin slid the driver's license into one of the slots, the registration tab into the other. He pressed a button below each slot. Inside the car a magnetic reader and auto-transmitter 'scanned' the magnetic symbols implanted in the tags. The information was fed instantly to Continental Headquarters Records division at Colorado Springs. In fractions of a second the great computers at Records were comparing the information on the tags with all previous traffic citations issued anywhere in the North American continent in the past forty-five years since the birth of the Patrol. The information from the driver's license and registration tab had been relayed from Beulah via the nearest patrol relay point. The answer came back the same way. Above the license recording slot were two small lights. The first flashed green: 'License is in order and valid.' The second flashed green as well: 'No previous citations.' Ben withdrew the tag from the slot. Had the first light come on red, he would have placed the driver under arrest immediately. Had the second light turned amber, it would have indicated a previous minor violation. This, Ben would have noted on the new citation. If the second light had been red, this would have meant either a major previous violation or more than one minor citation. Again, the driver would have been under immediate arrest. The law was mandatory. One big strike and you're out – two foul tips and the same story. And 'out' meant just that. Fines, possibly jail or prison sentence and lifetime revocation of driving privileges on the thruways.

Ben flipped the car-registration slot to 'standby' and went back to the teenagers' car. Even though they were parked on the service strip of the police emegency lane, out of all traffic, the youngsters stayed in the car. This one point of the law they knew and knew well. Survival chances were dim any time something went wrong on the highspeed thruways. That little margin of luck vanished once outside the not-too-much-better security of the vehicle body.

Martin finished writing and then slipped the driver's license into a pocket worked into the back of the metallic paper foil of the citation blank. He handed the pad into the window to the driver together with a carbon stylus. The boy's lip trembled and he signed the citation with a shaky hand.

Ben ripped off the citation blank and license, fed them into the slot on the patrol car and pressed both the car registration and license 'record' buttons. Ten seconds later the permanent record of the citation was on file in Colorado Springs and a duplicate recording of the action was in the Continental Traffic Court docket recorder nearest to the driver's hometown. Now, no power in three nations could 'fix' that ticket. Ben withdrew the citation and registration tag and walked back to the car. He handed the boy the license and registration tab, together with a copy of the citation. Ben bent down to peer into the car.

'I made it as light on you as I could,' he told the young driver. 'You're charged with improper use of the thruway. That's a minor violation. By rights, I should have cited you for illegal usage.' He looked around slowly at each of the young people. 'You look like nice kids,' he said. 'I think you'll grow up to be nice people. I want you around long enough to be able to vote in a few years. Who knows, maybe I'll be running for President then and I'll need your votes. It's a cinch that falling apart in the middle of 200-mile-an-hour traffic is no way to treat future voters. Goodnight, kids.'

He smiled and walked away from the car. The three young passengers smiled back at Ben. The young driver just stared unhappily at the citation.

Clay stood talking with the wrecker crewmen. Ben nodded to him and mounted into the patrol car. The young Canadian crushed out his cigarette and swung up behind the sergeant. Clay went to the control seat when he saw Martin pause in the door to the galley.

'I'm going to get a cup of coffee,' the older officer said, 'go to the john, wash my face and hands and then take the first shift. You keep Beulah till I get back.'

Clay nodded and pushed the throttles forward. Car 56 rolled back into the police lane, while behind it, the wrecker hooked onto the disabled car and swung north into the crossover. Clay checked both the chronometer and radiodometer and then reported in. 'Cinncy Control, this is Car Five Six back in service.' Cincinnati Control acknowledged.

Ten minutes later Ben reappeared in the cab, slid into the left-hand seat. 'Hit the sack, kid,' he told Ferguson. The chronometer read 2204. 'I'll wake you at midnight – or sooner, if anything breaks.'

Ferguson stood up and stretched, then went into the galley. He poured himself a cup of coffee and, carrying it with him, went back to the crew quarters. He closed the door to the galley and sat down on the lower bunk to sip his coffee. When he had finished, he tossed the cup into the basket, reached and dimmed the cubby lights and kicked off his boots. Still in his coveralls, Clay stretched out on the bunk and sighed luxuriously. He reached up and pressed a switch on the bulkhead above his pillow and the muted sounds of music from a standard-broadcast commercial station drifted into the bunk area. Clay closed his eyes and let the sounds of the music and the muted rumble of the engines lull him to sleep. It took almost 15 seconds for him to be in deep slumber.

Ben pushed Beulah up to her steady 75-mile-an-hour cruising speed, moved to the centre of the quarter-mile-wide police lane and locked her tracks into autodrive. He relaxed back in his seat and divided his gaze between the video monitors and the actual scene on either side of him in the night. Once again the sky was lighted, this time much brighter on the horizon as the roadways swept past Cincinnati.

Traffic was once again heavy and fast, with the blue and green carrying almost equal loads while white was really crowded and even the yellow 'zoom' lane was beginning to fill. The 2200-hours density reports from Cinncy had been given before the Ohio State–Cal football-game traffic had hit the thruways. Densities were now peaking near 20,000 vehicles for the 100-mile block of westbound NAT 26 out of Cincinnati.

Back to the east, near the eastern Ohio state line, Martin could hear Car 207 calling for a wrecker and meat wagon. Beulah rumbled on through the night. The video monitors flicked to the next 10-mile stretch as the patrol car rolled past another interchange. More vehicles streamed onto the westbound thruway, crossing over and dropping down into the same lanes they held coming out of the north-south road. Fifteen years on patrols had created automatic reflexes in the trooper sergeant. Out of the mass of cars and cargoes streaming along the rushing tide of traffic, his eye picked out the track of one vehicle slanting across the white lane just a shade faster than the flow of traffic. The vehicle was still four or five miles ahead. It wasn't enough out of the ordinary to cause more than a second, almost automatic, glance on the part of the veteran officer. He kept his view shifting from screen to screen and out to the sides of the car.

But the reflexes took hold again as his eye caught the track of the same vehicle as it hit the crossover from white to green, squeezed into the faster lane and continued its sloping run toward the next faster crossover. Now Martin followed the movement of the car almost constantly. The moving blip had made the cutover across the half-mile-wide green lane in the span of one crossover and was now whipping into the merger lane that would take it over the top of the police lane and drop it down into the 150–200-mile-an-hour blue. If the object of his scrutiny straightened out in the blue, he'd let it go. The driver had bordered on violation in his fast crossover in the face of heavy traffic. If he kept it up in the now-crowded high-speed lane, he was asking for sudden death. The monitors flicked to the next block and Ben waited just long enough to see the speeding car make a move to the left, cutting in front of a speeding cargo carrier. Ben slammed Beulah into high. Once again the bull horn blared as the cocoons slammed shut, this time locking both Clay and Kelly into their bunks, sealing Ben into the control seat.

Beulah lifted on her air cushion and the twin jets roared as she accelerated down the police lane at 300 miles an hour. Ben closed the gap on the speeder in less than a minute and then edged over to the south side of the police lane to make the jump into the blue lane. The red emergency lights and the radio siren had already cleared a hole for him in the traffic pattern and he eased back on the finger throttles as the patrol car sailed over the divider and into the blue traffic lane. Now he had eyeball contact with the speeding car, still edging over toward the ultra-high lane. On either side of the patrol car traffic gave way, falling back or moving to the left and right. Car 56 was now directly behind the speeding passenger vehicle. Ben fingered the cut-in switch that put his voice signal onto the standard vehicular emergency frequency – the band that carried the automatic siren-warning to all vehicles.

The patrol car was still hitting above the 200-mile-an-hour mark and was 500 feet behind the speeder. The head-lamp bathed the other car in a white glare, punctuated with angry red flashes from the emergency lights.

'You are directed to halt or be fired upon,' Ben's voice

roared out over the emergency frequency. Almost without warning, the speeding car began braking down with such deceleration that the gargantuan patrol car with its greater mass came close to smashing over it and crushing the small passenger vehicle like an insect. Ben cut all forward power, punched up full retrojet and at the instant he felt Beulah's tracks touch the pavement as the air cushion blew, he slammed on the brakes. Only the safety cocoon kept Martin from being hurled against the instrument panel, and in their bunks Kelly Lightfoot and Clay Ferguson felt their insides dragging down into their legs.

The safety cocoons snapped open and Clay jumped into his boots and leaped for the cab. 'Speeder,' Ben snapped as he jumped down the steps to the side hatch. Ferguson snatched up his helmet from the rack beside his seat and leaped down to join his partner. Ben ran up to the stopped car through a thick haze of smoke from the retrojets of the patrol car and the friction-burning brakes of both vehicles. Ferguson circled to the other side of the car. As they flashed their handlights into the car, they saw the driver of the car kneeling on the floor beside the reclined passenger seat. A woman lay stretched out on the seat, twisting in pain. The man raised an agonized face to the officers. 'My God, my wife's going to have the baby right here!'

'Kelly,' Ben spoke into his helmet transmitter. 'On the double. Maternity!'

The dispensary ramp was halfway down before Ben had finished calling. Kelly jumped to the ground and sprinted around the corner of the patrol car, medical bag in hand.

She shoved Clay out of the way and opened the door on the passenger side. On the seat, the woman moaned and then muffled a scream. The patrol doctor slid her hand under the woman's skirt and laid her palm on the distended belly. 'How fast are your pains coming?' she asked. 'About every two minutes,' the white-faced girl gasped. Clay and Ben had moved away from the car a few feet.

'Litter,' Kelly snapped over her shoulder. Clay raced for the patrol car while Ben unshipped a portable warning light and rolled it down the lane behind the patrol car. He flipped it to amber 'caution' and 'pass.' Blinking amber arrows pointed to the left and right of the halted passenger vehicle and traffic in the blue lane began picking up speed and parting around the obstructions.

By the time he returned to the patrol car, Kelly had the expectant mother in the dispensary. She slammed the door in the faces of the three men and then she went to work.

The woman's husband slumped against the side of the patrol vehicle. Ben dug out his pack of cigarettes and handed one to the shaking driver. He waited until the man had taken a few drags before speaking.

'Mister, I don't know if you realize it or not, but you came close to killing your wife, your baby and yourself,' Ben said softly, 'to say nothing of the possibility of killing several other families. Just what did you think you were doing?'

The driver's shoulders sagged and his hand shook as he took the cigarette from his mouth. 'Honestly, officer, I don't know. I just got frightened to death,' he said. He peered up at Martin. 'This is our first baby, you see, and Ellen wasn't due for another week. We thought it would be all right to visit my folks in Cleveland and Ellen was feeling just fine. Well, anyway, we started home tonight – we live in Jefferson City – and just about the time I got on the thruway, Ellen started having pains. Honest to God, officer, I was never so scared in my life. She screamed once and then tried to muffle them, but I knew what was happening and all I could think of was to get her to a hospital. I guess I went out of my head, what with her moaning and the traffic and everything. The only place I could think of that had a hospital was Evansville, and I was going to get her there come hell or high water.' The

53

young man tossed away the half-smoked cigarette and looked up at the closed dispensary door. 'Do you think she's all right?'

Ben sighed resignedly and put his hand on the man's shoulder. 'Don't you worry a bit. She's got one of the best doctors in the continent in there with her. Come on.' He took the husband by the arm and led him around to the patrol car cab hatch. 'You climb up there and sit down. I'll be with you in a second.'

The senior officer signaled to Ferguson. 'Let's get his car out of the traffic, Clay,' he directed. 'You drive it.'

Ben went back and retrieved the caution blinker and reracked it in the side of the patrol car, then climbed up into the cab. He took his seat at the controls and indicated the jump seat next to him. 'Sit down, son. We're going to get us and your car out of this mess before we all get clobbered.'

He flicked the headlamp at Ferguson in the control seat of the passenger car and the two vehicles moved out. Ben kept the emergency lights on while they eased carefully cross-stream to the north and the safety of the police lane. Clay picked up speed at the outer edge of the blue lane and rolled along until he reached the first 'Patrol Only' entrance through the divider to the service strip. Ben followed him in and then turned off the red blinkers and brought the patrol car to a halt behind the other vehicle.

The worried husband stood up and looked to the rear of the car. 'What's making it take so long?' he asked anxiously. 'They've been in there a long time.'

Ben smiled. 'Sit down, son. These things take time. Don't you worry. If there were anything wrong, Kelly would let us know. She can talk to us on the intercom anytime she wants anything.'

The man sat back down. 'What's your name?' Ben inquired.

'Haverstraw,' the husband replied distractedly, 'George

Haverstraw. I'm an accountant. That's my wife back there,' he cried, pointing to the closed galley door. 'That's Ellen.'

'I know,' Ben said gently. 'You told us that.'

Clay had come back to the patrol car and dropped into his seat across from the young husband. 'Got a name picked out for the baby?' he asked.

Haverstraw's face lighted. 'Oh yes,' he exclaimed. 'If it's a boy, we're going to call him Harmon Pierce Haverstraw. That was my grandfather's name. And if she's a girl, it's going to be Caroline May after Ellen's mother and grandmother.'

The intercom came to life. 'Anyone up there?' Kelly's voice asked. Before they could answer, the wail of a baby sounded over the system. Haverstraw yelled.

'Congratulations, Mr Haverstraw,' Kelly said, 'you've got a fine-looking son.'

'Hey,' the happy young father yelled, 'hey, how about that? I've got a son.' He pounded the two grinning troopers on the back. Suddenly he froze. 'What about Ellen? How's Ellen?' he called out.

'She's just fine,' Kelly replied. 'We'll let you in here in a couple of minutes, but we've got to get us gals and your new son looking pretty for papa. Just relax.'

Haverstraw sank down onto the jump seat with a happy dazed look on his face.

Ben smiled and reached for the radio. 'I guess our newest citizen deserves a ride in style,' he said. 'We're going to have to transfer Mrs Haverstraw and, er, oh yes, Master Harmon Pierce to an ambulance and then to a hospital now, George. You have any preference of where they should go?'

'Gosh, no,' the man replied. 'I guess the closest one to wherever we are.' He paused thoughtfully. 'Just where are we? I've lost all sense of distance or time or anything else.'

Ben looked at the radiodometer. 'We're just about due south of Indianapolis. How would that be?'

'Oh, that's fine,' Haverstraw replied.

'You can come back now, Mr Haverstraw,' Kelly called out. Haverstraw jumped up. Clay got up with him. 'Come on, papa,' he grinned, 'I'll show you the way.'

Ben smiled and then called in to Indianapolis Control for an ambulance.

'Ambulance on the way,' Control replied. 'Don't you need a wrecker, too, Five Six?'

Ben grinned. 'Not this time. We didn't lose one. We gained one.'

He got up and went back to have a look at Harmon Pierce Haverstraw, age five minutes, temporary address, North American Continental Thruway 26-West, mile marker 632.

Fifteen minutes later mother and baby were in the ambulance heading north to the hospital. Haverstraw, calmed down with a tranquilizer administered by Kelly, had nearly wrung their hands off in gratitude as he said good-bye.

'I'll mail you all cigars when I get home,' he shouted as he waved and climbed into his car.

Beulah's trio watched the new father ease carefully into the traffic as the ambulance headed down the policeway. Haverstraw would have to cut over to the next exchange and then go north to Indianapolis. He'd arrive later than his family. This time he was the very picture of careful driving and caution as he threaded his way across the green.

'I wonder if he knows what brand of cigars I smoke?' Kelly mused.

The chrono clicked up to 2335 as Car 56 resumed patrol. Kelly plumped down onto the jump seat beside Ben. Clay was fiddling in the galley. 'Why don't you go back to the sack?' Ben called.

'What, for a lousy twenty-five minutes,' Clay replied. 'I had a good nap before you turned the burners up to high. Besides, I'm hungry. Anyone else want a snack?'

Ben shook his head. 'No, thanks,' Kelly said. Ferguson finished slapping together a sandwich. Munching on it, he headed aft into the engine room to make the midnight check. Car 56 had now been on patrol almost eight hours. Only 232 hours and 2000 miles to go.

Kelly looked around at the departing back of the younger trooper. 'I'll bet this is the only car in NorCon that has to stock twenty days of groceries for a ten-day patrol,' she said.

Ben chuckled. 'He's still a growing boy.'

'Well, if he is, it's all between the ears,' the girl replied. 'You'd think that after a year I would have realized that nothing could penetrate that thick Canuck's skull. He gets me so damn mad sometimes that I want to forget I'm a lady.' She paused thoughtfully. 'Come to think of it, no one ever accused me of being a lady in the first place.'

'Sounds like love,' Ben smiled.

Hunched over on the jump seat with her elbows on her knees and her chin cupped in both hands, Kelly gave the senior officer a quizzical sideways look.

Ben was watching his monitors and missed the glance. Kelly sighed and stared out into the light-streaked night of the thruway. The heavy surge of football traffic had distributed itself into the general flow on the road and while all lanes were busy, there were no indications of any over-crowding or jam-ups. Much of the pattern was shifting from passenger to cargo vehicle as it neared midnight. The football crowds were filtering off at each exchange and exit, and the California fans had worked into the blue and yellow – mostly the yellow – for the long trip home. The fewer passenger cars on the thruway and the increase in cargo carriers gave the troopers a breathing spell. The men in the control buckets of the 300- and 400-

ton cargo vehicles were the real pros of the thruways; careful, courteous and fast. The NorCon patrol cars could settle down to watch out for the occasional nuts and drunks who might bring disaster.

Once again Martin had the patrol car on autodrive in the center of the police lane and he settled back in his seat. Beside him Kelly stared moodily into the night.

'How come you've never gotten married, Ben?' she asked. The senior trooper gave her a startled look. 'Why, I guess for the same reason you're still a maiden,' he answered. 'This just doesn't seem to be the right kind of a job for a married man.'

Kelly shook her head. 'No, it's not the same thing with me,' she said. 'At least, not entirely the same thing. If I got married, I'd have to quit the patrol and you wouldn't. And secondly, if you must know the truth, I've never been asked.'

Ben looked thoughtfully at the copper-haired Irish-Indian girl. All of a sudden she seemed to have changed in his eyes. He shook his head and turned back to the road monitors.

'I just don't think that a patrol trooper has any business getting married and trying to keep a marriage happy and make a home for a family thirty days out of every 360, with an occasional weekend home if you're lucky enough to draw your hometown for a terminal point. This might help the population rate, but it sure doesn't do anything for the institution of matrimony.'

'I know some troopers who are married,' Kelly said.

'But there aren't very many,' Ben countered. 'Comes the time they pull me off the cars and stick me behind a desk somewhere, then I'll think about it.'

'You might be too old by then,' Kelly murmured. Ben grinned. 'You sound as though you're worried about it,' he said.

'No,' Kelly replied softly, 'no, I'm not worried about it.

Just thinking.' She averted her eyes and looked out into the night again. 'I wonder what NorCon would do with a husband–wife team?' she murmured, almost to herself.

Ben looked sharply at her and frowned. 'Why, they'd probably split them up,' he said.

'Split what up?' Clay inquired, standing in the door of the cab.

'Split up all troopers named Clay Ferguson,' Kelly said disgustedly, 'and use them for firewood. Especially the heads. They say that hardwood burns long and leaves a fine ash. And that's what you've been for years.'

She sat erect in the jump seat and looked sourly at the young trooper.

Clay shuddered at the pun and squeezed by the girl to get to his seat. 'I'll take it now, Pop,' he said. 'Go get your geriatrics treatment.'

Ben got out of his seat with a snort. 'I'll "pop" you, skinhead,' he snapped. 'You may be eight years younger than I am, but you only have one third the virility and one tenth the brains. And eight years from now you'll still be in deficit spending on both counts.'

'Careful, venerable lord of my destiny,' Clay admonished, 'remember how I spent my vacation and remember how you spent yours before you go making unsubstantiated statements about my virility.'

Kelly stood up. 'If you two will excuse me, I'll go back to the dispensary and take a good jolt of male hormones and then we can come back and finish this man-to-man talk in good locker-room style.'

'Don't you dare,' Ben cried. 'I wouldn't let you tamper with one single, tiny one of your feminine traits, Princess. I like you just the way you are.'

Kelly looked at him with a wide-eyed, cherubic smile. 'You really mean than, Ben?'

The older trooper flushed briefly and then turned quickly into the galley. 'I'm going to try for some shuteye.

59

Wake me at two, Clay, if nothing else breaks.' He turned to Kelly, who still was smiling at him. 'And watch out for that lascivious young goat.'

'It's all just talk, talk, talk,' she said scornfully. 'You go to bed, Ben. I'm going to try something new in psychiatric annals. I'm going to try and psychoanalyze a dummy.' She sat back down on the jump seat.

At 2400 hours it was Vincennes Check with the density reports, all down in the past hour. The patrol was settling into what looked like a quiet night routine. Kelly chatted with Ferguson for another half hour and then rose again. 'I think I'll try to get some sleep,' she said. 'I'll put on a fresh pot of coffee for you two before I turn in.'

She rattled around in the galley for some time. 'Whatcha cooking?' Clay called out. 'Making coffee,' Kelly replied.

'It take all that time to make coffee?' Clay queried.

'No,' she said. 'Im also getting a few things ready so we can have a fast breakfast in case we have to eat on the run. I'm just about through now.'

A couple of minutes later she stuck her head into the cab. 'Coffee's done. Want some?'

Clay nodded. 'Please.'

She poured him a cup and set it in the rack beside his seat.

'Thanks,' Clay said. 'Goodnight, Hiawatha.'

'Goodnight, Babe,' she replied.

'You mean "Paul Bunyan," don't you?' Clay asked. '"Babe" was his blue ox.'

'I know what I said,' Kelly retorted and strolled back to the dispensary. As she passed through the crew cubby, she glanced at Ben sleeping on the bunk recently vacated by Ferguson. She paused and carefully and gently pulled a blanket up over his sleeping form. She smiled down at the trooper and then went softly to her compartment.

In the cab, Clay sipped at his coffee and kept watchful

eyes on the video monitors. Beulah was back on autodrive and Clay had dropped her speed to a slow 50 as the traffic thinned.

At 0200 hours he left the cab long enough to go back and shake Ben awake and was himself reawakened at 0400 to take back control. He let Ben sleep an extra hour before routing him out of the bunk again at 0700. The thin, gray light of the wintry morning was just taking hold when Ben came back into the cab. Clay had pulled Beulah off to the service strip and was stopped while he finished transcribing his scribbled notes from the 0700 Washington Criminal Control broadcast.

Ben ran his hand sleepily over his close-cropped head. 'Anything exciting?' he asked with a yawn. Clay shook his head. 'Same old crap. "All cars exercise special vigilance over illegal crossovers. Keep all lanes within legal speed limits." Same old noise.'

'Anything new on our hit-runner?'

'Nope.'

'Good morning, knights of the open road,' Kelly said from the galley door. 'Obviously you both went to sleep after I left and allowed our helpless citizens to slaughter each other.'

'How do you figure that one?' Ben laughed.

'Oh, it's very simple,' she replied. 'I managed to get in a full seven hours of sleep. When you sleep, I sleep. I slept. Ergo, you did likewise.'

'Nope,' Clay said, 'for once we had a really quiet night. Let's hope the day is of like disposition.'

Kelly began laying out the breakfast things. 'You guys want eggs this morning?'

'You gonna cook again today?' Clay inquired.

'Only breakfast,' Kelly said. 'You have the honors for the rest of the day. The diner is now open and we're taking orders.'

'I'll have mine over easy,' Ben said. 'Make mine sunny-up,' Clay called.

61

Kelly began breaking eggs into the pan, muttering to herself. 'Over easy, sunny-up, I like 'em scrambled. Next tour I take I'm going to get on a team where everyone likes scrambled eggs.'

A few minutes later Beulah's crew sat down to breakfast. Ben had just dipped into his egg yolk when the radio blared. 'Attention all cars, Special attention Cars Two Zero Seven, Five Six and Eight Two.'

'Just once,' Ben said, 'just once, I want to sit down to a meal and get it all down before that damned radio gives me indigestion.' He laid down his fork and reached for the message pad.

The radio broadcast continued. 'A late model, white over green Travelaire, containing two men and believed to be the subjects wanted in earlier broadcast on homicide, robbery and vehicular homicide, was involved in a service-station robbery and murder at Vandalia, Illinois, at approximately 0710 this date. NorCon criminal division believes this subject car escaped filter check and left NAT 26-West sometime during the night.

'Owner of this stolen vehicle states it had only half tanks of fuel at the time it was taken. This would indicate wanted subjects stopped for fuel. It is further believed they were recognized by the station attendant from video bulletins sent out by this department last date and that he was shot and killed to prevent him giving alarm.

'The shots alerted residents of the area and the subject car was last seen headed south. This vehicle may attempt to regain access to NAT 26-West or it may take another thruway. All units are warned once again to approach this vehicle with extreme caution and only with the assistance of another unit where possible. Acknowledge. Washington Criminal Control out.'

Ben looked at the chrono. 'They hit Vandalia at 0710, eh? Even in the yellow they couldn't get this far for another half hour. Let's finish breakfast. It may be a long time until lunch.'

The crew returned to their meal. While Kelly was cleaning up after breakfast, Clay ran the quick morning engine-room check. In the cab, Ben opened the arms rack and brought out two machine pistols and belts. He checked them for loads and laid one on Clay's control seat. He strapped the other around his waist. Then he flipped up a cover in the front panel of the cab. It exposed the breech mechanisms of a pair of twin-mounted 25-mm auto-cannon. The ammunition loads were full. Satisfied, Ben shut the inspection port and climbed into his seat. Clay came forward, saw the machine pistol on his seat and strapped it on without a word. He settled himself in his seat. 'Engine-room check is all green. Let's go rabbit hunting.'

Car 56 moved slowly out into the police lane. Both troopers had their individual sets of video monitors on in front of their seats and were watching them intently. In the growing light of day, a white-topped car was going to be easy to spot.

It had all the earmarks of being another wintry, over-cast day. The outside temperature at 0800 was right on the 29-degree mark and the threat of more snow re-mained in the air. The 0800 density reports from St Louis Control were below the 14,000 mark in all lanes in the 100-mile block west of the city. That was to be expected. They listened to the eastbound densities peaking at 26,000 vehicles in the same block, all heading into the metropolis and their jobs. The 0800, 1200 and 1600 hours density reports also carried the weather forecasts for a 500-mile radius from the broadcasting control point. Decreasing temperatures with light to moderate snow were in the works for Car 56 for the first couple of hundred miles west of St Louis, turning to almost blizzard conditions in central Kansas. Extra units had already been put into service on all thruways through the Midwest, and snow-burners were waging a losing battle from Wichita west to the Rockies around Alamosa, Colorado.

Outside the temperature was below freezing; inside the patrol car it was a comfortable 68 degrees. Kelly had cleared the galley and taken her place on the jump seat between the two troopers. With all three of them in the cab, Ben cut from the intercom to commercial broadcast to catch the early-morning newscasts and some pleasant music. The patrol vehicle glided along at a leisurely 60 miles an hour. An hour out of St Louis, a big liquid-cargo carrier was stopped on the inner edge of the green lane against the divider to the police lane. The trucker had dropped both warning barriers and lights a half mile back. Ben brought Beulah to a halt across the divider from the stopped carrier. 'Dropped a track pin,' the driver called out to the officers.

Ben backed Beulah across the divider behind the stalled carrier to give them protection while they tried to assist the stalled vehicle.

Donning work helmets to maintain contact with the patrol car and its remote radio system, the two troopers dismounted and went to see what needed fixing. Kelly drifted back to the dispensary and stretched out on one of the hospital bunks and picked up a new novel.

Beulah's well-equipped machine shop stockroom produced a matching pin and it was merely a matter of lifting the stall carrier and driving the pin into place in the track assembly. Ben brought the patrol car alongside the carrier and unshipped the crane. Twenty minutes later, Clay and the carrier driver had the new part installed and the tanker was on its way once again.

Clay climbed into the cab and surveyed his grease-stained uniform coveralls and filthy hands. 'Your nose is smudged, too, dearie,' Martin observed.

'Go to hell,' Clay said grinning. 'I'm going to shower and change clothes. Try and see if you can drive this thing until I get back without increasing the pedestrian fatality rate.' He ducked back into the crew cubby and stripped his coveralls.

Bored with her book, Kelly wandered back to the cab and took Clay's vacant control seat. The snow had started falling again and in the mid-morning light it tended to soften the harsh, utilitarian landscape of the broad thruway stretching ahead to infinity and spreading out in a mile of speeding traffic on either hand.

'Attention all cars on NAT 26-West and East,' Washington Criminal Control radio blared. 'Special attention Cars Five Six and Eight Two. Suspect vehicle, white over green Travelaire reported re-entered NAT 26-West on St Louis interchange 179. St Louis Control reports communications difficulty in delayed report. Vehicle now believed . . .'

'Car Five Six, Car Five Six,' St Louis Control broke in. 'Our pigeon is in your zone. Commercial carrier reports near-miss sideswipe three minutes ago in blue lane approximately three miles west of mile marker 975.

'Repeating. Car Five Six, suspect car . . .'

Ben glanced at the radiodometer. It read 969, then clicked to 970.

'This is Five Six, St Louis,' he broke in, 'acknowledged. Our position is mile marker nine seven zero . . .'

Kelly had been glued to the video monitors since the first of the bulletin. Suddenly she yelled and banged Ben on the shoulder. 'There they are. There they are,' she cried, pointing at the blue-lane monitor.

Martin took one look at the white-topped car cutting through traffic in the blue lane and slammed Beulah into high. The safety cocoons slammed shut almost on the first notes of the bull horn. Trapped in the shower stall, Clay was locked into the stall dripping wet as the water automatically shut off with the movement of the cocoon.

'I have them in sight,' Ben reported, as the patrol car

lifted on its air pad and leaped forward. 'They're in the blue five miles ahead of me and cutting over to the yellow. I estimate their speed at 225. I am in pursuit.'

Traffic gave way as Car Five Six hurtled the divider into the blue.

The radio continued to snap orders.

'Cars 112, 206, 76 and 93 establish roadblocks at mile marker crossover 1032. Car 82 divert all blue and yellow to green and white.'

Eight Two was 150 miles ahead, but at 300-mile-an-hour speeds, 82's team was very much a part of the operation. This would clear the two high-speed lanes if the suspect car hadn't been caught sooner.

'Cars 414, 227 and 290 in NAT 26-East, move into the yellow to cover in case our pigeon decides to fly the median.' The controller continued to move cars into covering positions in the area on all crossovers and turnoffs. The sweating dispatcher looked at his lighted map board and mentally cursed the lack of enough units to cover every exit. State and local authorities already had been notified in the event the fugitives left the thruways and tried to escape on a state freeway.

In car 56, Ben kept the patrol car roaring down the blue lane through the speeding westbound traffic. The standard emergency signal was doing a partial job of clearing the path, but at those speeds, driver reaction times weren't always fast enough. Ahead, the fleeing suspect car brushed against a light sedan, sending it careening and rocking across the lane. The driver fought for control as it swerved and screeched on its tilting frame. He brought it to a halt amid a haze of blue smoke from burning brakes and bent metal. The white over green Travelaire never slowed, fighting its way out of the blue into the ultra-high yellow and lighter traffic. Ben kept Beulah in bulldog pursuit.

The sideswipe ahead had sent other cars veering in

panic and a cluster inadvertently bunched up in the path of the roaring patrol car. Like a flock of hawk-frightened chickens, they tried to scatter as they saw and heard the massive police vehicle bearing down on them. But like chickens, they couldn't decide which way to run. It was a matter of five or six seconds before they parted enough to let the patrol car through. Ben had no choice but to cut the throttle and punch once on the retrojets to brake the hurtling patrol car. The momentary drops in speed unlocked the safety cocoons, and in an instant Clay had leaped from the shower stall and sped to the cab. Hearing, rather than seeing his partner, Martin snapped over his shoulder, 'Unrack the rifles. That's the car.' Clay reached for the gun rack at the rear of the cab.

Kelly took one look at the younger trooper and jumped for the doorway to the galley. A second later she was back. Without a word she handed the nude Ferguson a dangling pair of uniform coveralls. Clay dropped the rifles and grabbed the coveralls from her hand and clutched them to his body. Still without speaking, Kelly turned and ran back to her dispensary to be ready for the next acceleration.

Clay was into the coveralls and in his seat almost at the instant Martin whipped the patrol car through the hole in the blue traffic and shoved her into high once more.

There was no question that the occupants of the fugitive car knew they were being pursued. They shot through the crossover into the yellow lane and now were hurtling down the thruway close to the 400-mile-an-hour mark.

Martin had Beulah riding just under 300 to make the crossover, still 10 miles behind the suspect car and following on video monitor. The air still crackled with commands as St Louis and Washington Control maneuvered other cars into position as the pursuit went westward past other units blocking exit routes.

Clay read aloud the radiodometer numerals as they

clicked off a mile every nine seconds. Car 56 roared into the yellow, and the instant Ben had it straightened out he slammed all finger throttles to full power. Beulah snapped forward as if she had been goosed by a blow-torch, and even at 400 miles an hour, the sudden acceleration pasted the car's crew against the back of their cushioned seats. The patrol car shot forward at more than 500 miles an hour, closing the gap on the speeding fugitive vehicle.

The image of the Travelaire grew on the video monitor and then the two troopers had it in actual sight, a white, racing dot on the broad avenue of the thruway six miles ahead.

Clay triggered the controls for the forward bow cannon and a panel box flashed to 'ready fire' signal.

'Negative,' Martin ordered. 'We're coming up on the roadblock. You might miss and hit one of our cars.'

'Car Five Six to control,' the senior trooper called. 'Watch out at the roadblock. He's doing at least 500 in the yellow and he'll never be able to stop.'

Two hundred miles east, the St Louis controller made a snap decision. 'Abandon roadblock. Roadblock cars start west. Maintain 200 until subject comes into monitor view. Car Five Six, continue speed estimates of subject car. Maybe we can box this bastard in.'

At the roadblock 45 miles ahead of the speeding fugitives and their relentless pursuer, the four patrol cars pivoted and spread out across the roadway some 500 feet apart. They lunged forward and lifted up to air-cushion jet drive at just over 200 miles an hour. Eight pairs of eyes were fixed on video monitors set for the 10-mile block to the rear of the four vehicles.

Beulah's indicated ground speed now edged toward the 550 mark, close to the maximum speeds the massive patrol vehicle could attain.

The gap continued to close, but more slowly. 'He's

firing hotter,' Ben called out. 'Estimating 530 on subject vehicle.'

Now Car 56 was about three miles astern and still the gap closed. The fugitive car flashed past the site of the abandoned roadblock and 15 seconds later all four patrol cars racing ahead of the Travelaire, broke into almost simultaneous reports of 'Here he comes.'

A second later Clay Ferguson yelled out, 'There he goes. He's boondocking, he's boondocking.'

'He has you spotted,' Martin broke in. 'He's heading for the median. Cut, cut, cut. Get out in there ahead of him.'

The driver of the fugitive car had seen the bulk of the four big patrol cruisers outlined against the slight rise in the thruway almost at the instant he flashed onto their screens 10 miles behind them. He broke speed, rocked wildly from side to side, fighting for control, and then cut diagonally to the left, heading for the outer edge of the thruway and the unpaved, half-mile-wide strip of land-scaped earth that separated the east- and westbound segments of NAT 26.

The white and green car was still riding on its airpad when it hit the low, rounded curbing at the edge of the thruway. It hurtled into the air and sailed for a hundred feet across the gently-sloping snowcovered grass, came smashing down in a thick hedgerow of bushes – and kept going.

Car 56 slowed and headed for the curbing. 'Watch it, kids,' Ben snapped over the intercom, 'we may be buying a plot in a second.'

Still traveling more than 500 miles an hour, the huge patrol car hit the curbing and bounced into the air like a rocket-boosted elephant. It tilted and smashed its nose in a slanting blow into the snow-covered ground. The sound of smashing and breaking equipment mingled with the roar of the thundering jets, tracks and air drives as the car fought its way back to level travel. It surged forward and smashed through the hedgerow and plunged down the sloping snow-bank after the fleeing car.

'Clay,' Ben called in a strained voice, 'take 'er.'

Ferguson's fingers were already in position. 'You all right, Ben?' he asked anxiously.

'Think I dislocated a neck vertebra,' Ben replied. 'I can't move my head. Go get 'em, kid.'

'Try not to move your head at all, Ben,' Kelly called from her cocoon in the dispensary. 'I'll be there the minute we slow down.'

A half mile ahead, the fugitive car plowed along the bottom of the gentle draw in a cloud of snow, trying to fight its way up the opposite slope.

But the Travelaire was never designed for driving on anything but a modern superhighway. Car 56 slammed through the snow and down to the bottom of the draw. A quarter of a mile ahead of the fugitives, the first of the four roadblock units came plowing over the rise.

The car speed dropped quickly to under 100 and the cocoons were again retracted. Ben slumped forward in his seat and caught himself. He eased back with a gasp of pain, his head held rigidly straight. Almost the instant he started to straighten up, Kelly flung herself through the cab door. She clasped his forehead and held his head against the back of the control seat.

Suddenly the fugitive car spun sideways, bogged in the wet snow and muddy ground beneath and stopped. Clay bore down on it and was about 200 yards away when the canopy of the other vehicle popped open and a sheet of automatic-weapons fire raked the patrol car. Only the low angle of the sedan and the nearness of the bulky patrol car saved the troopers. Explosive bullets smashed into the patrol car canopy and sent shards of plastiglass showering down on the trio.

An instant later the bow cannon on the first of the

cutoff patrol units opened fire. An ugly, yellow-red blossom of smoke and fire erupted from the front of the Travelaire and it burst into flames. A second later a man staggered out of the burning car, clothes and hair aflame. He took four plunging steps and then fell face down in the snow. The car burned and crackled and a thick funeral pyre of oily black smoke billowed into the gray sky. It was snowing heavily now, and before the troopers could dismount and plow to the fallen man, a thin layer of snow covered his burned body.

An hour later Car 56 was again on NAT 26-West, this time headed for Wichita barracks and needed repairs. In the dispensary, Ben Martin was stretched out on a hospital bunk with a traction brace around his neck and a copper-haired medical-surgical patrolwoman fussing over him.

In the cab, Clay peered through the now almost-blinding blizzard that whirled and skirled thick snow across the thruway. Traffic densities were virtually zero despite the efforts of the dragon-like snow-burners trying to keep the roadways clear. The young trooper shivered despite the heavy jacket over his coveralls. Wind whistled through the shell holes in Beulah's canopy and snow sifted and drifted against the back bulkhead. The cab communications system had been smashed by the gunfire and Clay wore his work helmet both for communications and warmth.

The door to the galley cracked open and Kelly stuck her head in. 'How much farther, Clay?' she asked.

'We should be in the barracks in about twenty minutes,' the shivering trooper replied.

'I'll fix you a cup of hot coffee,' Kelly said. 'You look like you need it.'

Over the helmet intercom Clay heard her shoving things around in the galley. 'My heavens, but this place is a mess,' she exclaimed. 'I can't even find the coffee bin. That steeplechase driving has got to stop.' She paused.

'Clay,' she called out, 'have you been drinking in here? It smells like a brewery.'

Clay raised mournful eyes to the shattered canopy above him. 'My cooking wine!' he sighed.

▼

The week Ben spent in the hospital Clay used to get Beulah back in road condition. By the time the senior officer had disrupted the hospital so much with his demands to be released, Beulah had a new bubble and a partial paint job.

'She's positively beautiful,' Ben said happily as the trio prepared to board the cruiser. He looked around at the snow-covered vehicle parked in the cold Kansas barracks area.

'Beulah's beautiful,' he said. He smiled at Kelly. 'You're beautiful, too. Even you look good to me,' he added to Clay. 'Come on. I'm sick of this winter weather,' he added. 'Let's roll out of here.'

Ten minutes later Car 56 was again rolling westward.

By late afternoon the thruway began its long gentle climb from the Kansas plains to the base of the Rockies and the Denver Control Center. The snow lay piled deeply on either side of the lanes and formed high walls in the median dividers. Dark, lowering clouds held a threat of new snow.

The radio blared. 'Car Five Six, this is Denver Control.'

'This is Five Six,' Ben replied, 'go ahead.'

'Five Six, Kansas City Control reports your vehicle out of service for seven days and refitted. Since you are in shape for full patrol, shift to NAT 85-North at Denver and terminate current patrol at Anchorage. Acknowledge.'

'So much for heroism,' Ben sighed to himself. 'Acknowledged, Denver,' he called.

'And you're the guy who was tired of winter weather,' Clay hooted.

Ben hummed happily to himself and eyed the chronometer in the center of the instrument panel. The night
sky 30 miles ahead glowed with the lights of San
Francisco and it was just a little past midnight. Car 56
was nearing the end of its nine-day patrol south from
Anchorage. If they could just have a few more hours of
relatively quiet traffic, they'd hit Los Angeles Barracks
about daylight and a five-day rest before the start of the
next leg of the patrol. To either side of the bubble
canopy that covered the cab, two rivers of moving lights
flowed with the police vehicle in the four variable-speed
lanes of the superhighway. But traffic densities were
relatively light on all four of the southbound lanes. They
were on NAT 99-South, stretching from Fairbanks to San
Diego. A half mile east of the high-speed southbound
yellow lane was NAT 99-North, four identical
half-mile-wide lanes of northbound traffic plus the
northbound police lane.

In the left-hand bucket seat Clay relaxed with a
cigarette. The lights of the much heavier northbound
traffic silhouetted his crop-haired head.

The 60-foot-long police cruiser glided smoothly down
the center red emergency lane of the thruway at a steady
100 miles an hour, just keeping pace with the vehicles in
the slow white lane a mile to the right.

'What's "fleshpot" mean, Ben?' the young Canadian
officer asked.

The senior officer turned his broad-planed face and grinned. 'You planning on finding one when we hit L.A.?'

Clay shrugged. 'I've heard the expression and it sounds interesting. Only trouble is that I've never been able to find out exactly what it means. But after ten days in this over-sized sardine can, almost anything would sound interesting.'

Below the chronometer the big radiodometer clicked off another mile marker as Car 56 rolled past the beamed signal from the automatic radio marker posts that lined the thruways from one terminal point to another. Beulah's crew was now 2904 miles and nine and a half days out of Fairbanks with a half a day and more than 400 miles to go to the end of the patrol.

Car 56 started a gentle climb into the hills to the north of the Golden Gate, and the tracks rumbled slightly as the roadway passed over a high culvert. Ahead, wisps of fog drifted into the great white beam from the three-foot-wide variable-intensity headlight strip across the cruiser's bow. Ben reached forward and shifted the light color spectrum into the yellow range.

A bank of speakers above their heads came to life. 'Frisco Control to Car Nine One One.' Car 911 came back with a 'Go ahead.' Frisco Control continued. 'You've got a bad one at Marker 3012. Cargo carrier took out a passenger vehicle in the blue. Take it Code Three. And watch the fog.'

'Car Nine One One on the way,' came the reply. Fifty miles ahead of Martin and Ferguson another NorCon police cruiser slammed forward, lifting from the roadway and its tracks as its fan-drive impellers roared into action under the drive of the pair of 150,000-pound-thrust engines.

The radio continued: 'Frisco Control to all cars on Nine Nine north and south from markers 2900 to 3100. Heavy fog conditions now exist. Yellow lanes closing in two minutes. Speed reductions in force throughout designated area. Observe caution.'

The last transmission was broadcast on standard, all-vehicle frequency and was received by all cars and cargo carriers as well as NorCon police cruisers and work vehicles.

The fog was getting thicker and Ben again shifted the spectrum of the headlight deeper into the yellow. Car 56 topped the hill, and the sky ahead was a solid glow of light from the buildings of Baghdad-by-the-Bay. But the fog obscured any details beyond the limits of the brilliant headlight. On either side of the police cruiser, only the lights of vehicles running close to the east and west edges of the green and blue lanes could be detected.

The white-lane traffic, with its 100-mile-an-hour speed limit, was lost in the fog as was most of the traffic in the green 100-to-150-mile-an-hour lane. To the left, the 200-mile-an-hour blue lane still carried its previous loads. Out beyond the vision of the police cruiser, huge flashing amber and then amber-and-red lights were in action in the ultra-high-speed yellow lane, warning drivers to slow down and shift back to the blue. Barriers had risen out of the cross-overs to prevent any further traffic from moving into the yellow lane.

Again Frisco Control came on the air on police frequency. 'All cars on Nine Nine north and south. Additional information last broadcast. Video monitors to infra in one minute. Repeating, video monitors to infra in one minute.'

Ben and Clay reached for their work helmets beside their seats and pulled them over their heads. Each officer flipped down the infra-red filter mask and Ben flicked a switch on the arm control panel on his seat. Above the regular headlight strip on Beulah's bow another strip, black to the naked eye, came to life, and a brilliant band of infrared light now cut through the night and fog. At the same instant, the video monitors shifted into the infra spectrum and the officers again had eyeball contact with the traffic.

'This is going to slow things down for a while,' Ben said. 'You hit the sack, kid, and I'll take it till three.'

Clay nodded and climbed out of his seat, first racking his work helmet back into place beside the seat. 'Want a cup of coffee before I turn in?' he asked.

'I could use one,' Ben replied.

The younger trooper turned to the door at the rear of the cab. He thumbed a switch killing the lights in the little galley just behind the cab before opening the door, then slid the door open and shut behind him before turning the lights back on.

Ferguson turned up the heat under the coffee flask racked on the range, then opened the door to the crew quarters. He sat on a bunk, tugged off his boots and then padded back in stocking feet to the galley to pour his partner a cup of now-hot coffee. Again he flicked off the lights in the galley before opening the door to the control cab. The glow of the city lights dimly illuminated the cab enough for Clay to make out the helmeted figure of the sergeant. He eased into the cab and set the coffee down in a recess in the arm of the senior officer's control seat. 'Watch it, Ben,' he warned, 'it's hot.'

'Thanks, Clay,' Ben said. 'See you at three.'

Clay slid back out of the darkened cab and closed the galley door behind him. In the crew quarters, he dropped onto the lower bunk, reached up and set the alarm chrono mounted in the bottom of the overhead bunk to awaken him for his next watch at 0300, then rolled over and shut his eyes.

The muted throb of the big diesels that drove Beulah's track assembly at speeds up to 200 miles an hour echoed faintly through the insulated walls of the bulkhead separating the engine room from the crew quarters. The sound lulled Clay to sleep in less than a minute.

Car 56 rounded a sweeping curve in the hills and a blaze of light struck the gunmetal blue hull as the lights of the Golden Gate Causeway came into view. Ben flipped up the infrared filters. Solid banks of mercury tubes lined the length of the causeway, cutting through the fog and turning night into day. The great bridge was in reality a roof over the bay, five miles wide. It was lighted underneath as well as above for surface shipping that sailed under its protective cover for miles around the old Embarcadero to South Bay. NAT 99 north and south soared across the bay and sped high above the eastern fringes of the great city, angling southeasterly toward the peninsula where it once again dropped down to the surface of the land. Although it was unseen from the heights of the thruway, Ben knew that a maze of lesser elevated highways crisscrossed the city 50 feet below, carrying local traffic to interchanges leading to the thruways and north, south and east out of the city. Another belt of light to the east was the five-mile swath of NAT 50, entering the city from across the continent.

He held Beulah at a steady 100 as she glided along the edges of the bay. The radio sounded briefly as Car 911 called for a wrecker and ambulance. Traffic densities continued to rise in the southbound lanes as Ben knew they would. At this time of night, traffic would be leaving the city, heading for the bedroom communities to the north and south. Traffic had been light coming into San Francisco from the Marin side. Now it would increase, and with the densities would come the problems.

The fog hung like a porous pillow over the city, muffling sounds and grudgingly giving way only to the banks of mercury tubes that lined the thruway and the city expressways and streets below. The intensities of light would continue the length of the peninsula to the southern limits of the city in the San José residential district. Then it would be infra driving until the fog lifted. The thruway curved gently to the right around the backwaters of the bay. Ahead, Ben saw the sweeping arches of the interchange that switched traffic from NAT 50 to NAT 99. He eased off power and let Beulah drop to a snail's pace as she approached the interchange.

Just past the merger lanes Ben pulled the cruiser off to the left-hand service strip and stopped. He pulled the work helmet from his head and ran his fingers over his crew-cut, then fished for a cigarette.

He thumbed the transmit button on his arm panel. 'Car Five Six to Frisco Control.'

'This is Frisco Control. Go ahead, Five Six.'

'I'm taking five at the Five Oh dash Nine Nine interchange,' Ben said. 'Looks like a lot of traffic coming from across the bay so I thought I'd watch it here for a while.'

'Affirmative, Five Six,' Frisco controller said. 'South Frisco Check estimates white density seven hundred; green, nine-fifty; blue, five hundred; yellow is closed to Gilroy. Report when you're rolling again.'

'Affirmative,' Ben replied. He jotted the densities in his log.

Ben wasn't too concerned about the green and white, but a 500 density in the blue on a foggy night could mean trouble. At least the ultra-high yellow, with its 500-mile-an-hour limit, was closed. He leaned back in his control seat and smoked quietly, keeping his eyes on the video monitors. Ben flicked the blue monitor to the block ahead, put the green and white on his own block. He started to cut out the yellow since that lane was closed, but decided to leave it on, set for the present block.

Moisture from the fog-wet night beaded the plastic canopy of the cruiser and glistened on the roadway. His eyes flicked from the monitors to the racing bands of lights on either side of the police vehicle. The brilliant lights of passenger cars and cargo carriers whipped past, leaving glowing dots of reddish light from their exhausts. Amber lights flashed up from the rear in the blue lane, and the massive bulk of a 500-ton cargo carrier whipped by at a steady 200 miles an hour. In the instant it vanished, the driver of the carrier must have caught a glimpse of the patrol cruiser's bulk parked beside the roadway. He flicked his running lights in a brief 'hello' as he passed.

When he had finished his cigarette and coffee, Ben eased Beulah back into the police lane and called Frisco Control. 'Car Five Six to Frisco Control. We're rolling.'

'Affirmative, Five Six,' Frisco acknowledged. 'The fog's getting thicker. Keep alert for any shipping that might wander in off the bay. Frisco out.'

Ben grinned and settled comfortably into the control seat. His fingers rested lightly on the twin control panel as he pushed Beulah up to a leisurely 75, easing into the center of the police lane. He glanced over at the radiodometer as it clicked to mile marker 2944. Out of the corner of his eye he caught a flash on his yellow-lane monitor. By the time he turned to look at the screen, the flash was gone. The senior patrolman started doing several things at once. Beulah surged forward under diesel drive to 150 miles an hour, Ben reached over and switched the yellow monitor to the next 10-mile scanning block and at the same time called Frisco Control.

The screen showed a lone vehicle barreling down the yellow lane, ignoring the flashing amber and red lights and arrows.

'Frisco Control, this is Car Five Six. I have a vehicle in the yellow,' Ben called.

'This is Frisco. The yellow is closed, Five Six. That car has no business in there. What's the location?'

Ben glanced at the radiodometer. 'He's past 2950 and he looks like he's wide open; probably near 2960 now.'

'Get him outta there, Five Six,' the Frisco controller said tersely. 'We've been routing into the yellow around 3012 to clear traffic for Nine One One's accident. That idiot may plow right into them.'

Ben slammed Beulah into high. The bull horn blared throughout the vehicle and Ben's safety cocoon snapped shut, locking him into his seat. In both the crew quarters and dispensary, similar horizontal cocoons slapped down on the sleeping forms of Clay Ferguson and Kelly Lightfoot. Car 56 lifted from the roadway on its airpad and in five seconds Beulah was hitting 350 miles an hour and still accelerating. From the bow, piercing red emergency lights flashed and both an outside and radio broadcast siren screamed. Beulah came roaring into the crossover to the blue lane as vehicles scattered to give her room. Still holding at close to 400, Ben sailed across the two-foot rounded curbing between the blue and yellow lanes and straightened out in pursuit of the racing vehicle. Ahead, the exhausts of the speeding car were visible to his naked eye. 'I've got him in sight,' Ben reported. 'He's on air jet lift and he's weaving all over the road. Looks like a drunk.'

'Get him, Five Six,' Frisco exhorted. 'But don't herd him into the blue. That's where the mess is now. Car Nine Eleven, Car Nine One One, this is Frisco Control.'

'Car Nine One One affirmative,' came the reply. 'We hear. We're trying to get these vehicles outta here, but I've got this wrecker and a pile of junk halfway across the lane. We'll try. But stop him if you can, Five Six.'

'Affirmative,' Ben replied. His foot jammed to the floor and Beulah rammed toward peak speed In seconds the cruiser was less than 200 yards behind the speeder. Ben opened his mike on standard frequency. 'You are directed to stop immediately. This is a Thruway Patrol order,' Ben said. He peered at the weaving vehicle. 'I repeat, you in the Cadillaire. This is a patrol vehicle. I order you to stop immediately.'

The speeding car veered off to the right but didn't slow its speed. Ben glanced up at the blue and yellow monitors. The lights of the accident scene ahead and the shifting traffic were just coming into view on the screens.

The patrolman whipped the cruiser abreast of the speeder and then pulled ahead. Beulah was hitting 590. Ben fingered the emergency afterburner and the cruiser jumped ahead. When Beulah was 100 yards in front of the Cadillaire, Ben touched another switch. Twin ports in Beulah's stern snapped open and a pair of flared nozzles popped out. Like a giant squid spewing inky secretion to blind its foe, a dense black cloud sprayed from the twin nozzles. Thousands of tiny, dark plastic flakes shot out under high pressure into the night air, and into the path of the speeding Cadillaire. The car plunged into the cloud, and the high-impact plastic slammed against the friction-heated face of the vehicle. The flakes were designed for adhesion only under heat and impact. The hurtling car created both forces and the plastic welded to the entire front surface of the vehicle, covering the driver's canopy, lights and prow, building up in a distorted mass around the nose of the car. Thousands more particles were sucked into the impeller air intake to adhere to the balanced fan blades and turn them into wildly vibrating clubs. The car veered and lost speed as the air-pad system fouled and then failed. Inside the now-blinded bubble, the driver panicked and hit the brakes the instant the wheels were back to the surface. Brake locks and wheel bearings glowed red under the sudden friction and more of the plastic particles built up along the underside of the Cadillaire, coating the wheels and wheel wells in a steady built-up mass of welded plastic until the wheels could no longer turn. A rear tire smoked and then blew. A second later the car rocked to a halt.

The moment the impellers of the Cadillaire fouled, Ben whipped Beulah to the left, angling for the outer railing of the lane. He fired all retrojets. Less than five miles ahead was the barrier that blocked the lane to allow traffic to be diverted around the cargo-passenger accident.

Ben, Clay and Kelly momentarily blacked out under the force of 10 G's as Beulah lost speed. The cruiser dropped to her tracks and brakes added to the retrojet effect. Sliding like a mammoth on ice, Beulah shrieked to a stop less than 100 feet from the barrier. The safety cocoons snapped open.

Before Ben could get the cruiser turned around and headed back to the stalled Cadillaire, Clay was out of his bunk and in his seat in the cab. 'What's up?' he asked. 'Speeder,' Ben snapped. 'Probably drunk.' He flicked to intercom.

'Kelly,' he called, 'you OK?'

'I'll be fine just as soon as I can pull my bra back up from my hips,' Kelly replied. 'You need me, Ben?'

'Better be ready,' he replied, 'I think this one's a drunk and I want him tested right now if he is. Also, he might be off his rocker. Stand by, Princess.'

Ferguson was down the steps from the cab deck to the side hatch, waiting for Ben to bring the cruiser to a halt. His helmet was on and he had buckled a pistol belt around his blue uniform coveralls.

'Frisco Control, this is Car Five Six,' Ben reported. 'We got 'em but you better get a surfacing and vacuum cleanup crew out here. We had to stop-cloud him and we dug up a little road getting ourselves stopped.'

'*Madre de Dios*,' Car 911's patrolman broke in. 'I theenk you never stop. I weel light candles to the Virgin for you, Five Seex.'

Benn grinned at the Spanish accent. '*Gracias, amigo*,' he called back. '*De nada*.'

Ben brought Beulah to a halt with her bow aimed at the Cadillaire. In the yellow glare of the headlight, a man staggered around the front end of the vehicle, pawing at the soft mass of warm plastic molded to the front of the car. 'Check the car, Clay,' Ben called as he headed for the man on foot.

Ferguson moved to the side of the car and flashed his light through the driver's open hatch. A woman sat in the front passenger seat and another couple was in the rear seat.

Ben approached the wavy-haired blond man at the front of the car. 'You the driver of this vehicle?' Ben asked.

The man spun around, a silly grin on his face. 'In a manner of speaking, you might say that t' be more correct, officer, I was the driver of this now thoroughly fouled-up Caddy.'

Ben eyed the man. The driver, dressed in a dinner jacket, pulled at his collar, knocking his tie askew. A jewel-studded watch flashed in the lights of the police cruiser as the man ran his hands through his hair.

'May I see your driver's permit, please?' Ben asked.

'Oh, come off it, officer,' the man smiled and slumped against the front of the car. 'We had a fine lil' run there for a while and you won. Not fairly, but you won, nevertheless. Good show. But let's not get stuffy about it, eh?'

'I repeat,' Ben said in a level tone, 'show me your permit. This is a thruway. I am a patrol officer. You have violated the law. And this is no game.'

The tall blond stared owlishly at Ben, a half-amused smile on his lips. 'You really are going to try to be stuffy about this, aren't you?'

Ben's mouth tightened. 'Kelly,' he called over the helmet intercom.

'I've been listening, Ben,' she replied. 'Bring him in. I'm ready for him.'

Ben reached for the man's arm. 'If you'll just come with me, mister.'

The man yanked his arm from Ben's grip. 'I'll thank you to take your han's off me, officer. I'm no common criminal, nor do I intend to be treated like one. That's the trouble with you public servants. Give you a little authority and you think you can treat anyone like a public enemy.' He straightened himself up with a dignified air that was marred by a sudden loss of balance that sent him stumbling into Ben's arms. 'Sorry,' he muttered. 'Must be all this fresh air. Not used to it in such big doses.'

Ben hauled the young man upright and turned him so that he was facing down the roadway in the direction of the barrier a mile away. He pointed toward the barrier and the traffic moving from the blue to the yellow lane.

'See that?' Ben asked. The man nodded mutely. 'Do you have any idea how fast you were traveling?'

The driver blinked and shrugged. 'Oh, three-fifty, maybe four hundred. But I had perfect control, absolutely perfect control,' he replied.

Ben snorted. 'I don't know if you have any idea how long it takes for a vehicle to come to a complete stop from four hundred miles an hour. For your information, you were traveling much closer to six hundred than four hundred. In any case, five seconds more and you would have slammed through that barrier and killed yourself and everyone in your car. That's bad enough, but in all probability you'd have taken out a half dozen innocent occupants in those other cars.'

'This is the yellow lane,' the driver cried indignantly. 'They have no business moving slow as that in this lane.'

'And if you had an iota of brains in your head,' Ben retorted, 'you'd have seen the signals ordering you off the yellow lane forty miles back and you'd have obeyed my orders to stop. Now come on.'

He took the man by the arm and led him around to the rear of the cruiser where Kelly had lowered the ramp leading into the dispensary. Kelly was waiting beside the surgery table, hypo poised. Beside the table stood the cruiser's diagnostican. At the sight of the table and equipment, the blond stopped and pulled back in Ben's grip.

'What's this?' he demanded.

'We have to run a blood-alcohol test,' Ben replied. 'Now if you'll just lie down on . . .'

The young man began struggling. 'Oh no you don't,' he yelled. 'I'm not going to be subjected to this kind of treatment. You'll hear about . . .'

Kelly had moved to his side and with a deft movement slipped his sleeve back. She pressed the hypo gun briefly against the skin. The man slumped in Ben's arms.

'Get him on the table,' Kelly ordered. Ben heaved the inert body onto the table and Kelly made the necessary attachments. A blood analyzer needle went into an arm vein and then Kelly punched a series of buttons. Inside the machine, muted clicks indicated the data was being punched onto tapes. One copy of the tape remained sealed-in the machine until the end of the patrol, when it was opened by a reviewing board. Another copy spewed from the keypunch orifice.

Kelly read the tape. 'Two point eight five seven,' she said. 'This guy's so drunk he should be dead.' Ben nodded grimly. 'Bring him around, Kelly.'

She picked up another hypo gun from a rack and sprayed it into the man's bared arm. In a moment his eyes flickered and then opened. He blinked and tried to sit up and then retched. Kelly shoved a pan under his chin a split second before he vomited.

When the spasm had passed, the man sat up. Ben looked at him with disgust.

'You want something for that hangover?' he asked. The man nodded. Kelly fired another hypo into his arm, and seconds later his face brightened. He smiled at Kelly.

'Great stuff, that,' he said. 'Should keep Florence Nightingale with me on all parties.'

'Now that you can think straight,' Ben said, 'let's get this on record. I'm Patrol Sergeant Martin. You are in the dispensary of Thruway Patrol Car Five Six and I now

86

formally tell you that you are under arrest. I am charging you with driving while under the influence of alcohol, reckless driving, ignoring instructions of the Thruway Authority, ignoring the lawful orders of a patrol officer and leaving the confines of your vehicle while on a thruway. I further warn you that anything you say can be used in evidence against you in a court of law.'

The man stared up at Ben in amazement. Suddenly he began to laugh.

'Why, you really think you're going to arrest me,' he said with a chuckle. He arose unsteadily from the table and grabbed for support. 'This is quite ridiculous, you know, but I suppose it is my fault. You obviously don't know who I am.'

'No, I don't,' Ben admitted, 'but that's what I've been asking you for the past ten minutes. Now may I see your driver's license, please.'

'By all means, officer,' the blond said with a pleasant and confident laugh, 'by all means.' He fished his wallet from a pocket and handed it to the patrolman.

'Please remove your license from the wallet, sir,' Ben requested. The man stopped laughing and stared at Ben's craggy face for a moment, then slid the metallic driver-permit tag from the wallet and handed it across.

'There you are, officer,' he said. 'Now you know. Kevin Shellwood. That's who I am.'

Ben took the license and pulled his citation book from a pocket. He slipped the tag into a pocket of the citation book and unclipped a stylus from his coveralls pocket.

'Hey, wait a minute,' the blond protested. 'Maybe you don't understand. I'm Kevin Shellwood.' He peered at Ben's unmoved face. 'Perhaps you've heard of my father. Quentin Shellwood? Shellwood Electronics? Chairman of the Continental Bank. President's right han' man? I'm his very own, lone and beloved son, tha's who I am.'

Clay appeared at the door of the dispensary. 'Ben, what

do you want me to do with those other people in the car? They're pretty loaded.'

'Be with you in a minute,' Ben said, writing on the citation pad.

'Now hold on there, sergeant,' Shellwood protested. 'Perhaps I did get a little out of line, but there's no need for all this difficulty. Really there isn't.' He fumbled with his wallet and withdrew a sheaf of bills and laid them on the surgery table.

'Let's be reasonable about this little matter,' he said. He pointed to the pile of bills. 'There's at least six thousand there. Now I know you ladies and gentlemen are notoriously underpaid public servants. Risk your necks and all that sort of thing, very little to show for it. This would make better than two thousand apiece and if you'll just give me your names, when I get to L.A. I'll double it. In cash, of course.'

The three crew members eyed Shellwood. The man moved forward with a confident smile. 'I'll just pick up my things now and get out of your way, officer. The girls have enough cash to get us a cab to L.A. No hard feelings, old boy.'

He stuck out his palm to shake Ben's hand. In the next instant a handcuff snapped on his wrist, he was spun around and the second cuff snapped on his other wrist behind his back.

Ben spun Shellwood back around. 'Mr Shellwood, I now further charge you with attempting to bribe three officers of the Thruway Patrol.'

Shellwood's face dissolved. 'You're making a bad mistake!' he shouted. 'You have no idea how bad a mistake you've made. You know you can't make this stick. My father is a very vengeful man. This will mean your jobs, you know that, don't you?'

Ben ignored his protestations and frisked Shellwood, removing his belt, lighter, watch and necktie. In the presence of the two other crew members, he counted the cash, then put the entire contents of the wallet and Shellwood's other possessions into a sealed plastic bag. He wrote a detailed receipt for the items and stuffed it into Shellwood's coat pocket.

'Clay,' Ben ordered, 'take Mr Shellwood forward and lock him up. Then meet me at the car and let's get this mess cleaned up.'

Ferguson took the stunned Shellwood by the arm and led him out of the dispensary and around to the front of the cruiser. The trooper palmed a panel and a door opened in the bow. Inside were two fold-up bunks, a toilet and water tap. There was no handle on the inside of the door. A single light was recessed into the ceiling next to a small covered grille. Ferguson unlocked the cuffs and shoved Shellwood into the brig and slammed the door before the man could protest or turn around.

Clay walked back to the disabled Cadillaire, where Ben was talking with the three occupants. 'Now you just stay in there, Mr Hawks, until we get this vehicle off the roadway. Then you and the ladies can leave. I'll see that you get transportation to the nearest phone. But don't get out of that car or I'll have to put you under arrest too.'

'But what about Kevin?' the man in the back seat asked.

'Mr Shellwood is under arrest,' Ben replied, 'and he'll have to remain in custody for the time being.'

'Why, that's utterly ridiculous, officer,' the woman in the front seat protested. 'You just don't arrest Kevin Shellwood like a common criminal. Why, he's a – a gentleman!'

Ben leaned down and looked intently at the woman. 'M'am,' he said quietly, 'I have no doubt that Mr Shellwood's a gentleman. But Mr Shellwood is also the gentleman who in another five seconds would have killed you like a bug squashed against a windshield.' He pointed to the barrier ahead.

The woman gasped and put her hand to her mouth, then lapsed into ashenfaced silence.

Ben walked around to the front of the car and jotted the license number on his citation pad. Before returning to the cruiser, he reached into the car and removed the car-registration tab from its rack on the dash.

Back in Beulah's cab, he got on the radio. 'Frisco Control, this is Car Five Six. Send me one wrecker and permission for three passengers to ride wrecker to nearest off-road phone. Also, I have the driver in custody on "DWI" and assorted other goodies. Where shall I take him?'

'Car Five Six, this is Frisco Control. Wrecker on the way with OK for riders. Where does your driver reside?'

Ben glanced at the license.

'One four two one Claremont Drive, Malibu Beach, California,' he replied.

'Have you checked for previous violations?' Frisco asked.

'Not yet.'

'Check it out and then report back.'

'Affirmative,' Ben replied. He slipped the driver's license from his citation pad along with the vehicle-registration tag and slotted them.

The light above the registration slot flashed green, but the light above the permit slot turned amber, indicating a previous minor violation.

Ben called back to Frisco. 'He's got a previous minor,' he reported.

'Take him on into L.A.' Frisco Control replied. 'The fog's lifting now and you can make good time down the red lane. I'll take you off the board except for a really bad mess since you're almost at the end of your patrol anyway.'

'Thanks,' Ben said with a touch of bitterness. 'If we hurry, we might get him down there and through court before we have to pull out again. This shoots any rest period for us. By the way, this guy says he's a wheel and that we can't do this to him.'

'They all say that,' the Frisco controller laughed. 'Who is he?'

'Kevin Shellwood,' Ben replied.

'Shellwood Electronics?' the controller asked.

'The old man's son,' Ben replied.

'My God,' Frisco replied, 'he really *is* somebody. You've bought yourself a bundle of trouble tonight. Lots o'luck.'

'Yeah,' Ben replied thoughtfully, 'thanks.'

▼

Ten minutes later the lights of a bulky NorCon wrecker cut down the police lane and swung to the left, guided by the flashing warning lights on Beulah. Clay watched with a grin as the two evening-gowned women and their well-lubricated escort gingerly stepped up into the hatchway of the wrecker. The wrecker's stern crane clamps swung out and locked onto the Cadillaire. The entire vehicle was lifted into the air and another magnaclamp slapped it tight against the rear of the wrecker. The vehicle swung around and headed back up the emergency lane.

Clay swung up into the cab and slid into his seat. Ben was still writing up his report. The galley door opened and Kelly came into the cab and plumped down on the jump seat between the two troopers.

Ahead, the last of the earlier accident debris had been cleaned up and traffic once again was moving along the blue. Car 911 rolled across the median and alongside Beulah. The senior trooper flicked the car-to-car radio.

'Real nice work, Ben,' he said. 'That could have been a

helluva mess if you hadn't corralled them before they hit the barrier.'

The younger Mexican trooper cut in. 'I theenk maybe you ride rodeo sometime, *amigo*,' he said, 'like, what you call it – bulldozering!'

Ben smiled. 'More like calf-roping. Well, we've got our calf thrown and tied. Trouble is that now this little calf is beginning to look more like a tiger cub.'

'So I heard,' 911's senior officer said. 'Sorry it had to be one of those, but if there's any question, we'll back you to the limit.'

Ben waved. 'Thanks. I think we'll roll it now. Will you take a look at that roadway where we stopped? I was serious when I told Frisco it might be torn up a bit. If it is, better get a surfacing crew on it tonight.'

'Right,' the other officer replied. 'We'll handle it. And thanks again.'

The other cruiser pulled away and rolled slowly to the scene of Beulah's gut-rending halt. As Clay put Beulah in motion he saw the side hatch open and one of the 911 officers start an inspection of the paving surface. Even light corrugations could cause problems to vehicles traveling in excess of 300 miles an hour.

Clay angled Car 56 back to the center police lane and again headed south. Ben completed his report and laid his clipboard down. Clay had the cruiser rolling at just over 100.

'Kick 'er in the pants, kid,' Ben said, 'but keep her in track speed.'

Clay pressed the foot feed and Beulah lunged up to 190. He eased back on the acceleration and held the car at 195, just under Code Three speed.

Kelly looked at Martin. 'What happens now, Ben?'

Ben settled back and fished out a crumpled pack of cigarettes and passed them to her. When they had lighted up, he smoked thoughtfully for a couple of moments before answering.

'We take our boy into L.A.,' he said, 'turn him over to the prosecutor and from then on it's out of our hands.'

Kelly hunched forward on the jump seat, chin in hands, and peered into the dark of the thruway.

'I hope it's that easy,' she murmured. 'I just hope it's that easy.'

They were out of the Bay area fog belt and traffic had reopened on all lanes. Beulah rambled along at a steady 195, moving faster than the white and green lane flow but still under the thundering speeds of the blue and yellow lanes to the left. The radiodometer clicked off better than three miles every minute, and at 50-mile intervals the cruiser flashed under arching crossovers that carried traffic across the police lane from green to blue and back. The radio chattered with instructions for other patrol units along the thruway. Just north of Bakersfield, Beulah rolled past another cruiser, idling along on patrol at a mere 100 miles an hour. Normally, one car never passed another without specific leap-frog orders from Control. But Car 56 was officially off the patrol board, barring major emergency. Dawn was beginning to lighten the eastern skies and already densities were building up for the work day in the sprawling metropolis of Southland. At mileage marker 3200 control shifted from San Francisco to Los Angeles. The L.A. controller came on the air at 0400 with the density reports for all thruways leading into the nation's largest city.

Kelly went back to her dispensary for another couple of hours' sleep, first stopping in the galley to put a fresh pot of coffee on the range for the two troopers.

Ben had taken over the controls and Clay pored over the patrol records, making final entries and notations for the engineering crews that would take Beulah for a checkup at the L.A. Barracks.

Suddenly the floor beneath their feet resounded to a pounding from the brig. Clay swung over and lifted the hatch that covered the grille in the ceiling of the detention cell. Kevin Shellwood peered up at them.

'Is the condemned prisoner allowed to have a final cigarette before the execution?' Shellwood asked.

Clay pulled out his pack and lighted a cigarette and then handed it down through the grille to the prisoner. 'Comfy down there?' he asked.

Shellwood dragged gratefully on the cigarette. 'Oh, it's delightful, just delightful,' he said. 'Although I can't say much for your taste in interior decorating. How about sending the hostess down to keep me company? Now that's one bit of decoration on this tub that I really approve of.'

'Sorry,' Clay quipped, 'the hostess doesn't mingle with steerage passengers. Next time, travel first class. Come to think of it, the only traveling you'll be doing from now on is as a passenger.'

He started to close the hatch. 'Wait,' Shellwood cried. 'You two still determined to take me in?'

Ben glanced down to the open hatch. 'We have no choice, Shellwood. I'm sorry.'

Shellwood shrugged. 'Oh well, have your fun now. I'll have mine when we get to your headquarters. Thanks for the cigarette. I may be able to do the same for you in a day or so.'

Clay slammed the hatch. 'I'd like to put my foot right through his smug face,' he growled. 'That kid is due for a big surprise when he shows up in court.'

'Don't let him get to you,' Ben said. 'His kind have always existed. They think that money and influence is the answer to everything and that laws are made for everyone else but themselves.

'As far as traffic laws are concerned, I guess before the thruways, a man with enough money and power could buy his way out of jams. Every state had different traffic laws and you had a thousand different enforcement agencies, from town constables to state troopers. The worst part, though, wasn't in the enforcement of the law – it was in the administration.'

'How so?' Clay inquired.

'Well, you get the same thing today off the thruways and on state highways where we have no jurisdiction,' Ben replied. 'No matter how diligent a cop is about enforcing the law, in the final analysis it's up to the judge to determine the degree of punishment. And with all kinds of pressures on local judges and each with his own interpretation of what the law means, a driver charged with reckless operation in one state could get off with a twenty-five-dollar fine and suspended sentence, but lose his license and get socked a couple of hundred bucks in the next state. And probably pull thirty days in jail.

'The same thing applies depending on who the defendant might be. A judge who is either elected to office or appointed at the pleasure of the current administration sometimes thinks twice before he throws the book at the mayor's son. But he doesn't have a bit of compunction about throwing the same book for the same charge under identical conditions at some poor slob who hauls garbage for a living.'

Even though Car 56 was officially off patrol, force of habit kept Clay's eyes flicking to the monitor screens in front of him. All lanes were filling fast, and already it was light enough to make out the shapes of the speeding passenger cars and cargo carriers. Most of the traffic now was passenger vehicles heading into the heart of the city to places of work. The big rigs did their traveling at night to hit the early morning dock loadings and there was just a scattering of trucks in the green and blue lanes.

He made an adjustment on his blue monitor to throw it into the block ahead and sat back. 'One thing I remember from the Academy,' he mused, 'was that no NorCon judge can sit in judgment if he has had less than ten years

95

of actual patrol duty. That makes real sense, when you think about it. A guy who has had to help scrape some citizen off the side of a cargo carrier has no illusions about the safety of the road when an idiot gets turned loose behind a control column.'

'That was the main purpose in setting up the NorCon courts,' Ben replied. 'We have no political allegiances to either state or country. Our appointments are for life or unless we're fired for real cause or resign.

'Also, its kinda nice to think that when you get too old to wheel one of these tin buckets around, there's a chance to move up the ladder to a quieter and better-paying slot. Not that I'll ever make it,' he added with a rueful smile.

The radiodometer clicked to 3310. They were inside the city limits of L.A. now and Ben eased back and let Beulah drop to 100 mph. Overhead, two heavy thruway air-survey jet 'copters lazed along 100 feet above the jammed thruway, watching the flow of traffic and sending a running report back to L.A. Control. Amber lights began flashing alongside the blue lanes, indicating overcrowding ahead and signaling a 50-mile-an-hour slowdown for all vehicles until the jam cleared. Barriers rose out of the crossovers to prevent more green speed cars from moving into the congested lane.

Suddenly the radio came to life. 'L.A. Control, this is Chopper Seven Seven. There's a light-over-dark-green sedan cutting back from the yellow at about marker 3340. He's going too fast.'

L.A. Control cut in. 'Car Four Twelve, this is L.A. Control. What's your location?'

'This is Four Twelve. We're at 3368.'

'Drop back and cut into the blue and stop that vehicle, Four Twelve,' L.A. Control ordered. 'Chopper Seven Seven continue to monitor.'

'That guy's gonna kill somebody,' the officer in the

aerial cruiser shouted. 'Get back fast, Four Twelve. He's cutting through traffic like a maniac.'

Ben reached down and opened the brig hatch. 'Lie down on your bunk, Shellwood,' he ordered. 'Don't argue or you'll be pasted against the bulkhead in just two seconds.'

Shellwood threw him one quick look and then leaped for the bunk.

Ben slammed the hatch and flicked his transmit switch. 'L.A. Control, this is Car Five Six. We are now at 3315. Shall we pursue?'

'Affirmative,' Control snapped back.

The bull horn blared throughout the car as Ben slammed all drives full forward. Safety cocoons snapped shut on both officers in the cab and around the reclining form of the prisoner in the brig bunk. Aft, in the dispensary, Kelly made a leap for a corner cocoon at the first note of the bull horn. With a screaming roar, Beulah's lift fans and jets thundered into action and rocketed the 250-ton police cruiser down the emergency lane.

Overhead, the two police air cruisers were hanging over the dense mass of traffic in the blue lane. 'Car Five Six, this is Chopper Four Two. Watch yourself when you come into the blue. There's no room for you at the crossover. Pick your own hole on the median.'

'Affirmative,' Ben replied. 'Where is the subject vehicle now?'

'He's at about 3355.'

'I have him on the monitor, Ben,' Clay said.

'Five Six, this is Car Four Twelve. We're coming north. Watch out for us.'

'Affirmative,' Ben called out.

'Watch out, you damned fool,' the voice of the air patrolman screamed. 'Oh my God, that does it.'

Five miles ahead of the hurtling police cruisers, a billowing ball of black smoke and red flame blossomed into the early morning sunlight as the speeder slammed into a jam of other cars. One explosion followed another in rapid succession until the entire blue lane seemed to dissolve into a blanket of fire and smoke. Ben cut power and punched the retrojets and Beulah came slamming back down onto her tracks at 200 miles an hour and then continued to lose speed.

A mile away, Car 412 came rushing into view, losing speed and turning at the same time that Ben began twisting Beulah toward the carnage on the highway.

'L.A. Control, this is Chopper Seven Seven. Get us everything you can. We've got a major fire and major injuries and fatalities. Divert all blue and yellow. Clear 'em fast.'

The two ground cruisers eased their way through the mass of halted and burning vehicles, trying to reach the heart of the holocaust. In the dispensary, Kelly unshipped the three collapsible auto-litters racked beside the rear ramp, then slipped on her work helmet and rolled her mobile field kit to the door.

Thick, oily smoke covered the entire scene, blinding the officers as they tried to probe their big car into the lane. The quiet morning air held not a breath of breeze to dispel the smoke.

'Choppers, this is Car Five Six,' Ben called. 'Can you get low enough for your fans to blow some of this smoke away?'

'We'll try,' came the answer, 'but it'll spread the flames too.'

'Foam it at the same time,' Ben answered back. 'We've got to see what we're doing.'

More explosions ripped the air and a huge chunk of metal came flying out of the smoke and slammed off the impervious hull of the police cruiser. Clay had already left his seat and was standing in a retractable fire-control turret rising out of the engine room. The cruiser's foam nozzles were already out. A smashed car blocked Beulah's way and Ben pivoted the huge cruiser to the left.

Subconsciously, he heard L.A. Control ordering cars, choppers, wreckers, fire equipment, ambulances and hospital units into the area. Three cruisers working NAT 99-North within a 50-mile radius of the disaster already had crossed the half-mile-wide divider and were racing to the scene.

Flames erupted from out of the smoke ahead of Beulah and, before Ben could give the order, Clay had the fire turret up and was laying a blanket of foam on the fire. The smoke began to billow downward and suddenly there was a clear view through the wreckage as the two police jet choppers hovered and turned their big blades on the fire.

To his right, Ben saw the other police cruiser 100 yards away, spewing foam over the burning cars and pools of jet fuel burning on the thruway. The two choppers man-euvered into position above the ground cruisers and kept blowing the fire away from the slow-moving police cars.

A figure burst out of the wall of smoke and flame ahead and ran staggeringly toward the cruisers, clothing in flames.

'Clay,' Ben yelled, 'hit him.'

In the fire-control turret, Clay slammed a valve back to minimal pressure and aimed the nozzle at the flaming figure. A thin stream of foam struck the man, knocking him down. He lay on the ground, writhing in pain. Ben brought Beulah to a halt.

'Kelly,' he roared, 'open it up. I'm going out and bring one in.'

The trooper jumped down the steps and out the side hatch of the cruiser, to be met by a roaring wall of heat. Above him, the chopper pilot kept a steady air current blowing the flames away from the car as Ben waded through the oxygen-absorbing foam to the body of the fire victim. He reached down to grab the man's body and bumped into Kelly fighting her way to his side with an auto-litter. Ben started to say something and then just heaved the body of the man onto the litter and nodded Kelly back toward the cruiser. The motor-driven litter with its radio homing device rolled through the muck to the rear ramp of the cruiser, with Kelly riding the rear bar. Ben fought his way back to Beulah under a covering canopy of foam from Clay's turret.

He slammed the door shut and scrambled back up the steps and into the control seat. Four more choppers arrived overhead and began dumping Bentonite and foam on the shards of burning wreckage. He moved Beulah ahead through the maze of smoldering and foam-covered vehicles.

'Car Five Six to Chopper Seven Seven,' he panted, 'how close are we now to the center of this mess?'

'Hard to say, Five Six,' the chopper officer answered. 'Looks like you're about a hundred yards north and a couple of hundred west. But this thing spread over into the yellow after that first impact. We've got a lot of equipment in here now. Looks like the fires should be out in another minute or two.'

'L.A. Control to Cars Five Six and Four Twelve. Hold your positions and prepare to assist ambulance and wrecker rescue operations,' came the next order. Ben acknowledged and brought Beulah to a halt again, another 100 yards closer to the heart of the disaster. The smoke had cleared to a thin haze and a quarter of a mile south of Car 412 Ben could see two other cruisers working their way toward them, squirting foam on the last wisps of fire that flickered from burning cars.

'Secure your turret, Clay,' Ben ordered, 'then let's see what we can do in this mess.'

The fire turret retracted into the hull and Clay moved up to the cab. As he was donning his helmet, Shellwood pounded on the brig hatch. Ben lifted the cover.

'What's happening, officer?' The frightened face of the prisoner peered up at him. 'I heard the explosions and then it got hot as hell down here. What's going on?'

Ben glanced at his partner. Clay nodded.

'There's been a major accident, Mr Shellwood,' Ben said. 'We've got people hurt, dead and dying all over the thruway. Both Trooper Ferguson and I will have to leave the car to assist. I don't like leaving you in there with no one to move the vehicle or protect you if anything else should happen, although I don't think it will. Now, I'll let you out of there temporarily, Mr Shellwood, if I have your word that you will not try to escape from custody. I might point out that it would be a very foolish thing for you to attempt, in light of the other charges against you, and that it would be very easy for us to find you again. Do I have your word?'

'You have it, I swear it,' Shellwood answered earnestly.

Ben nodded at the junior trooper. Ferguson slid down the steps and out the hatch. He opened the door of the brig and stood back. Shellwood stepped out and stopped dead, his face ashen as he surveyed what looked like a scene from Dante's 'Inferno.'

'Mother of God,' he gasped, 'this surely must be Hell.'

Clay took him gently by the arm and led him around to the cab entrance and helped him up the steps.

Ben was buckling his helmet chin strap. He indicated the jump seat between the two control seats. 'Sit there, Mr Shellwood, and don't touch anything or attempt to leave this cab. The only exception to this order is in the event that there should be another explosion and fire would again come close to the car. In that case, you may go back through this door,' he indicated the entrance to the galley, 'and follow the passageway back to the dispensary, where Officer Lightfoot will give you further instructions.'

Shellwood nodded and sat down, staring out through

101

the canopy bubble at the terrible scene. Ben jumped down the steps and out the hatch. Clay hesitated and then tossed Shellwood a pack of cigarettes. 'Here,' he said, 'the matches are on the arm of my seat.' He followed Martin out the hatch.

The heat, along with the smoke, had abated. Underfoot was a thick scum of foam and oil. The two officers skidded and slipped around to the rear of the cruiser.

'Kelly,' Ben called on his helmet radio, 'open up and send out the litters.'

A second later the dispensary ramp flipped open and the three auto-litters came rolling out, homing on the beacon signal in the patrolman's helmet. Kelly waved and turned back to the still form on the surgery table.

'Might as well start close and work our way out,' Ben said, indicating the nearest of the smashed and smoldering vehicles.

The two troopers plodded through the muck with the litters trailing behind. The closest vehicle was turned on its side. Clay clambered up and peered into the smoking interior. The charred bodies of two men lay huddled against the far side. Clay eased back to the ground. 'Two dead,' he said. 'None alive.'

They threaded their way around a pile of smashed pieces, kicking some out of the way to make room for the litters. Next was a tangled heap of what appeared to be two, perhaps three, cars. It was virtually impossible to distinguish the parts of one from the others. The topmost vehicle held the smashed and burned bodies of three more men. Ben squeezed between chunks of crumpled paneling to peer into the second car. The mangled body of a man was slumped over in the seat and there was another form beneath him. Ben squirmed farther into the window and reached down to tug at the body of the man. The body slid sideways to reveal a woman lying twisted and bleeding on the seat. Ben stretched and found her arm and let it trail through his fingers until he had her wrist. There was a faint pulse.

He worked his way back out and surveyed the wreckage. 'There's a woman alive in there, kid,' he said. 'Now the trick is to get her out.'

Clay turned and started back for the cruiser. 'I'll get Beulah and we'll lift that top car.'

'Never make it through this mess,' Ben said. 'Hold on.'

Overhead, the police choppers were hovering over the scene directing the stream of emergency vehicles arriving on the scene.

'Patrol Sergeant Martin to any chopper,' Ben called. 'Need an airlift immediately. We have an injured party under a pile of junk.'

'This is Chopper Nine Seven,' came the answer. 'Where are you, Martin?'

Ben pulled his flashlight from a pocket, flipped the red color shield down and aimed it in the general direction of the several hovering aircraft. One of them cut away and headed toward the two patrolmen.

'We have you in sight, Martin.'

The craft came to a halt above them, and in the same instant a magnaclamp descended on a cable. Clay scrambled to the top of the pile and grabbed the dangling clamp and guided it to one end of the smashed vehicle.

'Nine Seven to Four Four, get over here, Charlie, I need another lift on this one,' the chopper pilot radioed. Another 'copter swung toward them and a second cable and clamp came down. Clay slapped it against the opposite end of the car and then slid down off the pile.

'Haul away,' Ben called.

Both 'copters took up the slack in their cables and then with a slow increase of power, began to rise. There was the sound of metal being ripped apart and then the smashed car was swinging free, dangling beneath the two choppers.

'Set it down in the first clear spot you've got,' Ben ordered, 'and then stand by, please. We may need you again.'

Clay had jumped up onto the side of the overturned bottom vehicle and was tugging desperately at the smashed door. The two 'copters backed away to a nearby open spot on the roadway and then lowered the wrecked car to the ground. They cut their cable power and the clamps swung free as the choppers moved back over the troopers.

'I can't get this door open!' Clay yelled. He looked up at the clamp dangling over his head. 'Give me another clamp, chopper,' he called, 'then see if you can give this door a couple of jerks to swing it open. But don't pull too hard or you may drop the car on the woman.'

He secured the clamp to the smashed door panel and then backed off and grabbed a jutting piece of metal for a handhold. 'OK,' he called, 'try it.'

The winch operator on the hovering aircraft gave a tentative fast lift. The car shivered but the door remained stuck. 'Put a little slack in the cable,' Ben directed, 'and then take it up with a snap.'

The cable drooped, then suddenly snapped upward and the door ripped open and off. Clay made a dive for the opening before the cable had stopped swinging. The broken door made a slow arc and slammed the trooper in the back of the head as he started to kneel by the open door and he hurtled headfirst into the smashed vehicle. The broken door swung once more across the metallic surface of the vehicle, raising a sheet of sparks. The next instant the vehicle was enveloped in flames.

'*Foam it!*' Ben screamed to the chopper as he leaped for the burning vehicle. A torrent of foam descended from the two choppers and in the split second before the chemical blanket dropped on him, Ben caught a glimpse of a leaping figure, jumping up into the foam and toward the burning car.

The fire was out almost as quickly as it had started. Ben fought his way to the top of the car, pawing the blinding foam from his face. As he reached down to grope for Clay's form, the body of the patrolman was shoved up through the gaping door. Ben caught his partner under the arms and dragged him down from the vehicle. He laid him on one of the auto-litters and turned back to the car. The torn body of the woman was rising to meet him. A foam-covered face appeared at the opening.

'Any more?' asked Kevin Shellwood.

Ambulance crews continued to probe among the shattered pieces of vehicles spread for hundreds of yards across and up and down the blue lane and parts of the yellow. Overhead, police 'copters lifted wreckage from the roadway and deposited it in tragic heaps along the service strips bordering the police lanes. Other choppers lifted litters and swung them over to the huge hospital carriers where surgical teams worked to save the pitiful handful of survivors.

In the dispensary of Car 56, Ferguson was stretched out on one of the bunks, nursing a nasty lump on his head and a queasy gut. Kelly had flushed his stomach to clear the residue of foam that he had taken into his system before Shellwood pulled him out of the wreck.

The woman victim was pulled out after Clay had been transferred to a hospital carrier. The first victim, he of the flaming clothing, was dead. His body lay in the chill box of the same hospital carrier that had taken the woman.

Most of the debris had been cleared from the roadway behind Car 56 and Ben slid into his control seat and kicked Beulah to life. The big cruiser slowly pivoted and then rolled back toward the police lane. Ben eased the car over the rounded curbing and parked. The galley door slid open and Kevin Shellwood, dressed in a set of Clay's spare uniform coveralls, stepped into the cab.

'Feel much better after a shower and change of clothes,'

he said. He sat down on the jump seat and eyed Ben innocently. 'Got a cigarette, Sarge?'

Ben fished out a pack and the two lit up silently. The trooper studied the man for a few moments. 'That was a damned fool thing to do,' Ben said. 'I thought I ordered you to stay in this cab under any circumstances.'

'Oh, you did indeed,' Shellwood agreed amiably. 'Never did take well to orders, though. As you well know.' He paused and took a deep drag on the cigarette.

'As a matter of fact,' he continued seriously, 'I was sick unto death at what I saw. I just couldn't sit here and not do something. Not built that way. So I followed you. Good thing I did, eh?'

Ben sighed and snubbed out the cigarette. 'I can't deny that. But I'm afraid that it isn't going to do you a bit of good on your other charges.'

Shellwood smiled.

'Didn't expect it would with you, Sergeant. Once a cop, always a cop, I've heard it said. Might put in a good word for me, though. Could mean an extra candy bar on visiting days, hm'm'm?'

'I just can't seem to get it through your head that you're in serious trouble, young fellow,' Ben emphasized. 'I'll put your actions on my report, and I'll see that it's noted by the proper authorities. But I warn you that it probably won't have one bit of effect on the court's action on your other charges. Apart from that, let me say that I'm personally grateful for your assistance and I'm damned sure that Trooper Ferguson is equally grateful. But as for the rest of it, I dunno.' Ben shook his head.

Shellwood smiled good-naturedly. 'And I can't seem to get it through your head, Sergeant, that Kevin Shellwood just doesn't get into serious trouble. Hate to disillusion you and all that, but it just doesn't happen. And when we get to your bastille or wherever you're taking me, I don't want you to feel badly about what will happen then. Don't worry about me. There are things that can be accomplished that are beyond the wildest imaginations of a simple policeman.'

'Let me ask you one question,' Ben parried. 'Have you ever tangled seriously with the Thruway Authority before?'

Shellwood shook his head. 'Not seriously, Sergeant. Just that little thing about improper lane crossing. Got that minor on my tag simply because it wasn't worth quibbling about.'

Ben nodded. 'Then let me give you some of your own advice. Don't feel too badly about what does happen when we get to Los Angeles Barracks. And no hard feelings, either.'

The trooper swung around into his control seat. He glanced at Shellwood on the jump seat. 'I still have your word on remaining in custody?'

The young man nodded.

'Kelly,' Ben called on intercom, 'how's our patient?'

'A miracle has occurred, Ben,' she replied.

'You mean that door knocked some sense into him?' Ben quipped.

'There's even a limit to miracles,' Kelly said. 'Nothing could knock any sense into this dumb Canuck. No, what I meant is that for the first time in his life, his stomach is doing handsprings at the thought of food. Otherwise, he's the same wet-eared juvenile he was an hour ago.' Ben could hear some mumbling in the background that suddenly was shut off. 'Lie down, lunkhead,' he heard Kelly order, 'or I'll give you an enema.'

Ben grinned and shoved Beulah into gear. The car moved slowly into the police lane, threading its way through the parked wreckers and ambulances and hospital vehicles.

'L.A. Control, this is Car Five Six,' Ben reported, 'en route your headquarters.'

'Affirmative, Car Five Six,' L.A. Control came back, 'and thanks for the fast assist.'

'Glad we were handy,' Ben replied. 'How bad is the tally?'

'Not good,' L.A. controller replied. 'Right now it stands at 32 dead, 15 injured. We still haven't finished digging everything out. But you're clear to head home.'

Ben signed off and took a final look at the scene of the mass pileup. Television newsmen camped in 'copters, hovering around the outskirts of the area, shooting with long lenses. All traffic was shut down in both the blue and yellow lanes, and the green and white were jammed hull to hull and moving at a snail's pace past the scene of the disaster. It was now past seven in the morning and the real business rush was on. But there were going to be thousands of Angelenos late for work this morning.

As it did in San Francisco, NAT 99 soared high above and around the outskirts of Los Angeles – or, at least, what purported to be the outskirts of the metropolis that spread from the ocean eastward for 125 miles in one direction and was 85 miles across from north to south. Near the heart of the city, a ramp angled down to the right. Above it was a sign reading, LOS ANGELES BARRACKS.

Ben turned onto the ramp, and Beulah glided down in a steady spiral, passing levels of other thruways and then dropping lower to the levels of the state freeways. The ramp straightened out and then arrowed into a tunnel. Car 56 plunged into the brilliantly lighted tunnel and down into the bowels of the city. The tunnel leveled off for another mile and then climbed back up.

As suddenly as they had entered the tunnel, they emerged into a huge cavern. Other portals dotted the wall they had just come out from and police cruisers and service vehicles were moving in both directions from the portals. Above each smaller tunnel was a lighted panel designating which thruway it led to. Ben slowed Beulah to 35 miles an hour and joined the stream of police vehicles moving toward the Los Angeles Barracks parking area. Another mile and they emerged into daylight and the vast terminal of the Western Division of NorCon. Ben eased Beulah into the parking area, following the hand signals of a techmech waving him into position. The tech made a chopping motion and Ben stopped the cruiser. With a sigh, he reached over and thumbed the master switch. For the first time since leaving Fairbanks ten days earlier, Beulah's complete power plant went silent.

'How's the patient now?' Ben called out to Kelly on intercom.

'A better man than you'll ever be,' Clay answered in person as he walked into the cab. A neat surgical patch covered a small shaved spot on the back of his head.

Ben surveyed his grinning partner. 'You look OK. How do you feel?'

'Let's just say that Kelly's touch when she's ministering to your wounds is considerably lighter than when she's looking after me,' Clay replied. 'I don't see how that woman ever got to be a doctor. A vet maybe. A doctor, never.'

'In that case,' Ben said, 'I'll let you turn Beulah over to the tender care of the grease monkeys and I'll take Mr Shellwood to headquarters. See you at the BOQ in about an hour.'

Shellwood arose and Clay stuck out his hand. 'I'm sorry you're in a jam, Mr Shellwood,' Clay said, 'and I really mean that. I want you to know I'm real happy you decided to take a walk when you did.' The two men shook hands.

'Glad to be of service, Trooper,' Shellwood replied. 'Come see me on visiting days.' He glanced at Ben. 'Shall we go, Sergeant?'

Ben climbed from the bucket seat and reached into a compartment beside the instrument panel. He pulled out the plastic bag containing Shellwood's possessions. Then, leading the man by the arm, he climbed out of Car 56 and headed for Patrol Headquarters.

As Ben opened the door to the headquarters building, a battery of cameras began clicking. In the far corner of the big patrol dispatch room, TV crews aimed their portable transmitters at the door to catch the patrol sergeant and Shellwood as they entered. Ben stood aside and motioned to the younger man to enter the room. As Shellwood entered, three men in business suits stepped forward. The older of the trio was unmistakably Shellwood's father. He grasped the young man's hand.

'Kevin,' Quentin Shellwood inquired, 'are you all right? What the devil is this all about?'

'Hi, Dad,' Kevin smiled, 'I'm fine.' He turned to the other two men and nodded. 'Mr Quinn, Mr Hackmore, good to see the legal eagles on the job.'

Shellwood turned back to his father. 'I'm really fine, Dad. Just a little misunderstanding. Nothing to get excited about.'

The newsmen were crowding in, recorders and mikes thrust forward. 'Do you have a statement, Mr Shellwood?' one asked. Quinn, the older of the two attorneys, held up his hand to the newsmen.

'Mr Shellwood has no statement to make at this time,' he said. 'We'll have a prepared statement for the press in a little while.'

Ben indicated to Kevin to go to the dispatch desk, where the officer on duty was making hand signals. The dispatcher leaned across the counter.

'Captain Fisher is waiting for you in his office, Ben. He wants you and your prisoner in there immediately.'

Ben nodded and led Kevin Shellwood through the counter door toward the inner offices. The elder Shellwood and the two attorneys followed. Ben knocked on the patrol captain's door and then entered. As the five men entered the office, Fisher, wearing the street dress blue uniform of the patrol, arose from behind his desk. He leaned over and shook hands with Ben.

'Glad to see you, Sergeant, and my personal commendation for your work in that pile-up. I just got the report a few minutes ago.' The captain straightened up and his face went stony as he eyed the younger Shellwood. 'Is this your prisoner, Sergeant?' he asked coldly, surveying the blue patrol coveralls Kevin was wearing.

'Yes, sir,' Ben replied. 'Mr Shellwood rendered some valuable assistance during the disaster and, in the course of it, ruined his personal clothing. We loaned him the coveralls until he could obtain proper clothing.'

'I see,' Fisher said. 'I assume you have a full report in writing?'

Ben laid his citation book and report sheets on the captain's desk. Fisher picked up the citation and read it carefully, then read the narrative report.

'I have called you all into my office,' Fisher said when he finished reading, 'to confirm for myself the charges brought against the prisoner and to make it clear that despite any so-called social status the prisoner may have . . .'

'Just a moment, Captain,' the elder Shellwood broke in, 'my son is no common criminal and he is no prisoner, as you so grossly put it.'

Fisher glared at the father. 'Mr Shellwood, you are in my office only by my invitation and not because of any legal requirement. For your information, your son is charged with a series of crimes – and I repeat, crimes – that, according to the international statutes of the Thruway Authority, are most serious in nature.

'Your son is, and will remain, a prisoner in custody of this agency until such time as he appears before a court of proper thruway jurisdiction and is either admitted to bond, acquitted or sentenced. I hope this is quite clear.'

'How dare you speak . . .' Shellwood spluttered, his face darkening in anger.

Quinn laid a hand on the father's arm. 'Calm down, Quentin. You're only making things tougher for the boy. Now just be quiet and let us handle this.' He smiled at Fisher. 'We apologize for the interruption, Captain. Please continue.'

'As I was saying,' Fisher went on, 'despite any protestations to the contrary, the prisoner will be processed in the same manner as any other person in custody of this authority and charged in the same manner by an officer of this agency. Now if there are no further questions – Sergeant Martin, will you please take your prisoner to the detention facilities and book him?'

Quinn asked, 'May I have a moment to speak with Mr Shellwood please, Captain?'

Fisher nodded.

Quinn took Kevin by the arm and walked him to the far corner of the room, where he conversed rapidly and in a low voice with the younger man. Shellwood nodded several times and then smiled. He turned and walked back to Martin.

'Let's go, Sergeant,' he said.

Martin took Shellwood out a side door of the patrol captain's office and into a corridor leading to the detention rooms. Walking down the hall with the officer, Kevin asked, 'How soon do you think I'll get into court?'

Ben glanced at his watch. 'It's a little after nine right now, Kevin. I'd say that you probably will come in for a preliminary sometime before noon.'

'What's that mean?'

'At that time the judge can set your trial date, assuming that you plead "not guilty" and, at the same time, he can set bond if he feels you should be freed pending trial,' Ben answered.

'Is there a question of whether he will allow bond?' Kevin asked anxiously.

'Well, that's up to the judge,' Ben said. 'But just guessing that in light of the fact that there were no injuries or accident involved in your case and because of what you did later on, I'd say that he'll allow bond.'

They reached the end of the hall and Ben motioned Kevin through a door into the detention room. A patrol sergeant moved up to the booking desk. Ben laid the plastic sack with Shellwood's possessions on the counter together with a copy of the arrest report. The desk sergeant glanced at the report and then took Shellwood by the arm and led him to an upright metallic cabinet at one side of the room.

'Please stand inside the cabinet,' the officer directed, 'facing in this direction. Place your hands on the two arm rests you see at your sides and grasp the knobs.'

Satisfied that Kevin was in position, the desk sergeant punched a series of buttons. 'You can come out now,' he said a minute later. When Shellwood emerged from the cabinet, a complete body analysis had been recorded. He had been photographed, fingerprinted, retinal image recorded, bone and muscle structure detailed, dental work described and encephalic pattern graphed. All of the information had been simultaneously transmitted to Continental Headquarters Records division at Colorado Springs, to be taped into his file together with his license, violations and convictions. Kevin Shellwood had been booked.

The desk sergeant inventoried the contents of the plastic bag, gave both Ben and Shellwood receipts and then took Shellwood back through another door to the actual detention cells.

Ben headed back for the dispatcher's desk. The newsmen were still there, apparently waiting for Shellwood to re-appear. When Ben showed up without the man, they again crowded around him. 'Where's young Shellwood, Sarge?' 'Is it true he tried to bribe you?' 'How much did he offer?'

Ben held up his hand. 'Mr Shellwood has been detained in custody of the patrol until his appearance in court, probably later this morning. I'm sorry but that's all that I can tell you at this time.'

'Aw, come on, Sarge,' one of the TV newsmen called out, 'give us a break. We've been waiting since dawn. You can tell us a little more than that?'

Ben grinned at him and brushed the three chevrons on his sleeve. 'I've put in a good many years getting these stripes,' he said. 'Any discussion of any thruway violation case by an officer means automatic dismissal. Sorry, gents, I've got nothing more to add to what I've already told you.' He turned his back on the crew and signaled to the dispatcher.

The grumbling newsmen gathered up their gear and streamed out of the room in search of a new lead to the story.

A half dozen other patrol officers were checking assignments at the dispatch counter. On the wall behind the dispatcher, a mural-sized map of the western segment of the North American continent was emblazoned with lighted paths indicating the many thruways that criss-crossed the land. Varied colored lights and symbols along the thruways showed road conditions, repairs and other out-of-the-ordinary situations that would affect traffic on the roads. The outgoing patrol officers made notes on the changes in their patrol logs. On another wall was an illuminated dispatch board with car numbers, the names of the patrol crews to man those cars and their thruway assignment. Car 56 – Beulah – and her crew, wouldn't be back on the board for five days while the cruiser was given a thorough going-over by the shop crews and reserviced and resupplied. Three of the days ostensibly were for rest and relaxation for the crew before heading out on their next ten-day patrol.

One of the dispatchers came down the long counter at Ben's signal.

'Officer Ferguson is completing the cruiser report,' Ben told him, 'and he'll file our closing clearance in a few minutes. Tell him, please, that I'll be in the BOQ and also notify Medical Officer Lightfoot that I'd like to see her as soon as she is clear.'

The dispatcher nodded and Ben walked out of the building to head for the transient patrol quarters. The newsmen had vanished and only the blue coverall uniforms of patrol officers dotted the walks leading to the various buildings of the L.A. Barracks area. Ben waved at some friends and stopped to chat with two other officers before he got to the batchelor officers' quarters.

He stopped at the desk to register. The clerk assigned him to Room 218 and Ben walked up the stairs to the room. Sitting in the easy chair facing the door as Ben opened it was Hackmore, the younger of the two attorneys who had met with Shellwood at headquarters.

He smiled as Ben entered. 'Shut the door, Sergeant,' he said, 'and let's have a little talk.'

Ben stood in the doorway and eyed the man coldly. 'I don't know what you're doing here, mister,' he said quietly, 'but I have a pretty good idea what you're going to say. So I'll tell you right now – get out!'

Hackmore ignored the order. 'I'm not here on business, Sergeant, just a social call, you might say. I might add that if you think I came to talk about young Shellwood, you're wrong. I'm not the least bit concerned about that young man's future. It's yours I'm concerned with at the moment.'

Ben slowly closed the door and moved into the room. 'What about my future?' he demanded.

Hackmore took a notebook from an inner pocket and flipped it open. 'Sergeant Benjamin H. Martin,' he read, 'age, thirty-three, fifteen years on Thruway Patrol. Graduated in upper tenth of his Academy class. Promoted to sergeant four years ago. Four citations for heroism and meritorious service. Twenty-five hours completed in work toward Master's Degree in Transportation Administration. Salary, eight thousand five hundred annually. Unmarried. One sister, married, lives in Vermont. Brother-in-law is research engineer with Allied Computers. Parents dead.'

'You seem to have gone to a lot of trouble to learn all that in so short a time,' Ben said grimly. 'Why?'

'You're quite right, Sergeant,' Hackmore smiled, 'we have gone to a great deal of trouble to find out what makes you tick. In answer to your question, let's just say as I did before, we're interested in your future. It has some bright possibilities.'

Ben moved across the room until he was standing directly in front of the seated man. 'Mister,' he said levelly, 'my future has all the possibilities that my career can offer and that I'm qualified to take advantage of. Those are the only possibilities I'm interest in.'

'Oh, I wouldn't be so hasty,' Hackmore said. 'I can foresee a much brighter future for you. You are virtually a trained lawyer; you have sound education and training in mechanics and engineering, you specialize in administration and have demonstrated outstanding leadership qualities. All of these, plus several other attributes, would make you a valuable asset to any large corporation. As a matter of fact, that's exactly why I am here now.

'Our evaluation of your background shows us clearly that we would be making a grave error not to employ your professional services in one of our several subsidiary organizations. And I'm prepared at this point to offer you such a position with a starting salary of, say, twenty thousand a year for a starter. Plus a liberal expense account, of course.'

'I just told you,' Ben said, 'that the only career and only job I'm interested in is the one I currently hold. Now get out.'

Hackmore rose and stood facing the trooper. 'You realize that you're making a very unwise decision. I'll repeat the offer again and remind you that it is open immediately, but that it will only be open for,' he paused and glanced at his watch, 'the next two hours.'

Ben stood aside and pointed toward the door, the muscles in his jaw twitching in his effort to hold his temper.

Hackmore shrugged and started slowly toward the door. Halfway across the room he paused and turned back. 'Oh, by the way,' he said, 'I forgot to mention that Allied Computers is also a subsidiary of Shellwood Electronics.'

He consulted his notebook again. 'I believe your brother-in-law is still a research engineer for Allied?'

In two giant strides Ben was across the room and had Hackmore by the lapels of the man's coat. Lifting him bodily from the floor, he slammed the attorney back against the wall.

'You slimy bastard,' he snarled. 'Let me tell you something. That kid of Shellwood's has got more guts and decency than his old man and every one of his rotten "yes" men right down to the cruddy bottom of the barrel that you crawled from. The kid's in trouble, he's committed some serious offenses and he damned near killed himself and God only knows how many other people. But I think he realizes what he's done and he at least has the manhood to face up to his problem. And not all the dough that his old man could rake up can buy him out of this.

'Now as for you. If I find out that there's been so much as an eye blink in the direction of my brother-in-law or my sister, I'm personally going to find you and push your filthy mind right down into your equally cancerous guts.'

Still holding Hackmore by the coat, Ben reached for the door, flung it open and heaved the attorney out of the room with such force that he bounced off the far corridor wall. The lawyer slid to the floor just as Clay Ferguson rounded the corner. The young trooper paused for a moment and looked down at the disheveled and frightened man and then stepped carefully over his legs and turned into Martin's room.

'Company just leaving?' he inquired pleasantly.

▼

At 1130 Kevin Shellwood, flanked by the two attorneys, stood before Thruway Authority Justice James Bell. Spectators packed the austere thruway courtroom, as the news of Shellwood's arrest had been on the vidicasts for the past two hours. At the side of the bench, the court reporter sat with headset in place, riding volume controls on his taped recordings of the court proceedings. The crew of Car 56, dressed in their off-patrol dress tunics, sat beside the thruway prosecutor. An amber panel came to light over the judge's bench and the courtroom fell silent.

Justice Bell leaned forward and addressed Shellwood.

'Kevin Shellwood, you are charged with driving on North American Thruway Ninety-Nine-South in the vicinity of mile marker 3012, this date, while under the influence of alcoholic beverages. You are further charged with reckless driving, ignoring instructions of the Thruway Authority, ignoring the lawful orders of a Thruway Patrol Officer and of leaving the confines of your vehicle while on a thruway. And you are further charged with the attempted bribery of three officers of the Thruway Authority.

'At this point, I wish to advise you of your rights under this court. Although this court does not waive jurisdiction nor authority to the sovereign countries of the United States of America, the Republic of Mexico or the Commonwealth of Canada, you do not waive your constitutional rights as a citizen of the United States accused

118

in a court of law. You may be represented by counsel and may at this time enter a plea to the charges. In the event you should enter a plea of "not guilty" you are entitled to trial by jury or may waive such trial and be heard in trial by this court.

'Do you understand both the charges and your rights?'

Shellwood cleared his throat nervously and answered, 'Yes sir, I understand them.'

'Very well,' Justice Bell continued, 'how do you now plead to the charges against you?'

'If it please the court,' Quinn took a step forward, 'I represent Mr Shellwood in this matter.'

'Very well, Mr Quinn,' Bell said. 'Do you wish further time to confer with your client?'

'No, Your Honor,' Quinn replied. 'At this time, we wish to enter a motion for dismissal of the charges on the grounds of insufficient and improperly obtained evidence.'

Bell thumbed through the sheaf of papers on his bench, pausing to study one of them in detail.

'Mr Quinn,' he then said, 'I have here transcripts of all radio communications between Thruway Control points at both San Francisco and Los Angeles with Thruway Patrol Car Five Six in regard to this matter, together with transcripts of tapes recording conversations among the officers of this unit and the accused. I further have prints of video tapes taken during the conversations between these officers and the accused while in the dispensary of Patrol Car Five Six at approximately 0100 hours this date. I find them sufficient cause for action to hold the accused. Motion denied.'

Quinn flushed. 'In that case, Your Honor, we then wish to enter a plea of "not guilty" to all charges.'

Bell made notes on the papers before him. 'Very well, counselor. I assume then you will seek a jury trial?'

Quinn nodded.

'In that case,' Justice Bell said, consulting a calendar, 'I will set a trial date for three weeks from this day at 1000 hours. In view of the recommendation of the arresting officer, I will further admit the defendant to bail, although under any other circumstances I would refuse bond.'

Kevin flashed a quick smile of gratitude at Ben sitting at the prosecution table.

'I will set bond at twenty thousand dollars in cash or forty thousand property. You may post the bond immediately with the court clerk.

'Next case.'

Ben, Clay and Kelly got up quietly from the prosecution table and walked out of the courtroom just behind Kevin and his attorneys. In the corridor outside the courtroom, Clay paused and pulled out cigarettes and passed them around.

Young Shellwood was talking with his attorneys a few feet away. Hackmore nodded and then left them to enter the clerk's office. Shellwood walked over to the trio of officers.

'Thanks for the kind word, Sergeant,' he said to Ben.

'You're welcome, kid,' he said. 'I just wish you hadn't gotten yourself in such a bind.'

Kevin laughed bitterly. 'You know, strange as it may seem at this point, I wish the same thing. I'm just beginning to find out that there are some things that your old man's money and influence can't buy for you. There are some things you have to buy yourself – no matter what the cost.

'But, what the hell, it's done now. And Sergeant, remember what I told you this morning. Don't feel badly about the outcome of all of this. I'll never stand trial. You know that, don't you?'

'Oh, come off it, Kevin,' Ben exploded, 'you know damned well you will.'

Shellwood smiled and started to turn away. 'You just don't know the determination of us Shellwoods.

'Oh, and by the way, I want to sincerely apologize for your visitor this morning. I didn't learn about it until a while ago. I assure you that it will never go any further. See you around sometime.'

He waved and walked back to Quinn, and the two of them entered the court clerk's office.

Ben ground out his cigarette savagely on the floor. 'Come on,' he snarled at his crew members. 'Let's go get drunk. I need a strong mouthwash right now.'

An hour later Ben and Kelly were seated in a corner booth of a cocktail lounge. Three empty glasses were in front of Ben and much of the tension and anger had drained from him. Clay had had one fast drink with them and then pulled out a small address book and began thumbing through it rapidly.

He excused himself and went to the phones. A few minutes later he returned, reached over and drained the remainder of his drink and reached for his uniform cap. 'Got to run, you two. See you in time to roll.'

He waved the little address book at them and rolled his eyes up in mock agony.

'So much to do and so little time to do it,' he murmured as he hurried away.

Ben grinned at the departing trooper and leaned back comfortably in the deep airfoam cushions. 'That kid's been up all night, worked like a horse, been under heavy tensions for several hours, and look at him. Two gets you five he doesn't get any sleep for another twenty-four hours.'

'No bet,' Kelly replied. She leaned back and moved closer to the big trooper. 'Tired, Ben?'

He ran his hand over his head and sighed. 'I guess I am, Princess. I'm not as young as that kid, and this business is beginning to get to me. I've had some rough days since I

121

started on patrols, but God deliver me from another one like today.'

Kelly reached out and slipped her hand into his. She rolled her head to his shoulder. 'You could always ask to get off patrol, darling.'

Ben smiled down at the golden red hair resting against him and gently squeezed her hand. 'Sure I could. I could have been moved to a desk job a year ago if I had wanted to, but I'm not quite ready to be turned out to pasture just yet.'

'Oh, don't be silly,' Kelly retorted, sitting up and facing him. 'Of course you're not getting old. It's just that patrol takes so much out of a person that the human body and mind can only stand so much of it. Then something's got to give.'

'What about you?' Ben inquired. 'You've been riding the back end of these armored hearses for three years now and you get far more of the misery and pain than we do, right along with the rest of the dangers that go with the patrol. When are you going to quit?'

Kelly looked up into the bronzed face of the patrol sergeant. 'I'll quit when you do,' she said softly.

He studied her fine-boned face. His big hand came up and with tender touch, he lightly traced the lines of her cheeks and mouth. 'You really mean that, don't you, Kelly?' She nodded mutely.

Ben let his head sink back against the cushions and punched the autobar for another drink.

'Look, baby,' he explained, 'another year, maybe, and then I'll be ready to turn in my work helmet for a voca-writer. But right now, with the patrol expanding and the new designs in cars and engines that the industry is turning out, we're too short-handed as it is on experienced patrol officers.

'Right now the thruways are designed to handle traffic up to five hundred miles an hour. But already the new reaction

122

engines can push well past the six hundred mark without straining and will probably go to eight hundred under stress. We've got to make modifications in both roadway design and patrol equipment. On top of that, consider how we're set up right now. We've got the thruways with their four speed lanes. But how many drivers – especially those buying the new and hotter models – are satisfied any longer with drifting along in the white lane limits? Or even in the green? The bulk of the traffic is shifting to the blue and yellow and even the cargo carriers are hotter and are moving into the blue.

'The system has got to be modified and that just doesn't mean raising the speed limits in all lanes. The roadways themselves have to be redesigned for the higher speeds. And there are more ground vehicles using the thruways every day as the speeds increase. Air travel is picking up, but the average man still can't afford to buy or fly an aircar, chopper or jet for the entire family when for a tenth of the cost he can get the same space, and even speed, in a ground vehicle.

'We need more patrolmen, faster and better equipment – and the experienced officers to train them and work with them until they're ready to take over a cruiser by themselves. Clay is almost ready. Don't tell him this, but this is his last year on junior status. I hate to lose him, but I'm recommending him for his own car at the end of this tour. So you see, I just can't walk out of the cruiser and say "Chief, I've had it. Put me on a desk." I'm still needed where I am, at least for another year or so. Then we'll see what the shuffle turns up.'

He took a long drag on his drink and looked at Kelly. 'You understand, don't you Princess?'

Kelly sat with her head down, her face concealed. Without looking at Ben, she began talking.

'Ben,' she said, 'at the risk of losing all of my maidenly virtues, I want to ask you a direct question and I want a direct and honest answer.' She hesitated and then blurted out, 'Are you in love with me?'

Ben put down his glass and took her chin in his hand and raised her face.

'I love you more than anything in this world, Princess,' he said. Blissfully ignoring anyone who might have been watching, their lips met in a long and loving kiss.

Kelly finally sat back with a happy, glazed look on her face. Neither of them spoke for several minutes. Then the girl shook her head and smiled delightedly. 'Now that that's settled,' she said, 'a girl can settle down and do some planning.'

She leaned over and kissed him again.

▼

On the morning of their fifth day in Los Angeles, Ben Martin and Clay Ferguson were again standing in front of the dispatcher's counter in the barracks headquarters. On the assignment board was the illuminated line reading, 'Car 56 – Martin – Ferguson – Lightfoot.' In the next column was the assignment: 'NAT 70-E.'

Both officers had their log sheets out to make notes as the dispatcher punched up the mural map and NAT 70-E on the big board.

'This is a milk run for you guys this time,' the dispatcher said. 'Since you've got this court hearing coming up in a little more than a couple of weeks you don't get a full run. You get Seventy-E to Oklahoma City, a three-day layover and then right back here on Seventy-W.'

He picked up an electric pointer and began picking out salient trouble points on the route. There were very few discrepancy symbols on 70-E. He flicked the light at a stretch of the roadway just east of the Arizona state line.

'We've got crews working in the yellow on the outside rim just south of Kingman on the big curve.' He moved the light eastward. 'Gallup has been reporting some bad storms with lowered visibility between there and Albuquerque. Other than that, she's green all the way.'

The troopers picked up their clipboards and with helmets slung over their arms, headed out to the parking area where Kelly was already aboard Beulah and checking her supply inventory.

A half hour later Car 56 rolled off the line and down the incline to the thruway entrances. Clay at the controls angled Beulah toward the portal marked '70-E' and 10 minutes later the cruiser burst out into the bright sunlight and heavy traffic of the eastbound national thruway.

The patrol quickly settled down into almost humdrum existence. The weather was clear, and once beyond the sprawling limits of Los Angeles, the traffic thinned out to a mere 18,000 vehicles per 100-mile block. Ben took the first watch while Clay caught up on some sleep missed during the Los Angeles layover. Six hours and as many hundred miles later, they switched. Traffic was light enough for them to pull off to the service strip and stop for a leisurely dinner in the tiny galley.

As predicted, the winds blew and the sand flew as Beulah rolled across the wintry desert east of Gallup. Caution lights were flashing in all lanes, and Albuquerque Control had closed the yellow from Gallup to Grants. Visibility in the blowing dust dropped to less than a half mile, but the only trouble came when a huge cargo carrier tried to get out of the blue and missed a crossover. Car 56 rolling along slowly at fifty, came up on the unsuspecting carrier gingerly feeling its way down the dead center of the police emergency lane. Ben pulled Beulah alongside the carrier and flashed his red lights.

The cargo driver brought his vehicle to a halt. Ben turned the radio to standard all-vehicle frequency. 'You're lost, Mac,' he said good-naturedly. 'I hate to tell you this, but you're right in the middle of the red.' Both officers laughed at the gasp of stunned disbelief on the face of the trucker. They waved to him and grinned and he returned the wave. 'Follow us,' Ben instructed him, 'and we'll both see if we can find the edge of this road.'

With the cargo carrier close behind, Beulah eased over to the right-hand curb of the police lane until Ben found a crossover. He hit his tail lights in rapid succession and aimed a side spotlight to indicate the ramp. The trucker blasted his horn in thanks as he turned off the police lane into the green.

Ben moved Beulah out and the patrol continued.

Beyond Albuquerque, the dust and sand subsided. The great thruway arrowed mile after unchanging mile across the heart of the Southwest. Video monitor camera towers flashed by every 10 miles, a turret-like patrol checkpoint looming up from the side of the police lane every hundred miles. Beyond the outer and inner lanes were the winter-green, reclaimed wastelands of what had once been sage-brush and mesquite desert. Huge 200-inch plastisteel pipes crisscrossed the land, bringing desalined sea water from the oceans hundreds of miles away. Nuclear-reactor relay pumping stations sent the great torrents of life-giving waters surging across mountains and valleys to spill onto the mineral-rich sandy loam of the desert and turn it into the new salad bowl of the continent.

Five days out of L.A., Car 56 rolled down the patrol ramps and into Oklahoma City Barracks and a brief layover before the return trip. As the trio walked away from Beulah, service crews were already swarming over the big cruiser for a fast checkout and refueling.

'Man, what a pleasure jaunt that was,' Clay exclaimed happily. 'First time since I've been aboard that bucket I ever really had time to get more than a half decent catnap.'

'It was a milk run, wasn't it?' Kelly said, walking

between the two tall troopers. She smiled up at Ben and winked. 'Didn't seem like the sort of patrol that calls for very much experience, Sergeant.'

Ben smiled. 'Just the lull before the storm, kitten. You don't get many like this one. Enjoy it while you can.'

They checked into the dispatch office, cleared the log and were assigned quarters. Clay fished in his pocket for his address book. He flipped the pages and then headed for the phones. 'See you two Wednesday,' he called.

'Oh no,' Kelly moaned. 'Not in Oklahoma City too?'

'Oh, it's not what you think,' Clay called back. 'There's this nice old lady I met in San Francisco. I promised her that if I ever got into Oklahoma City I'd call up her niece and drop in and then report back to the little old lady whether her niece had grown up any since the last time she saw her. Just my bounden duty, you know.' He strode off to the phones.

Thursday morning Car 56 rolled back out of Oklahoma City Barracks, this time on 70-West, once again en route to Los Angeles. Clay slumped in his seat.

Ben looked over at him. 'Had the nice little old lady's niece grown any?' he asked.

Clay sighed happily. 'Full grown, dad. Full grown.'

Shortly after the cruiser hit the outer thruway, Oklahoma City Control was on the air.

'Oak City Control to Car Five Six.'

Ben acknowledged.

'Car Five Six, dispatcher says he had a telegram for you and forgot to deliver it before you got away. Sorry,' the controller said.

'Who's it addressed to?' Ben said.

'To "Patrol Sergeant Ben Martin."'

'Go ahead and open it, please,' Ben said, 'and read it to me. This is Martin.'

'Affirmative,' Oak City said. 'Message follows: "Original offer remains open for another forty-eight

127

hours. Additionally directed to offer post of Director of Transportation. Salary unlimited. Please contact me in Los Angeles."'

'Is that all?' Ben asked.

'Yep. It's signed, "Marvin Hughes, Personnel Director, Shellwood Electronics."'

Ben signed off and looked at his partner. Kelly had come up into the cab in time to hear the message.

'Ben,' she said, 'I'm scared of them.'

'The bastards didn't get the message,' Ben said grimly. 'I guess I'll have to spell it out for them, this time more emphatically.'

The weather continued to hold cold and dry all through Texas and New Mexico and even the winds had died away. Car 56 rolled slowly westward, pausing once to give assistance to a disabled cargo carrier. Once again it was an uneventful trip, with Kelly catching up on her medical journals and Ben and Clay taking easy six-hour tricks in the cab and time for letter writing and study of the thick blue manuals each officer had to absorb before promotions came.

A storm was gathering in the west when Beulah rolled into the outskirts of Flagstaff. It was close to 1700 hours of the third day out of Oklahoma City. The traffic was light and Ben gave the word to pull up for dinner. He pulled Beulah off onto the service strip between the police and green lane and then reached for the radio. 'Flag Control, this is Car Five Six. We are out to dinner in your fair city. Don't call us, we'll call you.'

'Right, Five Six,' Flagstaff Control came back. 'We'll send out the keys to the city and a bottle of dago red. Report in when you're back in service.'

With speakers mounted throughout Beulah's compartments and storerooms, control operators could reach the crew at any moment of the day or night wherever they might be in the vehicle.

Ben slid out of his seat and headed for the galley.

Dinner over, Kelly shoveled the dishes into the disposal unit and generally tidied up in the galley. Clay and Ben climbed back into their bucket seats and Ben reported Beulah ready to roll. Although it was still just a little after 1800 hours, the skies were fast darkening under the great mass of thunderheads and rain clouds moving closer from the west.

'Looks like we'll get rain,' Clay commented.

Ben shoved Beulah into gear. 'Water's always welcome out here, piped or natural.'

Car 56 rolled back onto the police lane and continued westward. Fifteen minutes later, the first great drops of rain splattered against the cab bubble and a minute later they were deep inside a downpour. Ben switched on the headlights and wipers as the rain thundered down. He pushed the speed up to 100 and the rain beaded off the rounded bubble. Traffic was increasing in both the green and blue while an occasional car flashed by in the yellow, its headlight whipping up from behind in the rain and then winking out suddenly as it passed the cruiser a mile to the south.

At 1900 hours Flag Control came on with the hourly density reports and weather picture. The storm, which had been moving eastward, was now stationary, and the forecasters were calling for it to shift back to the west once again. Thruway predictions were for rain to the Arizona line just east of Needles.

Beulah rolled around the edge of Kingman shortly after 2100 hours and suddenly the radio sounded.

'Car Five Six, this is Flag Control. Just a few minutes ago Ash Fork Checkpoint reported a red-and-white Travelaire moving west in the yellow at maximum speed. In this kind of weather and with the repairs on the yellow west of Kingman on the grade, you might see if you can spot this joker before he gets into trouble. This might also be the same vehicle reported stolen from this city about two hours ago and believed to have been taken by a teenager. If it is and it's the same kid, we've had trouble with him before. He likes nothing but speed. And he may have a girl friend with him.'

'Car Five Six affirmative,' Ben replied. 'We'll start looking for them right now.'

The senior trooper swung Beulah south and into a crossover to the blue lane. He increased speed to 300, and the safety cocoons snapped shut. Beulah's warning siren cleared the way for her as Ben tooled diagonally across the blue and into the yellow. Clay had his eyes fixed on the monitors. Using his arm panel controls, he kept the yellow monitor switching across its three positions from the 10-mile block to the rear, to the block the cruiser was in and then to the block ahead.

Just as Ben straightened the cruiser out in the yellow Clay said tersely, 'There he is. He's way ahead.'

His monitor was in the block ahead of them and Ben shifted his monitor to the same block. The red-and-white car was whipping through the blinding rain at better than 500 miles an hour.

He slammed Beulah into high and the mighty jets mashed the crew back against their seats as the cruiser accelerated. Kelly was safely enfolded in her station cocoon in the dispensary.

Only three cars were ahead of the cruiser as it flew on its airpad down the half-mile-wide, rain-slick roadway.

'We'll never catch him before he hits the curve, Ben,' Clay exclaimed. 'He's wide open and wheeling.'

Ben glanced at the tachometer. Beulah was fast reaching the 600-mile-an-hour mark and gaining. 'We're closing up.' He flicked on the standard all-vehicle transmitter.

'This is a Thruway Patrol car. The driver of the red-and-white Travelaire now west of Kingman on NAT seventy-W

130

in the yellow is directed to stop immediately. I repeat, driver of the red-and-white Travelaire in the yellow west of Kingman, you are directed to stop immediately. This is a Thruway Patrol order.'

'Ben,' Clay cried, 'he's almost into the curve. He'll never clear it at that speed. They haven't got the bank into the road yet.'

On the monitor screens the red-and-white car went hurtling into the curve at better than 500 miles an hour. The curve down the long Kingman grade was gentle but never intended for such speeds. As the two horrified officers watched on their screens, the light sportster began slewing sideways to the left, toward the outside of the curve.

The driver obviously was fighting to straighten out with short additional bursts of power, but the combination of the centrifugal force on the light car and the wet roadway and lack of surface adhesion on air drive made it impossible. The car's left jet burst into a blaze of flame as the driver kicked the full afterburner into action in a last desperate attempt to hold the vehicle on the road. Almost in slow motion on the monitor screens, the car went whipping sideways against the guardrail, hurtled up into the air and rolled over several times in midair before vanishing from sight down the side of the mountain.

Ben was already slowing Beulah while Clay took over the radio. 'Flag Control, this is Car Five Six. Our red-and-white Travelaire has just taken the rail at the Kingman curve, marker 2480. He's down the side of the hill. Get us a chopper on the double.'

'This is Flag Control. Chopper en route, Five Six, also ambulance and wrecker.'

Ben fought Beulah to a halt beside the smashed railing. Rain was still pouring down. He nosed the cruiser to the edge of the road and aimed a big flexible spotlight down the side of the hill, moving the beam back and forth. It came to rest on the shattered hulk of the car, several hundred feet down the rugged mountainside.

'Let's go,' Ben said quietly. 'Kelly,' he called on the intercom, 'get on your rain suit and your kit bag, although I don't think we'll need it. Clay, you work the winch.'

He slipped on his helmet and climbed down into the rain. Kelly came up wheeling the mobile aid kit. Ben opened a panel in the cruiser's nose and pulled out the end of a cable and magnaclamp. From another side of the compartment came a wide plastic web safety belt and a pair of harnesses. Wordlessly he and Kelly slipped into the straps and then hooked the medical kit to the belt. With the belt and harnesses secured to the cable, he gave Clay the order to lower, and the cable began to pay out down the side of the cliff. Ben kept an arm around Kelly as they backed down the almost vertical face of the slope, picking their way among the rocks and brush.

A hundred feet down, they reached the body of a young girl. Ben flashed his light on her head and quickly turned it away. 'Keep going down,' he said softly into his helmet mike.

Just short of 300 feet of cable were out when they reached the wrecked car. Ben called to Clay to hold them there and they inched their way to the car. It was wedged upright between two boulders. Ben turned his light inside. The driver was smashed down against the seat, his face turned to the night sky, and rain was pouring over his slack bleeding features.

Blood bubbled from his lips with his shallow breathing.

'Merciful God,' Ben gasped. 'He's still alive.'

Kelly was already shoving Ben aside and pushing her kit onto the seat. She whipped out a hypogun and pushed it gently against the youth's bared chest. 'Give me your light,' she snapped, 'and get that damned chopper here in a hurry with a litter.'

Ben leaned back out into the rain-swept night and eyed the sky. Only the lights of the cruiser were visible.

'Clay,' he called over the helmet radio, 'find out where that chopper is.'

A new voice broke in. 'This is Chopper One One Five. I'm about at marker 2475 Car Five Six and I have your lights in sight. Our litter is ready to go. Where is the victim?'

Now Ben could hear the roar of the chopper's jets in the night and its huge spotlight loomed out of the rain. He unclipped his smaller handlight from his belt and aimed its red beam at the approaching aircraft.

'Got you, Five Six,' the chopper pilot called.

The craft came rushing in, stopped and hovered outboard of the cruiser but not dropping lower into the gorge. 'We'll have to make the lift from here,' the chopper pilot called out. 'Too turbulent and too dark to take a chance on the side of the hill. Litter coming down.'

From the bottom hatch of the chopper the litter dropped swiftly on its cable, two small flashing lights winking at the front and back to mark it against the dark sky. It came to rest a few feet from Ben, and he reached out and pulled it toward him. 'Slack off,' he ordered.

Kelly had squeezed into the blood-smeared interior of the car and was working her arms around the boy's thighs. 'Get his shoulders, Ben,' she ordered, 'and let's get him out of here. He's in deep shock and his chest is crushed.'

The officer and the girl worked the inert form out of the wreckage and onto the litter. Ben pulled the plastic cover over the litter. 'Take him up,' he called. 'And then lower the litter back for a DOA. Clay, stand by to haul Kelly up.'

Kelly had closed her kit and hooked back onto the cruiser cable. Ben gave the word and the cable began hauling her back up the muddy, rocky slope.

The instant she was back on the edge of the road, Kelly slipped out of her harness and went racing back to the ramp where the litter hovered a few feet off the ground.

She snapped the wheels down from the side of the litter and, on command, the chopper lowered the litter to the ground. Seconds later it was up the ramp, into the dispensary and beside the surgery table.

The chopper hauled up the cable, affixed another litter and lowered it back down to where Ben was waiting. The senior officer caught hold of the basket and told the pilot to haul up slowly. When he came to the level where the dead girl lay, the litter was halted and Ben gently lifted the shattered form onto the litter.

'Take it up,' Ben called. 'I'll be hanging on for a hand up this slope.'

Inside the cruiser, Clay had come running through the car and strode into the dispensary as Kelly was wheeling the diagnostican into position.

'Let's get him on the table,' she ordered. She and the trooper lifted the unconscious youth from the litter to the table and Kelly slipped a plasma needle into a vein even before attaching the big machine. She sprayed another dose of heart stimulant into the boy and turned to the diagnostican.

The boy's eyes flickered open. He stared dully at the white ceiling of the dispensary, his eyes unfocused.

'Kelly,' Clay said, 'he's conscious.'

The medical officer whipped around and reached for the boy's pulse. She stared at his eyes and rolled the lids back, then quickly began making the diagnostic attachments. Minutes ticked by as the machine analyzed the damage. Kelly had slapped gobs of Regen jelly into the superficial wounds that showed while the machine continued its diagnosis. A green light came on when the diagnosis was completed and the last of the taped data spilled from an orifice.

The boy's eyes had closed and his breathing became more labored. Outside, a patrol ambulance came roaring to a halt, and a team of medical technicians came running into the cruiser dispensary. Wet, muddy and blood-splattered, Ben followed them into the car. While Kelly was reading the tapes, the techs were unlocking the table from the dispensary floor to wheel it out and into the ambulance.

Kelly glanced at the last few readings on the tape and leaned over and rolled the boy's head gently to one side. A stream of blood spilled down his neck from his ear.

She looked up at Ben and shook her head.

The medtechs wheeled the table and its still form out into the red glare of the ambulance's' warning lights.

The crew of Car 56 watched the table vanish into the other vehicle. Red sheets of rain splattered off the hull of the vehicles and the wet roadway.

'You can't win 'em all, but damn it,' Ben swore softly, 'why can't we win the ones with the kids in them?'

A moment later, the medtechs came racing back with a new surgery table for the patrol car. They rolled it up the ramp and Kelly grabbed it and waved. With Clay's help, she shoved it into the deck clamps, and the medtechs ran back for their own vehicle. Seconds later, the ambulance with the dying boy and the body of the girl was hurtling back down the police lane towards Ash Fork.

Ben recovered the cable and winch panel in Beulah's bow and then headed into the cruiser to the men's quarters to clean up and change into dry uniform coveralls.

The wrecker had arrived and the shattered hulk of the sports car had been hauled up the face of the slope. The crews were installing warning lights and temporary barriers along the smashed railing.

Ben got Flagstaff on the radio. 'Better keep the yellow closed until this storm moves and at least for the rest of the night,' he suggested. 'You might lose another one over the side in the dark. Stand by for registration check.'

Clay had removed the registration tab from the wrecked

car and was back in the cab. He handed the tab to Ben and then checked with Kelly to see if she was ready to roll. 'Go ahead,' the girl replied. 'I'm just cleaning up back here. But give me a couple of seconds' warning in case we have to go Code Three in the next few minutes. I've got some of my equipment unracked.'

Beulah rumbled across the Colorado River causeway shortly before two in the morning and the control shifted back to Los Angeles. At six in the morning, Car 56 jockeyed into a parking slot in the Los Angeles Barracks motor pool and the completion of the ten-day patrol. The two troopers spent a half hour with the maintenance crew chief going over a number of minor discrepancies in Beulah's operation.

'You might as well give her a real going-over,' Ben told the mechanic. 'God only knows how long we're going to be tied up here in L.A. I know it's going to be at least six more days and it could run twice that long. She's due for blade rebalancing in another four hundred hours, so I'd just as soon get that done now and get new throat liners installed at the same time.'

'While you're at it,' Clay added, 'we can use either a repolishing job on the cab bubble or a new bubble. That sandstorm scratched and pitted the hell out of the canopy and we're getting halation and streaking at night.'

The crew chief made notes and then began unlocking outside inspection ports for the start of the routine vehicle inspection. Ben and Clay collected their gear and headed for the dispatch desk. Kelly had already left the car to report to the medical section with her tapes and reports and would meet them later.

At the dispatch desk, Ben shoved the closed log across the counter to the corporal on duty. The dispatcher glanced at the car number on the log book and then punched Car 56 off the ready board. He turned and reached into a cubbyhole behind the desk and extracted a memo sheet.

'You and your crew are to report immediately to Captain Fisher,' he told Ben. He shoved the memo across the counter. Ben nodded and motioned to Clay.

'Will you call over to medical section and inform Officer Lightfoot to meet us here?' Ben asked the corporal.

'She's already been notified,' the man said, 'and she's on the way over here. Go on into the Old Man's office and I'll send her in when she arrives.'

Ben and Clay headed for Fisher's office.

▼

'We've had so-called VIP's on the docket before,' Fisher said, 'but never of the political and economic influence of the Shellwoods.'

He paused and studied the faces of the three crew members of Car 56 sitting across the desk from him.

'Since you left here ten days ago,' the captain continued, 'we've felt the start of the most vicious attack on the Thruway Authority since it was created. Old man Shellwood has unleashed every one of his hounds on us in an effort to save that kid of his from jail. And this is only the beginning. Before we get through the trial, not only the authority but the three of you are going to be subjected to the toughest fight you've ever been involved in.

'Just for a starter, Shellwood's attorneys are entering countersuit charging false arrest, brutality, usurpation of authority and cruelty in subjecting Junior to the perils of disaster in the pile-up that you handled while you had him in custody.'

Fisher got up from his desk and went to a window that looked out on the huge motor-pool area of L.A. Barracks. Scores of the sleek and massive blue thruway cruisers were parked on the line while service crews swarmed over them. He continued his monologue with his back to Beulah's crew.

'We've worked like dogs to build this agency up for the sake of the people,' Fisher murmured, 'and now one lousy individual is trying to tear it down for his own personal gain.

'When you leave here, you three are to report to the prosecutor's office. He wants to go over all of the arrest reports and the rest of the material that he'll be using when we go into court next Monday. I've gone over all of the tapes and your written reports and I'm satisfied that you acted not only with proper authority but with the degree of propriety that I expect of every thruway crew. But that may not be enough. There's more at stake here than a simple case of drunk-driving charges against an individual.'

Fisher turned to face them.

'Nobody loves a cop,' he said grimly. 'I don't have to tell you that. Everybody wants one in a damned big hurry when theirs tails are in the wringer, but for the rest of the time, we're just a bunch of bastards trying to persecute innocent people when we apply preventive measures before they kill themselves. There's been a lot of talk in Congress about the federal appropriations for Thruway Authority and about the abrogation of American constitutional rights to the authority. As usual, the people want to have their cake and eat it too. They knew they could never have had the road system that the thruways have given them on either a state or national financial basis and that the only way it could be realized was through a continental sharing of the costs among the three nations. Well, they've got the roads and now they want to pull out and stop sharing the cost of keeping themselves alive. And Shellwood's outfit is using every bit of anti-thruway feeling possible against us.'

The captain slammed his clenched fist against his desk. 'That son-of-a-bitch would kill off half the population of this continent if he thought it would keep his kid out of jail.'

Ben slumped in his chair, glumly surveying the mosaic pattern of the floor. 'What's it take to stop him?' he asked without looking up.

'Huh,' Fisher snorted, 'that's simple. We drop the charges against the kid and the old man grins and goes about his business. And he'll keep grinning until the kid goes out on the roads again and kills himself and probably some other people, too. Then the old man will scream for our scalps for not protecting his innocent child from the horrors of the thruway. But the point is that if he wins this one, it can destroy much of what we've worked like dogs to create. Our biggest gun in the fight to keep people alive on the thruways has been that the law is bigger than any one person or group of persons and that all violators are treated equally in the courts and on the roads. They know that their basic protection lies in the fact that major violators are barred from the thruways for life through impartial justice by our courts. Let there be a break in that faith and the entire system is weakened.

'Well, enough of this. You three are now on detail to the prosecutor's office until the completion of this matter. Keep me posted on what's happening.'

The trio saluted and left Fisher's office. At the prosecutor's office, Kelly and Clay were asked to wait in the anteroom while Ben was ushered into the inner office.

The thruway prosecutor was in his middle fifties, slightly balding and beginning to run to paunch. He came around the desk as Ben entered. 'I'm John Harvey, Sergeant,' he said with a smile, his hand extended. 'Welcome to the siege of Troy.'

He waved at a chair and Ben sat down. Harvey shoved a cigarette box across the desk and then reached for a thick file of papers and microtapes.

'I'm going to level with you, Martin,' Harvey said, tapping the pile of evidence. 'This is going to be a nasty one. I've set this interview up so that I can talk to each one

139

of you individually and then check each of your stories against the other and then each and all against the reports and tapes. Now don't get me wrong. I haven't the least doubt in my mind that you all have acted in the best possible manner. But if there are any minor technical discrepancies, I want to know about them and be ready to counter them before that battery of defense lawyers has a chance to nail you to the cross.

'Now let's start at the beginning and tell me the entire story as it occurred.' Harvey leaned back and lighted a cigarette and Ben began talking.

While Ben was relating the events of Kevin Shellwood's arrest and the subsequent events, Harvey made occasional notes. When Ben had finished, Harvey leaned forward.

'Is that the entire story?'

Ben hesitated, thoughtful. 'As far as the actual arrest and the details of the patrol, that's the story.'

'What's that mean?' Harvey queried.

'There have been a couple of things that may have bearing on the case that have occurred since we first pulled into L.A. with Shellwood.'

'Such as what?' Harvey asked with a raised eyebrow.

Ben related the visit to his room by Shellwood's attorney before the preliminary hearing.

'. . . and when I got through telling him off,' Ben finished, 'I threw the bastard out into the hall.'

Harvey leaned forward excitedly. 'Was there anyone else present while he was making the proposition?'

'No,' Ben replied. 'Officer Ferguson arrived just as I tossed the guy out into the hall, but I don't think he heard any of the conversation.'

Harvey sat back, disappointed. 'I really didn't expect anyone else to be there,' he said. 'Those people are too smart for that. You know, if we could prove any bribery attempt by either old man Shellwood or his attorneys, we could bring them to trial too. But that's too much to hope for.'

The two men smoked in silence for a moment. 'You said that there were a couple of things that might have bearing,' Harvey said. 'What's the other thing?'

'I got a telegram from Shellwood Electronics,' Ben replied, 'raising the ante and keeping the offer open.'

Harvey snapped upright in his chair. 'Where is the wire?'

'I don't have the actual wire,' Ben explained. 'It was relayed to me from Oklahoma City Control. The dispatcher forgot to deliver it before we pulled out and I had them open it and read it to me on the air.'

'By God,' Harvey exclaimed, 'that might be the answer to a tired old prosecutor's prayer.' He grabbed his desk communicator. 'Ruth,' he said to his secretary, 'get Oklahoma City Control headquarters right away and have them get hold of the original copy of a telegram addressed to Patrol Sergeant Ben Martin.' Harvey paused and looked up at Ben. 'What date was that sent to you?'

Ben told him.

'That was on the fifteenth, Ruth,' Harvey continued. 'Tell them I want that original, together with their log of the transmission to Car Five Six concerning that telegram and their sealed tape recordings of the transmissions on the next jet for L.A. Tell 'em I want the entire package here no later than 1300 hours this afternoon.'

Harvey sat back and smiled at Ben. 'I think somebody goofed,' he said happily. 'I'll give you ten-to-one odds that the wire was never supposed to have been sent. What probably happened is that Shellwood's lawyers had a contract and binding papers drawn up and given to the personnel section and then were going to contact you in person but without witnesses after you got back here to Los Angeles. Probably some overzealous apple-polisher in the personnel section, like the personnel manager, has taken it upon himself to get hold of you in hopes of currying the old man's favor. And if this is the case – and I'm almost positive it is – we have a chance.

'Now, how was that wire worded?'

'As nearly as I can remember,' Ben said, 'it said in effect that the original offer is still open for forty-eight hours and that they'd make me director of transportation with an unlimited salary. And I was to contact the personnel manager when I got here.'

'Fine,' Harvey said, 'just great. Get on the horn and call the guy right now and make an appointment. You are about to become the new Director of Transportation for Shellwood Electronics.'

Ben stared at the chubby lawyer. 'Are you out of your mind, sir?'

Harvey shook his head. 'I've never been more serious in my life. You're going to go down there and dicker with these people before their lawyers have a chance to realize what's happening. And you're not only going to dicker over your job – you're going to get plush offers for the other two members of your crew. After all, even with you out of the picture, we could still have a pretty good case against Shellwood with them on the stand. You've got to make the company see that and make them come up with a good offer. Then all three of you are going to take the jobs.'

'But that means resigning from the patrol,' Ben protested.

'It sure does,' Harvey said. 'I'll see that the papers for your resignation and discharges are drawn up right away. Now let's get the rest of that crew of yours in here. We've got some planning to do and not much time to do it.'

He barked into his intercom. 'Ruth, send in the other two officers and get in here with your vocawriter.'

When the crew of Car 56 was assembled in Harvey's office and when his secretary had adjusted her vocawriter mask, the prosecutor began outlining his ideas.

'Now if this works,' he said, 'by early afternoon you three should be discharged from the patrol and well on your way to becoming employees of Shellwood Electronics.'

'Now wait a minute,' Ben growled, 'I have no . . .'

'Shut up, Sergeant,' Harvey snapped, 'and don't interrupt me until I get through. Then you can talk.

'As I was saying. You three should all get pretty good offers. But they may be predicated on your full discharges from the patrol and they'll want to see physical proof of such discharges. We'll have them for the company to see.

'Ruthie, see that the paperwork is done within an hour on the discharges of Patrol Sergeant Benjamin Martin, Patrolman Clay Ferguson and Medical Officer Kelly Lightfoot. Also, draft up simple letters of resignation for their signatures. You know the wording, "for personal reasons, et cetera."

'When you get those done, have one of the other girls working on three arrest warrants. The usual forms. The charges will be identical for all three. Coercion and conspiracy to coerce and bribe and otherwise intimidate duly authorized officers of the Thruway Authority. The warrants and the charges are to be drawn up for the arrest of Quentin Shellwood, Paul Quinn and Theodore Hackmore. Have them ready for my signature before noon and I'll have the tongues ripped out of the heads of anyone in this office that lets one peep of this out until the warrants are served.'

Harvey paused and looked at the trio of patrol officers sitting with dazed smiles on their faces. 'Starting to get the picture now?' he asked. Ben nodded silently.

'That'll do for now, Ruthie. When you get back to your desk, get me the commissioner on the horn.' The secretary left the room.

'Now here's a list of a few gadgets I want you people to draw from the investigation section,' Harvey said, jotting information on a pad. 'You'll need it when you talk about your new jobs in a little while.'

▼

'Who may I say is calling, please?' the receptionist asked.

'Tell Mr Hughes that Ben Martin wants to talk with him. Tell him he sent me a wire in Oklahoma City a couple of days ago, just in case my name doesn't ring a bell with him.'

The visiphone screen went blank and Ben waited. When it lighted again the face of a man in his middle forties, sporting a small moustache, stared out at Ben.

'Ah, Mr Martin,' Hughes said, 'nice of you to call. And just where are you making this call from, if you don't mind my curiosity?'

'I'm downtown at a pay booth,' Ben replied, stepping back so that the busy street intersection could be seen over the visiphone.

'Excellent, Mr Martin.' Hughes beamed. 'I knew you would be a man of discretion. Now, just what is it you wished to speak about?'

'Is your offer still open?' Ben asked. 'I'd like to come in and talk to you about it.'

'It most surely is,' Hughes replied, 'and I'd be delighted to talk to you about it. I assume, then, that you are interested?'

'I'm interested,' Ben said guilelessly, 'but before I commit myself there are a couple of other details that I'd have to work out with you before we could come to any terms.'

Hughes's eyebrows raised. 'Matters of money?'

'Not exactly,' Ben said. 'I have a couple of friends who I feel would be invaluable not only to me as members of the organization but also invaluable to you as well. They are the other two members of my cruiser crew who were with me on the night we came down from San Francisco and have almost as much information about the incidents of that night as I do. I think you can see the wisdom of my point.'

Hughes nodded knowingly. 'I see the point quite well and as a matter of real coincidence, we had already made plans to assimilate these good people into our organization at the same time we procured your services. I'm way ahead of you, Mr Martin. Now there is just one little detail I would like to arrange before we get together for our talk.'

'What's that?'

'You realize, of course,' Hughes said smoothly, 'that we would be somewhat embarrassed by signing an officer of the thruway to contract while that officer was still in the service. Therefore, I must insist that you be discharged and have completely severed your connections with the authority before coming to final terms.'

Ben smiled. 'This time, we're way ahead of you. Our discharges are now being processed and will be ready this afternoon.'

'My, but you certainly must have been sure of us,' Hughes said.

'I was,' Ben replied laconically. 'You can't do without us and if you back out now, even though we might be out on our ears with the patrol, we could still be brought to the stand as witnesses.'

Hughes smiled and shrugged. 'Quite so, Mr Martin. I can see that you're going to be a big asset to us. You already think our way. Very well, how soon can we get together?'

'I'll be at your office in an hour with my crew,' Ben replied. 'If we can come to terms, we can wind it up this afternoon.'

Ben broke off the connection and walked out of the booth. The hot summer sun filtered down through the maze of overhead state and city expressways and the highest level of the Continental Thruway running abreast of the 20th level of the office buildings piercing the sky. He threaded his way through the pedestrians to an autocab parked at the curb. Kelly and Clay, both in civilian dress, as was Ben, waited for him.

145

'We go up to Shellwood in an hour,' Ben told them. 'Let's get a bite of lunch and go over the operation once more before we go into the lion's den.'

They left the cab and strolled down the busy thoroughfare to a nearby restaurant.

'That transceiver working OK?' Clay asked Kelly.

'It was a few moments ago,' she replied. 'You still there, Mr Harvey?'

Hidden under the copper-red waves of her hair, a tiny earpiece was stuck with collodiplast to her left mastoid bone. 'Just as though I were walking with you, Miss Lightfoot,' Harvey's voice sounded in her ear. 'We are monitoring all three of you loud and clear. And we've just had word that Shellwood Electronics is checking on your discharges and have been told they are being processed. The fish has taken the bait.'

'He's there,' Kelly told Clay.

▼

An hour later they were seated in Hughes's office in the massive Shellwood Electronics headquarters building on the outskirts of Santa Monica.

'You understand,' Hughes said, 'that the contracts will become effective immediately upon proof of your separation from the authority. Now here are the contracts we have drawn up for your approval.' He shoved three documents across the desk.

'You will note,' he continued, 'that the contracts specify that you will accept employment at any place the company desires to assign you and upon the immediate notice of such assignment. Of course, any financial inconvenience brought about by such a move would be borne by the company.'

'What's that mean?' Clay asked.

'Quite simply,' Hughes said, 'that we will have immediate assignments for both you and Mr Martin at our operational offices in Paris. Miss Lightfoot will join our medical staff in London.'

'All three of us out of the country before any trial date, eh,' Ben said with a knowing smile.

Hughes returned the smile. 'In the best interests of our organization, you understand.'

Harvey's voice sounded in Kelly's ear, 'Get those contracts on film.'

Kelly shoved her contract over to Ben and then took Clay's and pushed it to the senior patrolman.

'You're the brains of this outfit,' she said brightly. 'Does the picture look all right to you, Ben?'

Ben smiled at her and laid the three contracts side by side on Hughes's desk. 'Let's see how they compare,' he said. He pulled a pen from his pocket and went through the contracts rapidly, line by line. When he had finished, the contracts were on microfilm in the pen. 'They look fine to me and the money sounds quite acceptable.'

'Do we sign now?' Clay asked.

'There's just one more slight detail,' Hughes said. 'I have another document which needs your signature. I think that after you have read it, you'll understand the need for it.' He pushed a single printed sheet across to Ben.

Ben read the document aloud.

'We the undersigned persons do agree not to testify in any fashion whatsoever against any member of this company or any subsidiary corporation in consideration of contractual employment with this corporation or any subsidiary thereof.'

Typed in below the text were their three names and places for their signatures.

'Hell,' Ben exploded, 'if we sign this, then we become parties to a conspiracy.'

'You have a quick mind, Mr Martin,' Hughes said. 'I

147

fully realize that this paper wouldn't save anyone from prosecution. But it will assure us that if any member of our organization should be prosecuted on the testimony of any of you, all three of you will then be in the same boat. Just let's call it a little insurance.'

'Do your company attorneys know about this?' Ben asked.

'It was drawn up by them,' Hughes said haughtily. 'But I see no need to drag them into this discussion since we are doing so nicely.

'Now if you'll just sign both the contracts and this paper,' Hughes continued, leaning across the desk and pointing to the proper places. 'You'll get copies of the contracts after we have certified your discharge papers from the Authority. There is only one copy of this other little paper. We'll hang on to that for safekeeping.'

Ben held the camera-pen over the self-incriminating document.

Once again Harvey's voice sounded in Kelly's ear. 'Stand by to assist boarders.'

The door to the outer office burst open and three men strode in. One of them went immediately to the desk and seized the papers.

'What the devil's the meaning of this?' Hughes spluttered. 'You have no right in here. Put those papers down and get out.'

One of the intruders flipped open a leather case and held it up.

'Los Angeles Metropolitan Police,' the man said. 'You are under arrest, Mr Hughes.' He took the personnel manager by the arm.

Sixty floors above, in the same building, two other plain-clothesmen shoved their way past the receptionist in Quentin Shellwood's private suite of offices. A uniformed Shellwood security guard rushed up to block their path.

'You can't go in there,' he ordered.

148

'Want to bet?' one of the officers asked, pushing the man aside and flashing his identification. The uniformed guard continued to block the way. 'I don't care if you are L.A.P.D.,' he said, 'you just don't barge in on Mr Shellwood.'

The other officer displayed a badge and card case. 'FBI,' he said tersely. 'Now get the hell out of the way.' The guard paled and backed off. The two agents entered the inner sanctum.

Quentin Shellwood glared up at them from behind his desk.

'Who let you in?' he bellowed. 'Get out.'

The federal agent displayed his credentials. 'Please come with us, Mr Shellwood. We have a warrant for your arrest.'

Shellwood's face purpled. 'Just who the hell do you think you are, ordering me around? And what the devil are you arresting me for?'

The federal officer pulled out a warrant. 'I have a joint Federal and Thruway Authority warrant charging you with conspiracy to coerce and with bribery. Now will you please come with us?'

'I will not,' Shellwood shouted. 'I'll see you in hell before I leave here on some phony trumped-up charge.' He reached for the visiphone. The metropolitan officer reached out and clamped a hand on his wrist.

'Mr Shellwood,' he said softly, 'you can come with us in good order, or you can come along in handcuffs. It doesn't make a bit of difference to us. But you are coming. And you'll make no phone calls until you are at headquarters at which time you will be allowed to consult with counsel. Now what's it going to be?'

The executive glared at the pair for a second and then got up from his desk. 'Would it be all right with you gentlemen,' he asked sarcastically, 'if I call my wife and tell her that I may be late for dinner?'

'I'm sorry, sir,' the federal agent said, taking Shellwood by the elbow and leading him to the door. 'Perhaps you can contact your wife later.'

Shellwood shook his arm from the agent's grasp. 'Get your hands off me,' he snarled. 'I can walk by myself.'

Flanked by the two officers, the head of the nation's largest corporation walked out of his office before the wondering and stunned gazes of his staff.

A half hour later at the opposite side of the city, a similar scene was being enacted in the offices of the law firm of Quinn, Reynolds, Chase and Hackmore. Accompanying the metropolitan and federal agents were attorneys from the offices of the Thruway Authority and the United States Attorney for the State of California.

While the senior and junior partners of the firm were being taken into custody, other agents, armed with warrants, were moving down the line of vocawriters in the outer office, stopping at each machine to speak 35 words into each device. As each vocawriter spewed out its printed text, the agents checked it against a photocopy they carried. Halfway down the bank of machines one of the agents called out. 'Here it is.'

The other men crowded around him and compared the copy in his hand against the copy on the machine. It read: 'We the undersigned persons do agree not to testify in any fashion whatsoever against any member of this company or any subsidiary corporation in consideration of contractual employment with this corporation or any subsidiary thereof.' On both the photocopy and the text from the vocawriter, the tail of the letter 'y', wherever it appeared, was partially snapped off.

▼

The trial of Kevin Shellwood on the original charges of driving while drunk, attempted bribery, et cetera, opened the following Monday. It lasted less than a day.

In their individually sealed rooms, the 12 jurors watched the courtroom proceedings through special wide-angle video monitors and viewed and listened to voice and video evidence tapes on their individual screens. Neither the prosecution nor defense could see the jury nor gauge the effects their legal maneuverings were having on any one juror. Each of the jurors had been selected from the venire list, sight unseen, and had been challenged and questioned in the same manner.

Now the prosecution was in its concluding statements. Dumpy John Harvey faced the judge and the unblinking video eyes of the jury box.

'. . .and man has progressed from the primitive law of the jungle. I have no quarrel with Darwin's theory of the survival of the fittest. But there is also no question but that an entire ethnic and cultural group can survive as the fittest rather than any single individual whose claws and morals might be more deadly than those of his neighbor.

'Our laws are designed for the protection of the masses of humanity and for the preservation of our progress. There can be no doubt in your minds about the evidence presented in this case. We have shown beyond a shadow of doubt that Kevin Shellwood was intoxicated at the time of his arrest. We have given you graphic testimony of the danger to untold lives that he posed in his unwarranted and liquor-laden driving of a three-ton projectile down a thruway with the velocity of a medium-powered bullet. You have seen pictures and heard his actual voice as he attempted to bribe his way out of his crime. Yet the case of Kevin Shellwood can not stand of itself. In a few days, his father and his attorneys, together with other employees of the rich and powerful industrial empire of Shellwood Electronics, will come before another court and another jury to face additional charges of coercion and attempted bribery. Their alleged crimes are part of

Kevin Shellwood's story, for both father and son have attempted to set themselves apart from human society; have used money, influence and power in an attempt to corrupt society for their own ends. They have said in effect, "We recognize no law but that of the clan."

'Members of the jury, Kevin Shellwood is on trial here today, but at the same time, so are you, as representatives of the people. If Kevin Shellwood is freed of the charges against him, society has signed its own death warrant. The magnificent transportation system that a free people of an entire continent have created for their own benefits and safety will become an open invitation to murder by those with enough money to buy their way out of their crimes. You can have no choice but to find Kevin Shellwood guilty as charged. Thank you.'

Harvey bowed to the judge and went back to his seat.

At the bench, Thruway Authority Justice James Bell addressed himself to the dozen faces watching him intently on a dozen small monitor screens concealed in the rim of his desk. The faces of the jurors were hidden from all but the judge. He gave his charge to the jury. When he had finished, covers slid down over the video eyes of each juror's room. The jurors could discuss the case over a closed circuit that was unmonitored by any other source.

Across the big courtroom, Kevin Shellwood slumped in his chair at the defense table and eyed the trio of patrol officers from Car 56 at the prosecution tables. The younger Shellwood was flanked by three attorneys, but not Quinn and Hackmore. They sat in the spectators' section together with the senior Shellwood, freed under $50,000 bonds pending their trials.

Kelly Lightfoot leaned toward Harvey. 'What do you think Kevin will get if they find him guilty?'

Harvey shrugged. 'I dunno. That's up to the judge. My guess is that he'll throw the book at him on both sentence and fine and then possibly withhold some of the sentence. But you never know how these things will turn out.'

Kelly looked across the room at the obviously nervous younger Shellwood. 'I feel sorry for him,' she murmured.

'So do I,' Ben said, 'but not for the same reasons. He might have been a good kid at one time and he still may turn out all right after this is over. But I can feel a lot sorrier for the people that he might have killed. And when this is over, at least he'll be alive and won't kill himself or anyone else on a highway.'

The crew and Harvey got up and went out into the corridor for a smoke. They had just taken a couple of puffs when a muted buzzer sounded at the door to the courtroom. 'The jury's ready,' Harvey said, snubbing out the cigarette and hurrying back into the courtroom.

Justice Bell was re-entering the room and ascending the bench as the patrol crew walked back into the courtroom. The judge seated himself and then pressed a button on his bench. The 12 panels slid up from the jury videos. On the bench, the judge's monitors showed the faces of the jurors.

'Have you reached a verdict?' Justice Bell asked.

From a speaker over the bench, the voice of one of the jurors sounded. 'We have, Your Honor.'

Bell glanced up at the defense table, 'The defendant will rise and face the bench.' Kevin pushed his chair back and stood up.

'Members of the jury,' the judge said, 'how do you find?'

'We find the defendant, Kevin Shellwood, guilty as charged on all counts.'

Across the room the youth slumped and pressed his palms against the edge of the table. His head was bowed. In the spectator section, his father half arose from his seat but was pulled back down by the two lawyers.

Justice Bell addressed the jury. 'Is this the verdict of each and all of you individually and collectively?' he asked. 'I now poll you individually. Juror Number One, is this your verdict?'

From the speaker above the first video lens came the words, 'It is.' The justice continued through the 12. When all had agreed, the judge paused.

'I thank the jury for its verdict and now dismiss it.' The covers slid down over the video lens and the monitors on the bench went blank.

'The defendant will approach the bench.'

Kevin moved out from behind the defense table, two of his attorneys following him. He halted before the bench.

'Kevin Shellwood,' Justice Bell said, 'you have been found guilty of all charges against you. Do you have anything to say before the court passes judgment?'

Shellwood shook his head.

'Very well,' Bell said. 'I hereby sentence you to serve a term in the Thruway Correctional Institution at St Louis, Missouri, not to exceed five years on each count, the sentences to run concurrently. I further fine you the sum of twenty-five thousand dollars. However, upon recommendation of the prosecuting attorney and the recommendation of the arresting officer for your part in a disastrous situation on the thruways after your arrest, I am suspending two years of your correctional term. And I further direct that the final year of your term after time for good behavior has been deducted, be spent either on trustee status or under guard depending upon your honor, as an attendant crew member of a thruway ambulance team. Perhaps then you can witness the kind of tragedy that you came so close to creating.

'I further warn you that under the laws of the Thruway Authority, you are automatically barred for life from the operation of *any* kind of surface ground vehicle and that failure to comply with this law will bring not only reinstatement of your full sentence but an additional sentence of ten years in correction.'

The judge's expression softened.

'I should like to add this comment. I personally feel that you are the product of your environment and your family. It is unfortunate that you failed to learn at a much earlier age that laws are made for all people and that there is no such thing as a privileged class. I sincerely hope that, in your future dealings with your fellow men following your release, you will recognize this fact.'

Justice Bell raised his eyes and looked over the younger Shellwood's head to the spectator section where Kevin's father sat.

'It may come as a shock to some people to realize that in this complex society in which we live and this ever-growing technology that both serves and threatens mankind, there are still people to whom the service of humanity is more important than rising above that humanity.

'The trial is ended.'

Justice Bell rose from his bench and walked from the courtroom. Two thruway officers moved up and led Kevin Shellwood away.

The spectators filed out of the courtroom and the crew of Car 56 followed. As they moved past the row of seats where the elder Shellwood still sat, Ben glanced over at the older man. Quentin Shellwood caught the look and turned his face defiantly to the officer. Pure hatred glowed in the older man's eyes. Ben paused and looked steadily at Kevin's father for a moment and then sighed and hurried after his crew.

He caught up with them in the corridor. 'Come on,' he said, taking Clay and Kelly by their arms. 'We've still got time for lunch before we head back for the barracks. We'll probably be rolling by nightfall. And I gather from what the Old Man says, we draw the Miami run this trip.'

Clay looked up and stopped. 'No kidding, Ben. You really think we'll draw Miami?'

Ben nodded.

Clay fished in his tunic pocket and pulled out the little address book.

'What a break,' he murmured, thumbing through the pages. 'I didn't think I'd get to see her again this year. Now what was her last name. . . '

Thick, wind-driven snow sheeted across the half-mile-wide police lane of NAT 85-N. The Arctic-spawned blizzard sweeping down out of the Rockies buried the road-way under crystal-hard, wind-whipped granules of snow. Clay fought to keep the gargantuan cruiser from slewing on the slippery pavement.

'Miami,' he muttered, as he peered through the snow. 'Miami was supposed to be the next stop. I should have my head examined for ever believing we'd be lucky enough to pull the Miami run in the middle of winter.'

'I don't know what you're complaining about,' Ben chuckled. 'Maybe we didn't get the Florida run, but look at the nice warm sun you had in Mexico.'

'Oh, sure,' Clay responded. 'Two whole, wonderful days under the warm Mexican sun while I sweated in the motor pool with the techmechs on the new radar installation. What fun do I have to look forward to on my regular vacation? Two weeks in sunny Death Valley making an engine change?'

Ben grinned and tried to make out the shapes of the vehicles in the inside lanes bordering the police lane. He increased de-icing temperatures as snow began accumulating on the wiper blades. Then he switched slowly through the four video monitors, noting road conditions in each lane of traffic as it appeared on the pickups.

Beulah was clawing her way up the long incline of Raton Pass in northern New Mexico, heading for NorCon Inter-mountain Headquarters at Denver.

'There are times,' Ferguson grumbled, 'when I wish meteorology wasn't an exact science. Meteorology forecasts a blizzard and a blizzard we get. Whatever happened to the good old days when the weatherman used to be wrong on occasion?'

Ben smiled and kept his eyes on the monitors. 'Even in those days,' he said, 'when he was wrong it was always on the bad side of the weather. The forecast would call for sunny skies, folks would pile into the car and head out for a picnic, then the rains would come. Now the weather boys are more accurate. They call for foul weather and we get foul weather.' He shrugged.

As the thruway climbed higher into the pass, the snow fell thicker and the wind blew harder. Visibility dropped not only from the cab of the cruiser but on the monitors as well. The only traffic visible to the searching officers was the vehicles moving slowly northward and passing within fifty yards of the video towers in each 10-mile block.

A fleet of snowburners had been dispatched from Pueblo and Trinidad at the onset of the storm, but the snow was falling faster than the burners could melt it from the roadways. They did keep the snow depth down on all traffic lanes and the steady stream of vehicles at the lower elevations continued to pack it even more. The police lane went unattended since the huge patrol cars could move ahead through any kind of terrain barring quicksand. As a consequence, deep drifts were piled three to four feet high in the police lane.

The radio speakers behind the officers' heads blared. 'Trinidad Control to all cars on NAT Eighty-five north and south. Weather reports call for increasing snowfall for the next five hours between mile markers 1875 and 2050. Yellow lanes will close in five minutes. Speed in blue lanes limited to green limits. Repeating. Yellow lanes will close in five minutes. Speeds reduced in blue lanes to green-lane limits. Traffic in all lanes is cautioned to be alert for slow-moving snowburning equipment.'

Nearly a mile west of the laboring patrol cruiser, high-intensity warning lights were beginning to flash from arches between the video pickup towers in the highspeed yellow lane, warning drivers to take the next crossover back to the lower speed blue lane. Barriers rose up at all incoming crossovers to prevent cars from entering.

At the same time, flashing amber lights in the 200-mile-an-hour blue lane signaled the speed reduction to the 150 miles an hour permitted in the green lane to the east.

Beulah bucked a heavy drift and skidded sideways as Clay fought to straighten out the big vehicle. Tracks spun, then gripped, as the huge diesels growled and labored to move the 250-ton bulk forward.

'Kelly,' the younger officer called back to the dispensary, 'if I give you the signal, drop your rear ramp and jump out and push.'

At the rear of the vehicle, Kelly laid down her book and grinned. 'I've got a better idea, Canuck,' she answered. 'I've got a big whip, and since you're a native to this miserable kind of weather, Ben and I'll just put you in harness and you can mush along.'

'We could throw him a frozen fish from time to time,' Ben chuckled.

Car 56 was on the final day of its 10-day patrol that had begun 1900 miles south at Villahermosa, Mexico. In Denver the car would be serviced and resupplied for another 10-day patrol. And in Denver Patrol Sergeant Ben Martin would come to the end of the line; a line that had been drawn from Alaska to Guatemala; from Key West to Seattle; from Limestone to Laguna. It was a line that had been 15 years in the making, from academy cadet to rookie, to patrolman and finally, sergeant. Three quarters of that time had been spent inside the confines of a NorCon vehicle. In Denver Ben would complete his last regular patrol and report to the North American Continental Thruway Patrol Academy at Colorado Springs as a training officer.

But first, he had to get to Denver.

The first snow flurries had dusted the roadways just north of Santa Fe shortly after noon. By the time Beulah passed through Las Vegas, New Mexico, it turned into a steady fall, and by four in the afternoon the full force of the blizzard lashed at Raton. The trio abandoned all hope of reaching Denver by early evening.

The radiodometer in the center of the instrument panel clicked up to 1892 as the cruiser plowed past a mileage-marker transmitter. The sky had darkened fast in the late afternoon hours. Clay turned on the broad headlight.

Instantly visibility was limited to a blinding white wall of wind-driven snow illuminated by the high-intensity light. Clay immediately switched to the amber fog-and-haze spectrum but the net gain was negligible.

'This is getting real mean,' Ben said. He thumbed his radio.

'Car Five Six to Trinidad Control,' he called. 'Blizzard conditions at marker 1892 and no visibility under the lights. Recommend closing the blue and switch to infra monitoring. Acknowledge.'

'Acknowledged, Five Six,' Trinidad blared back. 'Stand by.'

Clay cursed softly as Beulah again slewed and skidded off a windblown snow hummock that sprang up out of the swirling, night-darkened storm.

'Trinidad Control,' the distant operator came back on standard thruway nonpolice frequency, 'to all vehicles on NAT Eighty-five North and South. Particular attention vehicles between mile markers 1875 and 2050. Due to blizzard conditions, blue lane will close in five minutes. All monitors will shift to infrared in two minutes. Drivers are urged to leave the thruway at the next community

160

turn-off unless travel is essential or emergency, due to hazardous road conditions.'

Ben had already slipped on his work helmet with its built-in shields. He flipped down his infra visor as Clay darkened the bubble cab and flicked on the two rectangular panels of infrared headlamps mounted about Beulah's cyclopean main light.

'I've got it,' Ben said, settling himself into his bucket seat and grasping the throttle controls.

Clay nodded and reached for his own helmet. As his infra shield slid down, the dark night and driving snow outside the bubble vanished as the broad infra lamps cut a swath into the early winter evening.

'That's a little improvement,' he commented, 'but it's not doing a thing about getting us to Denver any faster.'

'Be thankful for what you have,' Ben said. '"I used to complain because I had no shoes until I met a man who had no feet,"' he quoted. 'In other words, quit your bitching.'

Clay reached up and tuned the video monitor as the screens moved into the red spectrum. 'You know,' he said, 'I've been sort of ambivalent about this patrol ever since we left Villahermosa. I keep telling myself that "good old Ben" isn't going to be around after we get to Denver and I'm going to miss "good old Ben." Then you pop out with one of those idiotic, folksy bits of philosophy and I just can't seem to get to Denver soon enough.'

Ben grinned in the privacy of his helmet.

'After three years of trying to stuff some of my pearls of wisdom into that skull of yours,' he replied, 'I've earned my right to a one-way ticket away from this cast-iron kiddy car. From Denver on, you've lost your only hope of keeping the front office from finding out that you're really a road-sweeping jockey who has stowed away in a patrol car.'

Before Clay could retort, Ben cut off his circuit and thumbed Trinidad Control.

'Car Five Six to Trinidad.' He glanced at the radiodometer. 'Mile marker 1901. Traffic densities, please.'

'Trinidad to Five Six,' the reply came, 'densities light. Less than 100 in the green, estimated 150 to 200 in the white but moving off fast.'

The storm was pushing vehicles from the thruway to rest areas spaced every 25 miles. If the storm continued to grow in intensity, the traffic would fall even more while the danger of vehicles' becoming stuck in the deep drifts was increasing. Both troopers kept their eyes on the video monitors, watching for the unmoving point of light that would signal a stopped or stalled vehicle.

'Are we stopping for supper?' Kelly called.

'I don't think we'd better, honey,' Ben replied. 'This snow is getting damned deep and while I don't think we could bog Beulah down, I wouldn't want to take a chance. And I'd rather keep rolling in case we find someone out of action.'

'OK,' the redhead replied. 'I'll throw some stuff in the cookers and you two can take turns eating. I'll holler when it's ready.'

'Not too much for me,' Ben said. 'I'd just as soon have a quick snack and wait until we get into Denver for a real meal.'

'Thanks for nothing,' the girl snapped back. 'At last I've found out what you really think about my cooking. And I'm glad I learned the truth about you, Ben Martin, before I made the fatal mistake of cooking for you every day of my life.'

'Princess,' Ben grinned, 'when I marry you, it won't be for your cooking. Besides, not even you could be brazen enough to call tossing three trays of frozen junk into an oven "cooking."'

'Ignore him, Hiawatha,' Clay chimed in. 'We gourmets appreciate your culinary excellence. Just go right ahead and whip up a little seven-course snack for me. And don't forget that I like oil and vinegar on my salad and a very dry light wine with the entrée.'

'"Gourmet,"' Kelly snorted, 'that's French-Canadian for "pig," you stomach with ears. How do you want your steak? Medium charred or burned to a crisp?'

'After two years of eating your cooking, Doc,' Clay retorted, 'I've gotten to the point where I can't distinguish between your medium charred or your charcoal crisp. No wonder your ancestors wore buffalo blankets. After what their women did to the meat, they had to have something to show for their hunting efforts.'

Kelly stalked up the passageway, slamming the bulk-head doors behind her. She slammed into the galley and grabbed the handle of the door to the cab.

'Hold it, Princess,' Ben warned. 'We're in the red.'

Kelly's hand dropped from the door handle and she turned away, muttering darkly. No one entered the cab under infra conditions until lights had been extinguished in the interior of the vehicle.

She extracted a pair of frozen meals from the galley freezer and pushed them into the sonic cooker, then dug out a disposable soup container for Ben and tossed it into the cooker with the full dinners.

While the meals were heating, she brewed a fresh urn of coffee and found an opened box of crackers in the lazaret.

Beulah lurched and skidded sickeningly for a moment and Kelly grabbed for a handhold. While the patrol car's gyros kept it moving forward on even keel, the gyros did nothing at all for sliding side motions caused by the deep drifts and icy pack that now covered the five lanes of NAT 85-N to a depth of more than three feet.

In the darkened cab, Ben juggled foot pedals and armrest controls to keep the juggernaut moving. The diesels growled and surged as the four-foot-wide tracks clawed for traction in the treacherous snow and ice.

'We'll be lucky if we get into Denver by daybreak,' Ferguson said, 'at the rate we're going now.'

Although the infra beams illuminated a path directly ahead of the patrol vehicle in the police lane, there was no eyeball visibility to either side, and particularly to the right-hand green and white lanes where all traffic had been channeled. Clay's eyes were fixed on the two right-hand radar monitors.

As Beulah struggled up the snowbound mountain pass, the radio chattered with talk between Trinidad and Raton Controls and the several NorCon patrol vehicles on both the north and south banks of NAT 85. Sixty miles ahead, Car 245 was calling for a wrecker to tow a disabled passenger car in the green lane. Thirty miles south of Beulah another cruiser wanted to know what was holding up the snowburner he had requested earlier. Raton Control told the patrolman he'd have to wait his turn. The snowburner was working its way up to him.

Clay tapped Ben on the arm, pointing to the white lane radar screen.

'We've got one stopped,' he said.

'Which block?'

'Current block,' the young officer replied, 'about three miles ahead.'

Ben had already swung Beulah's nose to the right. The deepening snow covered the divider strip that separated the red police lane from the green lane immediately to the right. The only indication that the car had crossed the line came from the row of reflector markers banding the divider strip and mounted on high posts. Clay flicked on the brilliant red emergency lights recessed into the stern and sides of the cruiser, to keep vehicles from plowing into them in the dark and snow.

The green monitor now showed virtually no traffic in the current block and the white lane monitor was bare of vehicle blips with the exception of the unmoving spot that marked the stopped car or cargo carrier.

Beulah surged diagonally across the green lane and into the white, gaining a mile on the stopped vehicle in the slanting drive.

'He looks like he's almost off the right-hand edge of the lane,' Clay said. 'Keep bearing right.' On the monitor screen the motionless blip appeared dead ahead. The patrol car rumbled through the driving wind and snow.

'Half mile to go,' Clay called out.

Ben eased off the throttles to avoid coming up on the car and skidding into the stalled vehicle.

'Let's go back to white light.' Both officers threw back their infra helmet shields as Clay thumbed the main headlamp and illuminated a blinding sheet of driven snow.

The diesels growled as Ben let the cruiser crawl the last few yards to the stopped vehicle. Clay peered through the bubble and then shot a quick glance at the monitor. It showed the stalled vehicle to be within 10 feet of the police car.

'Where the hell is it?' Ferguson asked, again straining to penetrate the blinding snow. Ben braked to a halt. He turned a mobile spotlight to the front and moved it in a slow semicircle. It swept over a mound of snow. Ben brought the beam back.

'That's got to be it,' he said, 'under that drift.'

'I'll get the shovels,' Clay said, rising from his seat.

Ben backed away from the snow-covered vehicle, then swung left and eased alongside the mound and slightly ahead of it, placing Beulah's big hull in the path of the blizzard and giving some protection against the full force of the wind.

Kelly came into the cab and scanned the silent mound for some trace of engine exhaust. Ben flipped on another pair of side spotlights and focused them on the mound, then rose from his seat. Kelly handed him a snow parka and turned back to the main passageway. She squeezed against the bulkhead as Clay hurried back with the shovels and his own parka.

'I'll get the dispensary ready,' she said. 'You want to bring them in the back ramp?'

Ben shook his head. 'Better to keep in the lee of the car. If there's anyone still alive in there we'll carry him in through the passageway.'

Clay dropped down the three steps to the side hatch. It slid open and a cloud of snow feathered up into the cab. The younger trooper stepped from the car and sank waist deep into the drift. Both men closed the facepieces of their work helmets and began shoveling and tunneling into the snow. Despite the protection of the massive patrol car, the wind still whipped blasts of snow across their path.

They worked silently, fighting their way into the mound. Ben's shovel struck metal. 'Here it is,' he said. He turned the blade of the shovel and scraped away more snow on a rounded blue metal surface.

'I think we're standing almost on top of it,' he said. Clay moved to his side and began shoveling down along the slope of the metal.

Glass came into sight and Clay stooped and pawed at the window. The spotlights were not aimed low enough. He turned a handlight into the cleared area of the glass. The beam swept across a luggage-strewn back seat and then to the front. A man slumped over the control wheel.

'Looks like just one guy,' Clay reported, 'and he's in the front seat. We're at the back window.'

Both troopers now cut through the snow to the front door. Clay grabbed the door handle while Ben cleared enough snow back to get it open. Ferguson tugged, but the door remained closed.

'I can't get the damned thing open,' he grunted, bracing a foot against the car.

'Must be frozen tight,' Ben said. 'Back up a second.'

The sergeant reversed his shovel and smashed the handle against the glass. A dozen blows at the safety glass opened a hole big enough to admit the handle of the shovel. Ben levered the shovel between the door and post and then leaned. 'Now pull,' he ordered.

There was a sudden snap and the door came open. Ben dropped his shovel and moved around to help Clay, who was already reaching for the still form of the driver. They pulled the man out into the snow.

'We can't carry him up out of this hole in this stuff,' Ben said. 'We'll just have to drag him. It couldn't hurt him any more than he is now, if he's still alive.'

The troopers clamped hands under the driver's armpits and wormed and slid their way up and out. Slipping and stumbling, they dragged the man to the open patrol-car hatch. Seconds later they had him in the cab and the hatch closed again. Another thirty seconds and the driver was stretched out on the dispensary treatment table and Kelly was ripping open his clothing to get a stethoscope on the cold chest.

'He's alive,' she snapped. 'Help me get him out of these clothes.'

Five minutes later the two troopers were back in the cab, leaving the medical officer working over the unconscious driver.

Ferguson had the man's clothing and began going through the pockets for identification. Coins, keys and a wallet came out of the pants. Clay laid them on the console and reached for the shirt.

'What the hell!' he exclaimed. Ben spun around and then grunted in surprise.

Clay opened the familiar blue plastic ID case of a North American Thruway Patrol officer. A silver NorCon badge glistened in its place on one cover while the identity card sealed into the other cover displayed the face of the unconscious man in the dispensary.

'Christopher Arnold Peale,' Ben read aloud, 'patrolman fourth, age twenty-three, date of rank. . . .' He studied the card. 'Hell,' he muttered, 'this guy's just a rookie. I wonder what the devil he was doing out here and in civvies at that.'

Clay was going through the man's wallet. 'Find anything else?' Ben asked.

Ferguson shook his head. 'Nope, just the usual stuff. Driver's license, service card and some cash. Nothing more of NorCon.'

Ben slid into his seat and thumbed the intercom.

'Kelly,' he called, 'how's he doing?'

'He's alive, but just,' she replied. 'The diagno calls it severe exposure, slight anoxia and possibly some bad frostbite. We've got to get him to the hospital as quickly as possible. Know who he is yet?'

'Hold onto your hypo,' Ben replied, 'he's a NorCon trooper.'

Kelly gasped as Ben cut out of intercom to radio channel.

'Trinidad Control,' he called, 'this is Car Five Six.'

'Go ahead, Five Six.'

Ben glanced up at the radiodometer. 'We have just recovered a man from a stalled vehicle at marker 1934. He is in serious condition from exposure and other problems. Our medical officer advises immediate hospitalization. Is there any possibility of an airlift?'

'Negative on airlift,' Trinidad replied. 'We're under total blizzard conditions here and no visibility. I'll get an ambulance team moving your way, Five Six, and suggest you head this way wide open. In other words, take it on Code Three status.'

'We'll try,' Ben replied, 'but in this stuff we'll be lucky if we can manage a Code One-and-a-half. Ask that ambulance to give me a running marker count. I'd hate to become a patient myself.'

Clay dropped into his seat and began backing and turning Beulah out of her snow pocket.

'Did you hear Trinidad?' Ben called to Kelly.

'I heard,' she replied. 'Give me three minutes to get my patient into a treatment shell and then you can lift.'

From the ceiling of the dispensary a body-mold safety cocoon lowered over the still form on the table. Kelly made a series of rapid connections, gave one last check glance at the table and then backed into the near corner of the compartment.

'All set,' she called.

While Kelly had been preparing her patient, Beulah had clawed her way back across the white and green lanes and lurched around, heading north again in the police lane.

'Let's lift,' Ben called out. He slammed the throttles forward and the patrol car's tracks spun, then grabbed the snow. Gathering speed like a drunken gooney bird, the gargantuan vehicle roared down the blizzard-swept lane. Both officers were back under infra hoods. Ben kept his eyes flicking back and forth from the radar scopes to the tachometer. At 100 miles an hour there was a perceptible lightening as the car lifted on its tracks. Still the speed increased. At 150, Ben had lost so much traction that the nose began slewing dangerously.

'Stand by,' he called.

He made the manual shift to air-cushion drive. The warning horns sounded and cocoons snapped shut. Beulah lifted, then fell sickeningly as the mighty fans ripped the snow cover from the pavement. The tracks touched in a grinding shriek, and then the car lifted again. Gathering speed, it roared blindly into the night, leaving in its wake a blizzard a hundred times more dense than the storm through which it bored.

Under zero visibility conditions and with an ambulance heading south from Trinidad in the same lane, Ben had no intention of moving any faster than necessary to maintain air drive.

The half-mile-wide lane was a blurring strip of white and black through the infra shield. Ben's eyes never wavered from the roadway.

'Read 'em off to me,' he ordered.

The radiodometer was clicking off the mile markers every 15 seconds. Clay began calling off the numbers every five miles. Car 56 had been just over 80 miles from Trinidad Control when it left the snowbound car. They would reach Trinidad in less than 20 minutes without a rendezvous with the ambulance.

'Car Five Six to Trinidad,' Ben called. 'Has that ambulance left yet?'

'Affirmative, Five Six,' the dispatcher replied. 'Ambulance Six One is now en route.'

'Marker one nine five zero,' Clay called out.

'Car Five Six to Ambulance Six One,' Ben called, 'what is your marker and your speed?'

'This is Ambulance Six One,' the reply came. 'We were north of Trinidad when we got the call. I'm now at marker two zero one five, speed two zero zero miles.'

Ben did some quick figuring.

'OK, Six One,' he said, 'let's hold speed for seven minutes, then start groping. We can't see a half mile ahead in this stuff. Also, let's read off markers in case my subtraction is off.'

'Will do, Five Six,' the ambulance driver replied. 'Reading by fives. Now, marker two zero zero five.'

'Car Five Six now at one niner five five,' Clay cut in.

Fifty miles north of Beulah the long and lower ambulance thundered blindly through the storm to meet the oncoming patrol car.

As Clay and the ambulance co-driver exchanged closing marker numbers, Ben kept his eyes straining into the storm.

'I wonder what idiot decided that no one would ever need a monitor in the red lane,' he muttered unhappily.

While four video and radar monitors scanned the traffic lanes, the middle lane was a blank – apparently on the assumption that police and emergency vehicles knew where each other was at all times.

'One nine eight zero,' Clay read off.

'One niner niner two,' the ambulance called out.

Almost in chorus, Ben and the ambulance driver called out to each other, 'Down track.'

Both vehicles slowed, came off air drive and thumped and lurched into the snow on tracks, speed dropping with every yard. At eight miles apart they were down to a hundred miles an hour, at five miles down to fifty and still slowing. Now safety cocoons were open.

A moment later, Clay caught the faint glimpse of light in the distance.

'Going white,' he said and threw up his infra shield while hitting both the front lamps and the blood-red flashing emergency light on the bow. Through the blinding snow he could see the answering red flash of the approaching ambulance.

'We've got you in sight,' Clay said, 'so just hold fast there and we'll back into your stern ramp.'

Ben maneuvered Beulah into position and cut drive. The two mammoth vehicles sat back-to-back in the blizzard.

In Beulah's dispensary, Kelly had unlocked her mobile treatment table with its still-unconscious patient. She moved to the back bulkhead and opened the ramp almost at the instant the ambulance ramp came down. Even before both doors were fully recessed, a pair of medtechs ran out of the ambulance and into the patrol-car dispensary. They wheeled the treatment table down one ramp, up the other and into the ambulance. As they vanished into the maw of the medical vehicle, a second team of techs wheeled a fresh treatment table on a return course into Kelly's dispensary. Ten seconds later it was locked into place and the team had returned to the ambulance. Both ramps and doors closed. An instant later the ambulance swung around the patrol car and again headed north, this time racing for the general hospital in Denver.

In the cab, Ben and Clay listened as the ambulance reported to Trinidad. Ben waited until the ambulance signed off then cut in.

'Car Five Six to Trinidad,' Ben paused and winked at Clay. 'The patient's name is . . . NorCon Patrolman Fourth Class Christopher Arnold Peale, age twenty-three. No other information available.'

'I thought you said you had the driver of the stalled vehicle as a patient,' Trinidad dispatcher came back. 'How did one of your crew wind up. . . . Hey, that's not one of your people. You kidding me, Martin?'

'Nope,' Ben replied. 'We're just as confused as you are. This kid was carrying the ID we gave you and his mug matches his card. He was wearing civvies and driving what looked to be a dark blue, two-door Spartan. We didn't take time to dig down to the plates or really look too closely at the car. You'll have to get a snowburner in there before anyone can tell for sure. But what a trooper would be doing in that car at this time, we don't know.'

'We'll check it, Five Six,' Trinidad said. 'Continue patrol. Meteorology reports wind velocity now down to 30 knots and dropping fast as the cold front moves eastward. Snow will continue but with decreasing fall, ending about 2200 hours. All traffic except white now closed from your position to marker 2090. White densities Trinidad-Pueblo less than 100.'

'There's still lots of snow on the road,' Ben said, 'so we'll keep an eye out for any more stranded and strayed rookies.'

If the wind was diminishing, it was not apparent from where Beulah was parked. Falling snow still sheeted blindingly across the face of the patrol car.

172

'It occurs to me, Mr Ferguson,' Ben said, 'that all of a sudden I'm hungry. And since there's no practical reason for both of us to be in the dark, I'm going back and eat and then you can come back.'

'One more day,' Clay growled, 'and I get rid of you. Then I'll be the prima donna of this bucket and I'll eat first.'

Ben grinned and slipped out of the cab into the tiny galley. As the doors closed, Clay switched back to infra light and Beulah again lumbered forward on the last leg of the patrol to Denver.

Ben peered into the warming section of the oven where the precooked trays had been shunted automatically from the sonic cooker. He hefted the coffee maker from its rack and nodded with satisfaction, then eased down the narrow passageway to the dispensary.

Kelly was absorbed in the task of realigning the diagnostican and didn't hear him enter. He slipped behind her and placed a kiss on her tanned neck just beneath the short waving cap of copper-red hair. She spun around and Ben hugged her to him. Her head went back and her eyes closed as he bent to kiss her. Her arms slid up around his neck.

It was Ben who broke away.

'Enough,' he gasped laughingly. 'If we keep this up we may never be welcome again in the dispensary of NorCon Car Five Six.'

'Stuffy,' Kelly murmured through half-closed eyes. 'Clay's got to keep driving and there isn't anyone else aboard. I think you're just afraid of me.'

She reached for him but Ben backed away.

'Oh no, Princess,' he said. 'Just a little more and you'd walk out of this dispensary more a woman than a girl.'

'So?' Kelly smiled seductively.

Ben grinned and glanced at the medical cots racked along the wall.

'Can you imagine what it would be like to be caught like that when Clay got a code call?' he asked.

Kelly paused thoughtfully and then broke in spasms of laughter.

'The cocoons,' she gasped hilariously, 'I forgot those goddamned cocoons. Oh, darling, I think it would be tremendous. Making love at 500 miles an hour, locked in a cocoon with you.'

'You might think it's tremendous,' Ben laughed, 'but I've got a feeling it would be downright disastrous, to say nothing of being just plain injurious. Come on, you evil-minded wench, let's get something to eat.'

Kelly headed toward the galley, still laughing.

▼

It was after two in the morning when Car 56 rolled into the lighted patrol assembly yard at Denver Regional Headquarters. Ben tooled Beulah easily through the ranks of parked patrol vehicles, service carriers and medical vehicles parked in military rows. Ahead, a techmech signaled with a traffic wand. Beulah rolled up to the gesturing man, pivoted sharply to the right and slid into the designated parking slot.

Ben's hands went to the console to begin cutting power. His hand hovered over the board for a full five seconds as he suddenly realized that for him, this was the end of his thruway patrol days. He sighed, reached, and Beulah's deep-throated purr died away.

He left Clay to complete the end-of-patrol report and went back to the cramped crew quarters. His two dress-blue uniforms, with their big yellow slashes of chevrons, hung in the locker beside two extra sets of work coveralls. Ben slid a bag from under his bunk and tossed in his dirty uniforms.

Since Car 56 was a Los Angeles-based vehicle, the crew

174

maintained so-called permanent quarters there. He'd have to send out for the rest of his gear from his room-and-bath home in the bachelor officers' dorm. Normally it took him less than five minutes to pack his patrol gear, ready to check out. Tonight he moved slowly, trying to put off the moment that would end an almost ingrained way of life. Everything was in the bag and there was no longer any excuse to linger. Bag in hand, he went forward.

Clay was standing beside the step leading down to the side hatch. His work helmet was neatly racked behind the right-hand junior seat. Ben set his bag down and removed his own helmet from the opposite bucket seat. Then he unracked Clay's helmet and moved it over to the left-hand seat. He turned and stuck out his hand.

'She's all yours, Mr Ferguson,' he smiled. 'Roll the hell outta her.'

Clay gripped the outstretched hand.

'I've always wanted to have a command seat,' the younger officer said, 'and I knew that by the grace of God and a not-too-demanding front office, I'd get it someday. But damn it, Ben, this just isn't the way I had envisioned it. It just isn't going to seem right to be sitting in your seat.'

Ben laughed and slapped Clay's shoulder.

'It's your seat now,' he said, 'and you've earned it. The one thing I'm really thankful for is the fact that I don't have to be around to hear you playing the Old Philosopher to the poor rookie who's going to be sitting next to you.' He paused. 'Better still – thank God I'm not that rookie. I'd probably kill you.'

Both men laughed and swung down out of the car. Kelly came around the rear of the vehicle with a small overnight bag in hand.

'You two go ahead and sign out,' Clay said. 'I'll pre-scribe treatment for Beulah and be along in a couple of minutes.'

He turned and began going over the vehicle report with the waiting techmech.

Kelly tucked her hand under Ben's arm and the two of them moved off toward the dispatcher's office. At the end of the row of vehicles, Ben stopped and looked back at Clay gesturing to the techmech and pointing to Beulah's tracks.

'He'll be a good command officer,' he mused aloud.

Kelly tightened her grip on his arm. 'You're going to be a fine senior officer, Ben,' she said.

Ben smiled down at her. 'You mean a fine rookies' wetnurse, don't you?'

'I don't care what they have you doing,' Kelly said happily. 'You'll do the best job they've ever seen.'

'You know,' Ben said, 'one of the reasons I'm going to marry you is that you're bigoted.'

They turned into the long dispatch office and went to the counter. Ben reached for the officers' checklist, signed off patrol, then slid the book down to Kelly. One of the dispatchers came over.

'Sergeant Martin?' he inquired.

Ben nodded.

The man turned back to a desk and picked up a heavy folder.

'These are for you,' the dispatcher said, handing Ben the folder. 'You're to report to Captain Maxwell at 0900 hours today. The other orders are in the folder and he'll fill you in on the rest.'

'Were there any orders waiting for me?' Kelly asked.

'You're Miss Lightfoot, aren't you?' the dispatcher queried. 'No ma'am, no written orders, but you're to report to Captain Maxwell at the same time along with Sergeant Martin.'

'Thanks,' Ben said, turning to Kelly. 'Want a cup of coffee before we sack out?'

'I could use it,' she replied.

'Tell Officer Ferguson that we'll wait for him in the snack room,' Ben told the dispatcher.

Ten minutes later the three were sprawled tiredly in the lounge, mugs of steaming coffee before them. Ben broke the seal on the folder and extracted the sheaf of papers. He glanced at the first couple of sheets and then handed them to Kelly while he studied the other papers.

'Anything unexpected?' Clay asked. Ben shook his head.

'Not really,' he replied. 'I'm to report to the Academy as an instructor. Most of these are the usual forms on quarters, change of status, clearances, so on. It doesn't spell out just what I'll be doing, but I guess Maxwell will tell me that in the morning.'

Kelly glanced at the first of the two sheets Ben had handed her, then turned to the second. Her eyes moved quickly over the page. She let out a whoop and hurled herself at Ben, arms around his neck and hugging him delightedly.

'You're an inspector, darling,' she cried happily. 'I'm so proud and happy for you.'

She sat back and glared at him. 'Ben Martin, how could you just look at those promotion orders so calmly and not say a word?' she demanded.

Ben smiled and pulled her to his shoulder.

'It just goes to prove, Princess,' he said, 'that if you are pure of heart, you will triumph.'

'I guess that makes me the first permanent patrolman first class in the history of NorCon,' Clay sighed.

'I said "pure of heart," Ben quipped. 'I didn't say a thing about pure of mind.'

'So there's hope,' Clay said. He set his empty coffee mug on the table and got to his feet. 'Let me know when you have to leave for Colorado Springs. I'll hang around in the morning and wait until I hear from you, Ben, before I make any plans. I may go on down with you and spend a couple of days at the school and then go over to the lodge and ski for the rest of the break period.'

Ben and Kelly sat quietly for a moment after Clay left. Her head was on his shoulder.

'You know your conduct is scandalous, Miss Lightfoot,' Ben said softly. 'Patrol officers do not make love to each other in public. It gives the organization a bad name.'

'This officer does,' Kelly said, snuggling closer. 'Besides, I don't plan on being an officer much longer. I've got a new career as a wife all mapped out.'

Ben smiled down gently at the copper-haired girl. 'You still plan to resign even if you get assigned to the school?'

'Oh, I might be willing to stay on awhile in that case,' she replied. 'But only if it doesn't interfere with my job of making you happy.'

She pulled away and looked up at Ben. 'Can we be married right away, darling?' she asked anxiously.

'Just as quickly as we get settled,' Ben replied. 'We'll know more after we talk with the captain later this morning. If we both draw the school, then I'd say let's get married just as fast as Colorado law permits.'

'It takes three days,' Kelly recited quickly, 'and you have to have a blood test.'

Ben grinned. 'You seem to be mighty well versed on Colorado law, Princess.'

'Would you like to know what the laws are in all the other states and Mexico and Canada?' Kelly asked, laughing. 'I've made it a point to become an expert on marriage law. I never knew when or where I might find you in a weakened moment and I wanted to be prepared when you succumbed to my fatal female fascination.'

'That fascination, baby, will be pretty dull if you don't get some sleep,' Ben said, glancing at his watch. 'Now let's turn in and grab a few hours' rest. The day begins early and we may have a helluva lot to do before it's over.'

He pulled her face to his and her arms went round his

neck as their lips met. Kelly pulled away finally. She rested her hand lightly on his cheek and looked deeply into his eyes.

'I love you, Ben,' she said softly.

Then she jumped up and walked quickly from the room. Ben waited until she was out of sight and then headed for the transient quarters.

▼

A bright winter sun dazzled across the white-covered roofs of the compound and sent melting snow pouring down the sides of the parked patrol vehicles as Ben and Kelly crossed the yard to Captain Maxwell's office in the administration building.

The deep rumble of diesels echoed across the yard as techmechs revved engines on the service line. Ben and Kelly cut through the line of parked vehicles and then paused to let a returning snowburner growl past on its way back to the road-maintenance section. Two patrol units rolled down the line, heading out for the tunnel ports to their respective NAT assignments. When they had passed, the man and woman hurried across the ramp to the pedestrian walk beside the buildings.

They turned into the headquarters and went to the reception desk.

'Officers Martin and Lightfoot to see Captain Maxwell,' Ben told the uniformed girl at the desk.

She touched a button on the panel beside her and ducked her head into the Hide-a-speak receptacle. When she raised her face she smiled at Ben.

'You're to go right in, Inspector,' she said, emphasizing his title. 'Right down the corridor to Room Forty-one eleven.'

Ben and Kelly walked into Maxwell's office. The senior officer was talking on the visiphone as they entered. He smiled and waved them into chairs by his desk. A moment later he broke off the connection and swung around and stood up. Ben jumped to his feet.

'Don't you even know what your rank is, Inspector?' Maxwell boomed as he shook hands with Martin. '"Officer Martin" indeed.'

He turned to Kelly. 'I'd guess that this promotion doesn't make you angry, Miss Lightfoot,' he said smiling. 'If my grapevine information is correct – and in twenty-four years on this force I've never known it to be wrong – you're about to become Mrs Martin. Congratulations to you both.' He waved Ben back into the chair. 'Sit down, sit down, we've got a lot to talk about.'

Maxwell sank back into his own chair and fished out a cigarette.

'You had time to look over those orders, Ben?' he asked.

'I've been through them, sir,' Ben replied, 'but they still don't tell me a helluva lot. I know that I'm reassigned to the Academy and that I'm to be a training officer. Beyond that, I'm in the dark. There was no fixed reporting date on the orders.'

Maxwell nodded.

'That's true,' he said. 'I thought that perhaps you might like a few days' rest before reporting down there. How long a rest you take will be up to you, after we go over the job we have in mind for you. We can always cut a supplemental order and back-date it to cover the time from now until you show up at Colorado Springs.'

He turned to Kelly. 'But first, let's see what we can do for Officer Lightfoot.'

Kelly smiled happily. 'I suppose you've seen my request for transfer, Captain?' Maxwell nodded. 'That's about all that I had in mind. If I can be reassigned to the Academy,' she continued, 'I'll stay on the force. If not, I'll resign and become just plain Mrs Martin.'

'I can't imagine anything about you ever being "plain,"
Miss Lightfoot,' Maxwell chuckled. 'But I'm afraid that
I've got bad news for you at the moment. And at the same
time, I've been asked to make a request of you since we had
anticipated your plans to a certain degree.'

Kelly's eyebrows rose quizzically.

'We've got a special assignment for Ben,' Maxwell continued, 'and we would anticipate that we can arrange a
transfer for you to the Academy in about thirty to forty-five
days; perhaps less. But this would work out about right for
both of you inasmuch as I can promise you that the minute
Ben gets to Colorado Springs, he's going to find himself
immersed in this job day and night. He has a lot of catching
up to do and then he'll be turning to a radically new
operation. At the end of the first month or so, he should
have the sweat labor worked out, and from then on, you
two could look to as about as normal a life as any of us in
this weird business can expect.'

He paused as he studied Kelly.

'Now for the request,' he said. 'As you're probably
aware, we've been expanding the force during the past
year. We're still below the number of officers and units that
we'd like to have, but it has been an improvement. But as
with every expansion, there are always areas that fail to
keep pace with the advance.

'In this instance, it's medical officers. Right now, we're
short nearly twenty qualified medtech officers to man the new
patrols that we want to get on the road. I've got the vehicles
and I've got the male officers, but I can't put them out on the
road without a well-trained gal riding dispensary with them.
Just four days ago Kansas City reported to us that they've
signed up the last of the girls to fill out the cars. But it will be
some time before they're ready to go out on patrol by
themselves. As a result, I just can't afford to lose another
trained officer like you, if there's any way I can persuade you
to stay on the road for at least another month or so.'

Maxwell leaned forward and reached for the cigarettes on the desk. 'I know you two want to be married and I also know that you don't want to be separated. But Kelly, when Ben gets to school, even if you were there, you'd see damned little of him for at least a month. That's why I'm asking you to stay with your car for another month. Then I'll guarantee your transfer to the Academy.'

He paused and surveyed the olive-skinned girl. 'What do you say?'

'I can't say that I'm overjoyed,' Kelly said dryly, 'but if I were sure that the transfer would come through when you say it will, I suppose that I really have no choice in the matter.'

'You could resign,' Maxwell said levelly.

'I know that, Captain,' Kelly replied. 'I also know that I've got an investment in this outfit just as much as you have. I may not like this too well but I understand the need. I'll stay on if you can assure me of the transfer.'

'When we made the decision to move Ben to the school,' Maxwell said, 'I was informed of the, er, shall I say status of you two. That was just two weeks ago. As soon as I had verified my source of information, I notified the commandant to put one of his junior medical techs in patrol training status since she had never been on the road. This was to make the vacancy for you, Kelly.'

'My God,' the girl gasped, 'does everyone in NorCon know about Ben and me?'

'Hell, no,' Maxwell chortled. 'Why, I'd bet you anything that I could call up New York dispatch right now and there'd be at least two techmechs there who hadn't heard about it.'

Both he and Ben roared with laughter as the girl's face crimsoned.

'Now that that's settled,' Maxwell said, still chuckling, 'we can get back to Ben.'

'One last thing, Captain,' Kelly interrupted. 'Since I'm

going to stay on patrol, I'd like to remain assigned to Car Five Six. Even though Ben is going off, I work well with Trooper Ferguson and I sort of feel at home there after all these years.'

'Of course,' Maxwell said. 'I thought I made that clear. Ferguson will be taking command of the car and it might be good for him to have you aboard at the start in any case. He's going to be busy enough breaking in a new officer without having to worry about having a new medic aboard at the same time.'

He turned to Ben. 'By the way, I've got his promotion orders here. You gave him a pretty strong recommendation, Ben. After I read your report I felt that we should have boosted him up to a least a lieutenant, instead of a mere corporal.'

'He's a good officer, Captain,' Ben replied with a smile. 'I'm happy to see him get the command and the stripes. He's earned them both. When does he learn about the stripes?'

Maxwell fished in his file box and extracted an envelope. 'One of the responsibilities and pleasures of having the rank of inspector in this outfit,' he said, 'is handing out promotions. I thought you might like to give these to him yourself as your first official duty in your new rank.' He shoved the envelope to Ben.

'And while you're at it,' he continued, 'you might get the proper rank insignia on your own uniforms, Inspector.'

Ben grinned. 'I'll have them on by noon.'

'Good,' Maxwell grunted, pawing through the papers on the desk. 'Now let's take up this job we've got lined out for you.

'A lot of this you already know, Ben, but bear with me and let's review a little of the situation. We've found out over the past two or three years that we're in a losing race with the car manufacturers and the driving public, so far as equipment and road conditions are concerned.'

The problem area Maxwell outlined was fast becoming a bitter fact to every patrol officer riding the big cruisers.

When the thruways were first conceived, engineers designed a road system that could take almost saturation traffic in controlled speed lanes up to 500 miles an hour. The designers assumed that any time a traveler wanted to go faster than that, he'd take to the air. But they overlooked the economics of the future as well as the psychology of the human animal. The human mind has always been prey to the illogical. When a jet or rocket developed engine trouble, its chances of getting down safely were minimal. The air transport of the age was too fast, the landscape was too crowded. And the news media still gave max publicity to the air accidents, even though five times as many people were being killed on the roadways.

The illogical result was the reluctance of the average person toward personal piloting in favor of the cheaper ground car.

'Your average motorist,' Maxwell said, 'still thinks than if something goes wrong on the thruway while he's driving his souped-up Meteor Eight he can just coast to a stop. We know better. He doesn't consider what happens to him when he's traveling at any speed in excess of a hundred miles an hour and loses control of his vehicle or the driver next to him loses control. He completely overlooks the fact that his chances of survival are even less than if he were in the air. Now combine this false thinking with the vehicular industrial capacity as compared to the air-transport industry and you find that John Q. can still purchase and operate a ground vehicle for less money than an air car. But the mere fact that he's on the ground doesn't mean that he wants to travel any slower than if he were flying. Oh, no. He keeps trying to push his foot into the mixer to get that last erg of power out of his beat-up wagon. The automotive industry knows which side its chrome is polished on and it strives to please. Net result: faster and faster models coming down the road each year and more of 'em.'

He paused for breath and then jabbed a finger at the wall map of the western divisions of NorCon.

'Where does that leave us?' he asked. 'We now have roads designed for a maximum speed of 500 miles an hour while the newer-model cars and even some of the carriers coming off the lines have test ratings of up to 800 and 900 miles an hour. As an experienced officer, Ben, you know damned well that when Junior gets into the family bus and knows that it'll do 800, he's damned well going to try and wring it out, with one eye on the road and the other on his tachometer. The road isn't designed for that speed; there's too much traffic and, until the road is revamped, we have the job of trying to nail Junior before he kills himself and about fifty or more innocent persons. But what do we have to work with?

'When they designed the thruways they laid plans for the patrol. And quite logically, they decided that if 500 was to be the top allowable speed for motorists – and remember that they hadn't even come up with the 500-miler at the time – then it made good sense to build a police vehicle that had a 600-mile-an-hour speed. And that's just what we have today. A 600-mile-an-hour patrol car incapable of overtaking at least twenty percent of the newer cars on the road today and becoming more obsolete with each new model offered to the public.

'That's where you come in, Ben.'

Maxwell got up and went to the wall at his right. He flipped a switch and a screen lighted on the wall. Centered in the picture was what looked like a blunt-nosed guided missile lying on its side. A high vertical fin topped a pair of short horizontal flaps at the rear and, apart from a small wedge-shaped, flat-topped plexisel canopy at the front, the projectile-like vehicle was smooth-skinned. It bore the color and markings of NorCon Police and on its side was the designation XV-4. Ben and Kelly stared at the picture.

'There's your new baby, Ben,' the captain said softly, 'and she's hot and deadly.'

There was a full minute of unbroken silence as the trio gazed at the sleek image. On closer inspection, Ben noted a track system beneath the low-slung vehicle.

'My God, Captain,' he breathed, 'what is it?'

'This,' Maxwell said, pointing to the picture, 'is Experimental Vehicle Number Four. The first three killed their test crews. This one stands up. It is nuclear-powered, monotracked with a dual impeller air-lift system with lateral control ducts. It has been tested on the straight-away at 1400 miles an hour. It has a lift capability of twenty feet for short periods. It carries a crew of three, just like the standard cars, but it has been completely redesigned inside. With a reactor drive, it eliminates large fuel-tank requirements. Since we wanted it light enough to move and to lift, we've sacrificed much of the machine shop and some other ancillary equipment. That way, we've cut the weight from the present 250 tons to under 150. It has high maneuverability under certain speeds.'

'Sounds and looks good,' Ben said doubtfully.

'Almost. It has one major drawback,' Maxwell said dryly. 'We haven't found a way to stop the son-of-a-bitch in under ten miles at top speed.'

'But I thought you said this had been tested and it held up,' Kelly protested.

'That's just what I did say,' the captain replied. 'We've tested it under test conditions—not on the thruway. And it does hold up in that it doesn't blow up, fall apart, burn up or roll over. It just doesn't stop, that's all.'

'And you're going to put Ben in that,' Kelly cried angrily. 'Over my dead body.'

'Now hold on, young lady,' Maxwell cautioned. 'We have no intention of sending Ben out on the road while

186

the car is in this condition. We know how to lick this retrodrive problem and it's being fabricated right now. When it's finished it will be installed and then we'll see how she works. If it does the job we think it will, the next step will be road-testing. But not until we're positive we aren't going to wipe out half of a Sunday churchgoing traffic jam.

'But while the retros are being completed, we can still go ahead with driver-training programs on the test field, holding the car down well under max speeds and having ample room to stop in. This is what Ben will be doing. This way, by the time the car is ready for road-testing, and hopefully is successful, we'll have a cadre of trained young officers to man the cars right away.'

'I still don't like the idea,' Kelly said doubtfully, 'but I guess I haven't anything to say about it.'

'Now, Baby,' Ben smiled gently at her, 'the captain has spelled it out and it makes good sense to me.' He looked back at the picture on the wall. 'I thought I was going to be retired to a classroom. This makes it a much better job.'

'In a sense, you are being retired to a classroom,' Maxwell said. 'It's just that your classroom is capable of going 1400 miles an hour. You're still going to be the teacher.'

'If I'm going to be the teacher,' Ben said, 'I'd better get my tail in high gear and get down to Colorado Springs and start learning something about my subject. I hate like hell to stay only one lesson ahead of my students.'

'We'd like you to get on the job as soon as possible,' Maxwell repeated, 'but since I have a pretty good notion of what a grind this is going to be, I think it's just as important that you show up rested and a little relaxed. Take a few days' leave, take in a few shows and a moderate quantity of stimulants and then head for the Academy.'

He smiled at Kelly.

'I have a feeling you two don't need any more stimulants than each other, right at the moment.'

He arose and walked around the desk.

'Talk it over,' he said, holding out his hand to Ben, 'and call me up later in the day when you decide how much time you want. I'll get the orders issued then.'

▼

It was after ten o'clock when Ben and Kelly emerged from Maxwell's office. 'Let's get Clay,' Ben said as they walked down the corridor. 'He'll want to know our plans and I want to spring the promotion on him.'

'If I know that Canuck,' Kelly said, 'he'll probably just be rolling out of bed about now, if at all.'

Ben paused at a vacant desk in the front reception room and dialed the transient officers' quarters for Clay's room. The phone rang but once and Ferguson answered.

'This is a surprise,' Ben said. 'Kelly didn't think you'd be out of the sack yet.'

'When a man assumes command responsibility,' Clay retorted, 'he can't be lolling around in the sack all day.'

'How long have you been up?' Ben asked.

'About three minutes.'

'Since you're so eagerly assuming command responsibility,' Ben laughed, 'we'll meet you in the central mess in ten minutes. I'll even buy you breakfast – or lunch, if you want it.'

'I wouldn't accept this from a common patrolman,' Clay said, 'but since you're now wearing brass, Inspector, I shall be delighted to let you pay for my steak and eggs. See you in ten.'

Ben chuckled and hung up. He and Kelly strolled down the sun-warmed walk toward the mess hall, dodging dripping rivulets of melting snow from the rooftops. Kelly walked with eyes cast down, wrapped in her thoughts. She reached for Ben's hand and squeezed it tightly.

'What's that for, Baby?' he asked.

She turned a worried face up to him and stopped. She studied his craggy features and his smiling dark eyes.

'I love you so much, Ben,' she finally spoke.

'I know that, sweetheart,' he said gently. 'Why so solemn about it?'

'I'm worried, darling. I know I'm probably just acting like a woman – and a woman in love, at that. But I can't help myself. I don't like this job you're getting, and what's worse, I know there isn't a thing I can do to keep you from it.'

'You are being feminine and possessive,' Ben said, 'and I love you for it. But believe me, Baby, I love you just as much as you love me and I have no intention of getting myself into anything that's going to hurt either of us. I'll get a much more detailed briefing and solid instruction when I get to the Academy and I'm sure that they wouldn't have gotten this far without complete confidence in the safety of the car.'

'Captain Maxwell admitted that it killed the first three crews,' Kelly retorted.

'That was before this car was developed,' Ben replied. 'That's just one of the calculated risks that have to be taken when they develop a new car or a plane or a rocket. The guys who piloted the thing knew what the percentages were. Now I know what they'll be on this car. The blowups are a thing of the past. Quit worrying, kitten. I plan on making you wait on me hand and foot when I get to be eighty.'

Kelly smiled. 'That's a wonderful thought, Ben. I'll push your wheelchair around and you'll reach out and try and pinch my bottom every so often.'

She sighed, tucked her arm in Ben's and they turned on down the walk again.

Kelly glanced up and noticed they were passing the base-personnel store. She tugged at Ben and they turned into the store.

'Come on, darling,' she said, 'Let's buy you those inspector's tabs. I want to buy them for you and I want to pin them on your collar.'

Ben glanced down at the broad yellow chevrons on his arm. 'You'll have to take these off first,' he said.

Kelly purchased a half dozen sets of the silver diamond-shaped tabs that denoted inspector rank in NorCon. Ben smiled as she excitedly reached for the tabs and turned to pin them on.

'Hold it, Baby,' he exclaimed, 'these stripes have to come off first.'

'Have you got a pair of snippers, please?' Kelly asked the clerk.

'I've got some, miss,' he answered, looking at Ben's faded blue uniform jacket, 'but I don't think they'll do you any good. Those stripes have been on the inspector's sleeve for quite a while, it would appear to me, and when you cut them off you're going to have a dark outline left on the sleeve.'

'Hm'm'm,' Kelly mused, studying Ben's uniform, 'you're right. Well, in that case, Inspector, you're just going to have to buy some new uniforms. It's about time, anyway. Those are beginning to get frayed and they're about two shades too light.'

'Hey, wait a minute,' Ben protested. 'I came in here so you could buy me some tabs. I didn't bargain on buying a whole new wardrobe to go with the tabs.'

'Oh, quit your arguing, Ben Martin,' Kelly exclaimed, 'and get back there and start trying on jackets.'

A half hour later they emerged from the store. Ben was resplendent in a new uniform jacket and trousers, and the new silver tabs sparkled on his collar. Kelly had insisted that the tailor fix one pair of trousers immediately so Ben could be properly dressed. The other uniforms would be ready later in the day.

Clay was already in the mess and eating when they walked in. He looked up as they sat down at the table.

'You two have the lousiest notion of how long ten minutes are,' he said grumpily. 'I've been here at least . . .' He noticed the new uniform. 'Well I'll be damned,' he exclaimed, 'look at you!'

'It's not my idea,' Ben grinned, pointing at Kelly. 'She's the one who's taking this thing seriously.'

'On you it looks great,' Clay said. He stood up and extended his hand across the table. 'Congratulations, Ben. Or do I have to say "Inspector, sir"?'

'Since this is a rather loose organization,' Ben replied, 'we usually get away with a first-name basis with anyone who is within two grades of our own. So let's keep it "Ben," shall we?'

Clay sat down and picked up his fork, a frown on his face. 'In that case, forgive the familiarity, Inspector,' he said. 'We patrolmen know our place.'

'I didn't notice any undue familiarity, Corporal,' Ben said unsmilingly.

Clay shoveled a forkful of eggs into his mouth, still frowning. Gradually, his eyebrows rose as he realized what Ben had said. He looked up.

'What did you call me?'

'Why, I believe I called you by your rank, Corporal,' Ben smiled and shoved the envelope with the promotion orders across the table.

Clay ripped them open and scanned the sheet. 'Well I will be a son-of-a-bitch,' he breathed. 'I made corporal.' He broke into a broad grin. 'This had to be your doing, Ben,' he said happily. 'Thanks, old friend. Thanks a lot.'

'Don't thank me,' Ben said. 'You earned them or you wouldn't have them.'

'This is fine,' Clay repeated in a happy daze, 'just fine. You make inspector and I get Beulah and stripes. This is a helluva fine day.'

He smiled happily at his two friends and then suddenly his face sobered. 'Hey, what did Maxwell have to say?'

191

Ben turned to Kelly. 'Want coffee?' She nodded. 'Wait until I get us coffee,' he told Clay, 'and then I'll tell you the whole story.'

After lunch, Ben called Maxwell and asked for a week's delay before reporting to the Academy. The trio decided to spend half of the time in Denver, catching up on good restaurants and entertainment and then going to Colorado Springs to ski until the time was up. Ben wanted to head for school immediately, but Kelly vetoed him.

'You're going into a terrible grind, Ben,' she insisted, 'and you'll probably not get any rest for at least a month. You're going to take a few days off now. Besides, I want some time with you before I have to leave you, darling.'

Six days later the three of them drove through the main gates of the North American Thruway Patrol Academy. Built on the site of the former Air Force Academy, the glistening steel-and-stone buildings nestled in the shadows of the lofty Rockies. The small but elite corps of cadets was housed in two large dormitories while the rest of the vast complex was devoted to a classroom university center, shops and a training field that was in reality a cut-out segment of thruway extending eastward along the base of the mountains for 25 miles. It was on this complete reproduction of a thruway that the cadet officers were training in driving and traffic procedures.

They climbed out of their rented runabout in front of Academy headquarters. A squad of second-year cadets marched down the open field in front of the door. The trio stopped to watch. As they came abreast of the officers, the upperclassman in command snapped a salute.

Kelly rammed elbows into both Ben and Clay. 'Return his salute, ninnies,' she whispered fiercely. Ben and Clay whipped their hands up and the squad moved smartly past.

'Good Lord,' Ben said, 'I'd forgotten what this place was like. It's been so damned long since I was a cadet I'd forgotten that they play soldier here. That's one thing I'm not going to like.'

At the door to headquarters, Clay stopped.

'Kelly and I will take a walk around the grounds, Ben,' he said. 'You go ahead and report and we'll meet you back here in a half hour or less. If you're not through by then, we'll wait inside for you.'

A young cadet whipped to attention and carried Ben's orders into the commandant's office. A moment later he returned and ushered Ben to the CO's door. Ben knocked, then entered and closed the door.

The tall, white-haired officer behind the desk arose. 'Welcome, Inspector Martin,' he said, walking around the desk to shake hands. 'I'm Commandant Ellington.' The double stars shone on the older man's collar. 'Glad to have you here. We've been waiting for you so that we could get the Bomb program going. Sit down,' he said, signaling Ben into a chair beside the desk.

'The "Bomb" program, sir?' Ben inquired. 'I don't believe I understand.'

The commandant's eyes twinkled. 'That's our name for the Ex Vee Four,' he said. 'And when you see it, you'll agree with us. Captain Maxwell called me earlier in the week and said that he had briefed you on the program.'

'Yes sir, he did,' Ben said, 'but he left a lot of questions to be asked after I had time to digest what he had given me.'

'I'm sure of that,' the older man said, 'and we'll try to answer those questions for you just as fast as we can. I'm very anxious to get this driver program started. We did a lot of screening, Inspector, until the front office selected you. You should be very proud of your record. You were picked for this job for some exceptional qualities and you are the final choice out of a full survey of virtually every officer on the force.'

'Thank you, sir,' Ben said. 'I just hope I can do the job.'

'I'm sure you can,' the other man said. 'Now, are there any immediate questions that perhaps I might answer? Before you ask them, though, let me tell you that I'm just the man who tries to keep things running smoothly here. Tomorrow you'll meet the brains behind this project and they'll be far better equipped to answer your questions than I.'

'I have one pressing question,' Ben said, 'and I'm sure you can answer this one. How are they picking the people who are going to be trained under the program and how many of them can I expect in the initial group?'

'Well,' the commandant said, settling back in his chair, 'first off, let me explain the "how" in choosing the cadre. With all due respect to the gray I see in your hair, Inspector, when you've driven the Bomb I'm sure that you'll agree that for day-in and day-out operation, it's a job for the young. It takes too much out of an older man for him to last long.

'This creates a dilemma for us. We need the younger officer for his stamina and reflex abilities, but we need the older officer for his wisdom and experience in patrol work. Obviously we can't have both, so we have picked the one officer on the force who has shown the highest degree of ability and maturity and we're putting him in charge in hopes that he will be able to rub some of his characteristics off on the young people who will be manning the Bomb.

'We've screened these kids without regard to rank or seniority. We were concerned with their reflex time, their mechanical knowledge, driving aptitude and their classroom grounding in basic nucleonics. That's about as far as we've gone. Since they are all working patrol officers, they are graduates of the Academy and as such have certain basic skills and discipline as well as training common to all patrol officers.

'That's how we're choosing them. As for how many,

you will train an initial cadre of twenty. The ten scoring highest in your sight will become car commanders on ten Bombs while the remaining ten will take the right-hand seats.'

'That makes sense,' Ben said. 'When does the training start?'

'Just as soon as you say you're ready,' the commandant replied. "You'll need time to familiarize yourself with the Bomb and to lay out a course of instruction for your cadre. Since this is basically a driver program, you shouldn't have to spend much time on general patrol procedures. But I do insist that you make a full determination of each of the officers you will be training. I want you to be satisfied not only with his driving ability but also with his sense of judgment, both as a driver and as an officer. We've issued orders for the first five trainees to report to the Academy not later than the first of next week. If you think you are ready by that time, then go to it. If you want more time to familiarize yourself with the Bomb, don't hesitate to say so. We can keep the young gentlemen busy at many other tasks until you are certain of yourself. Take what time you honestly feel you must have, but please, Inspector, no more than that. We need these kids ready to go just as soon as we can get this final bug out of the Bomb.'

The commandant rose from his chair and Ben jumped up.

'I know you're anxious to get a look at the Bomb,' the older man said, 'so why don't we do that now? I'll call my staff car.'

Ben glanced at his watch. 'Sir, if you don't mind, Corporal Ferguson, who has been my junior officer and is now taking command of my old car, and Miss Lightfoot, our medical officer, came up with me. I wonder if we might take them with us? I know that Ferguson wants to see the Bomb. They're walking around the grounds and were to meet me back here in about another ten minutes.'

'Fine,' Ellington said. 'I'm in no rush. While we're waiting for them, I'll introduce you to the headquarters staff. Come on.'

As they started out the door Ellington was talking half to himself. 'Lightfoot, Lightfoot.' Then he smiled at Ben. 'Of course. That's the young lady who's wearing your ring. Of course, she must see your new assignment.'

The Bomb was parked off by itself in the school motor pool; a destroyer disdainfully looking down its deadly snout at the nearby company of dreadnoughts.

The driver brought the staff car to a halt a dozen yards from the nose of the XV-4. Ben and Clay eyed the sleek vehicle critically. Kelly shuddered.

'There it is,' Ellington spoke up. 'The Bomb. Five feet longer, five feet lower, a hundred tons lighter and two and a half times faster than anything that the patrol has ever had.'

'That's not a patrol vehicle,' Kelly exclaimed coldly. 'That's a weapon.'

Ellington looked at the girl. 'Perhaps you're right, Miss Lightfoot, perhaps you're right. But if it is a weapon, it's one to be used to fight death, not to cause it.'

Without taking his eyes from the Bomb, Ben opened the door of the staff car and slid out. He moved toward the experimental vehicle. Clay jumped out and followed. The commandant and Kelly waited beside the staff car.

Silently the two patrol officers prowled the circumference of the Bomb. It hovered like a missile in its launcher, poised and balanced on the broad split track that ran two thirds of the length down the hull. Just forward of the track, a bottom panel of the hull swung down to the ground. Steps on the inner side of the panel gave access to the interior. More than 50 feet away, at the other end of the track, a second hatch opened into the dispensary.

The two men completed their circuit of the vehicle and then peered up into the open forward hatch. Neither made a move to enter. The only sounds were the weird whistles of the wintry mountain wind surfing down the snow-covered slopes beyond the school grounds. The officers stood looking up into the white-lighted interior of the cab, then turned and walked back to the commandant and the girl.

'What do you think of it?' Ellington asked, a half-smile playing at his mouth.

Ben turned and looked back at the Bomb before answering. He studied the 65-foot length of the vehicle from blunted snout to towering tail fin, his eyes traveling slowly down the length of the hull. He turned back to the commandant.

'I have a feeling,' he said, 'that you don't want patrol officers driving that. This was left over here from the days of the Air Force Academy. You want a rocket pilot.'

The commandant smiled. 'Remember back to the first time you were introduced at close range to a standard cruiser, Ben?'

Martin nodded.

'What went through your mind in that first glance?'

'My first thought was,' Ben replied, 'that if I ever got one of those monsters rolling fast enough I'd never be able to stop it.' He paused and then began to laugh as the analogy struck him.

'See what I mean,' Ellington chuckled, 'nothing ever really changes.'

Riding back to the lodge in town after their inspection of the Bomb, the trio was silent and subdued. Clay pulled into the driveway in front of the lodge and stopped.

'I've had enough of this fresh-air bit,' he turned to the couple beside him. 'I think I'll check out right now and head back up to Denver and hit the clubs again. We've still got three more days before we check out, Kelly, so why don't you stay over and come up the morning we're set to roll? I'll make sure that your supply list is put

197

aboard, so there's no need for you to come up ahead of time.'

He reached over and took Ben's hand.

'You're going to have some job taming that beast,' he said quietly. 'Do it the easy way, Ben. That's no gadget to be playing loose with. I've gotten used to having you around. Let's keep it that way.'

Ben gripped the younger officer's hand. 'Now look who's lecturing,' he teased gently. 'Thanks, Clay. I plan to keep it easy. See you when you get back in town from patrol. Take care of this gal for me and be kind to Beulah.'

Kelly and Ben slid out of the car and Clay waved and drove off.

The couple went through the lobby and up to Ben's room.

'I could use a drink,' he said lightly. 'How about you, Princess?'

He sloshed whiskey into a pair of glasses and reached under the service table for the auto-ice drawer. Kelly was sprawled tummy-down across the foot of the bed, her face set and drawn. Ben handed her the glass and sat down on the edge of the bed beside her.

She sipped at the drink and then let her head and arms dangle down to the floor, putting the glass down.

'Ben,' she called in muffled tones, head still down and half hidden in the covers, 'I want to get married.'

He put his hand on her back and stroked gently. 'We are going to be married, sweetheart,' he said. 'A month isn't going to be so long.'

She rolled over on her back and put her head in his lap. 'I don't want to wait a month. I want to be married right away. Please, darling. We can run out to the school dispensary in the morning and get the blood tests before you report for duty. I can pick them up in the afternoon and go down and buy the license. We could be married before I report back to Denver.'

Ben smiled. 'I thought you wanted a big church wedding, with flowers and bridesmaids and things?'

She sat up and threw her arms about his neck and buried her face in his chest.

'I don't give a damn about that,' she wailed, 'I just want you and I want you now. Oh, darling, I'm so frightened.'

Ben put his drink on the side table and took her in his arms.

'There's nothing to be frightened of,' he soothed her, kissing her eyes. 'I promise you nothing is going to happen to me. You think that I'd take any chances now that I've got you?'

Kelly's head rolled back in his arms. 'I want you, darling. I want you to have me. I don't care about anything but you and I'm so scared. Ben, hold me, darling. Don't leave me. Please don't leave me.'

The warm softness of her body pressed against him as they sank back onto the bed. He held her tightly to stop her shivering.

Three days later they were married by a justice of the peace.

They stood in the cold dawn of their wedding night, waiting for the Denver shuttle to begin loading. The first rays of the cold winter morning sun glinted on the tiny diamond gold band on Kelly's finger. She nestled tightly to Ben's side.

'I'll call you the minute we stop, darling,' she said. 'And I'll write to you every day and then mail the whole batch of them to you at the first stop. And you write to me. I want a bag of letters waiting for me the minute I set foot out of the car.'

'Yes ma'am, Mrs Martin.' Ben squeezed her to him.

The doors of the shuttle slid open and people moved quickly into the car.

'Oh, darling,' Kelly wailed, hugging Ben desperately, 'I love you so much. Please take care of yourself.'

Ben tipped her head up. Tears welled from her eyes as she lifted her face to his. Then she broke away quickly and ran into the car. The doors slid shut and an instant later the shuttle whipped out from the platform. Ben hunched his shoulders deeper into his topcoat and walked back down the station steps and into the cold morning.

▼

'Since your pile is hot all the time,' Sgt Lee Hathaway said, 'there's no lag time in getting under way or in acceleration. We've built a controlled damping effect into the thrust load so that you can't smear yourself and crew over the nearest rear bulkhead by sudden power surges.' He reached over from his right-hand seat in the cab of the Bomb and touched a control button lightly. 'This is what we laughingly call the air-cushion braking control on this monster.'

Ben grinned at the slightly-built test driver who was his checkout instructor.

'At any speed up to about 800,' Hathaway continued, 'the present retrodrives work pretty good. But you've got to remember, Ben, that the streamlining on this buggy has eliminated a lot of the frontal resistance you found in the standard cruisers. You could be balling along at 600 in the big boys and just take your hand off the power controls and the bulk of the front of the car would drop your speed almost instantly by a hundred miles an hour. You haven't got that here, so you've got to have an anchor to toss out.'

Lee reached up and pulled his work helmet down onto his head and settled back in his seat. Ben's helmet was already on. The Bomb was sitting at the edge of the Academy motor pool. To their right, four standard patrol cruisers, with cadets at the controls, were rumbling out onto the training thruway.

'All right, Inspector,' Lee said, 'let's see you drive this thing.'

Ben pressed lightly on the power grip at the forward edge of his right arm rest. Noiselessly, the Bomb rolled toward the gate. Without the deep-throated sound of the diesels, the only noise was the muted rumble of the broad, splitband track grating on the pavement. At low speeds, the heavy shielding completely silenced the noise of the reaction drives thirty feet behind the control cab. Ben increased power and touched his steering pedals lightly. One side of the split track locked momentarily and the huge vehicle turned. Almost imperceptibly, the towering vertical stabilizer also turned.

The Bomb rolled onto the red lane at a quiet 75 miles an hour.

'Remember,' Lee said, 'that to all intents and purposes, this car handles exactly like a standard up to 600. You go into automatic synchro airlift drive at 200. You have both track and retrodrive for braking under that speed. Use retros only above 200 and, until we get the new retro system installed, you're red-lined at 750.'

Ben increased pressure on the power grip and there was a noticeable lightening and rising as the torpedo-shaped vehicle gained speed. The radiodometer clicked off five miles and the Bomb hit 200. The familiar bull horns blared and reinforced cocoons snapped shut over the two men. Front and back fan ports snapped open and twin columns of air pressure lifted the rocket from the ground. The reaction motors cut to thrust drive from the two gaping throats at the rear of the vehicle. Even through the heavy shielding and the encasing cocoon, Ben could hear the high-pitched whine of the drives. Ahead, a standard patrol unit was speeding along at just under air-drive pace. Ben touched his foot pedals and the slim vehicle whipped too far to the right.

'She's sensitive as an oversexed virgin,' Lee cautioned. 'Don't overcontrol.' Ben corrected and the Bomb raced past the standard unit.

'Remember I said this handles *almost* like a conventional car under 600,' Lee said. 'Now let me show the differences and the things this will do that you can't in a standard.' The Bomb was now hitting 300 miles an hour. 'I'll take it,' Lee said.

Ben's hands came off the controls and Lee increased speed. They were coming up fast on another standard cruiser directly ahead. Lee held the XV steady at 600 miles an hour and Ben began trying to shrink back into his seat as they bore down on the bulky vehicle in front of them. Fifty feet before they collided with the rear of the other car, Lee touched a button. The Bomb bounced twenty feet into the air on a tremendous surge of impeller power. Lee's fingers danced on the console. The lift cut off the split second he applied full thrust. The manned projectile sailed four feet above the standard unit and an instant later the lift cut back in as the vehicle began to sink to the paving. It righted itself and quickly sank back to the normal three-foot air-pad clearance above the roadway. Speed had increased to 650 and they were coming up fast on the end of the training thruway. Lee shifted slightly to the left out of the path of the vehicle behind them and touched retrodrive. Ben felt the G-force shove him against the front of his cocoon. A moment later the tracks touched and Lee was in a full braking pattern. At a leisurely 100 miles an hour, the Bomb swung into the long sweeping curve that led into the opposite straightaway back to the motor pool.

'Well I'll be goddamned!' Ben exclaimed. 'We leapfrogged the son-of-a-bitch.'

Lee grinned at him. 'And that, my friend, is one of those minor differences I mentioned.'

'I still don't believe it,' Ben said, 'even after seeing it happen. Now tell me how the hell you did it.'

'It's all done with your fingers,' Lee explained. 'When they designed the Bomb, they recognized the fact that while it would have all the speed they needed, it would lack maneuverability at those speeds. There's always the odd idiot who either ignores your emergency run signals or just freezes up in the middle of the road. So what do you do if you're clocking better than 800, coming up on one of those clowns? You can't turn because before you could correct, you'd be two miles out in left field. So you go over him. But it takes a little finger work because you have to cut your lift as you leap frog or you might squash him like a bug.

'This is just something you're going to have to practice and get the feel of it.'

By the end of the week, Ben was handling the Bomb as though he had been driving it all of his career. Away from the controls, there were long hours with the techreps and the nuclear engine teams, in study on procedures and technical repairs and adjustments.

From the factory came a report that the new retrodrives had been successfully static-tested and would be ready for shipment within another week. A single-lane, high-speed test run had already been built, extending 40 miles beyond the curve, and in line with the center lane of the training thruway. The braking system would be tested on that stretch.

After ten days of intensive work, Ben reported to the commandant's office.

'I'm as ready as I'll ever be,' he told Ellington. 'I can start the slow work with the trainees any time.'

'You feel certain of yourself?' the older officer asked searchingly.

'I don't intend to try any high-speed runs, if that's what you mean,' Ben replied, 'but by the time they're ready for that, I'll be ready. We're going to lose at least a week right after we start, sir, while the Bomb is being fitted out with the new retros and then tested. Then I'll have to run her to speed myself. I figure that I can get at least a week's slow time with the trainees and then put them in the hands of the techreps and shop people for that other week. It'll save us training time.'

'Fine,' Ellington smiled. 'The first five are already on the post and will report to you at eight tomorrow morning at the motor pool.'

Ben was just opening the door to his room in the officers' quarters when the visiphone sounded. He hurried to the screen and opened the circuit. Kelly's happy face filled the screen.

'Oh, darling, I've missed you so much,' she said. 'You look so good and so damned far away.'

'I've missed you just as much, Baby,' Ben replied. 'Where are you?'

'We're in Chicago,' she answered. 'It was a nothing trip. Just the usual troubles and no big ones. We'll be here two days and then I guess we go to New Orleans. But I don't want to talk about that. I want to talk about you, about us. Tell me everything that you've been doing and how the job is going and, oh, darling, I want you so badly.'

▼

The five young officers were sprawled on chairs in the motor section building when Ben arrived. One of them, a stocky, good-looking blond boy, was telling a story and the others were grouped around him, heads bent to catch the punch line.

Ben stood quietly in the doorway and studied each of the men thoughtfully.

'. . . so when the girl came out of the barn the next morning,' the blond storyteller said, 'the farmer asked her how she made out. "Fine" she said, "but that one bastard in the fur coat was the damnedest cheapskate I've ever met."'

The four listeners guffawed and the blond boy watched their reactions with an amused smile.

Ben shut the door. 'Good morning, gentlemen.'

The laughter broke off and the five jumped to their feet, facing him.

The young man who had been telling the story took a half step forward, saluted and replied, 'Good morning, Inspector.'

Ben returned the salute. 'At ease, gentlemen,' he smiled. 'I'm Ben Martin, and since you are all working officers and not cadets, I think we can do without the military aspects of this job. We might have to put on an occasional show if any of the youngsters are around. But otherwise, let's keep it informal.'

The quintet visibly relaxed. All five were dressed in offduty uniforms. 'I hope you all brought work coveralls with you,' Ben said. There was a nodding of heads. 'Good. Then I suggest that the first thing you do is get into them and then report back here to me with work helmets. And before you go, I understand the training office has issued you class cards, since we do have to keep some sort of training records. Will you please give me those cards now, before you go to change clothes.'

He began taking the proffered cards.

'John Quinton,' Ben read the first card. 'Yes, sir,' a tall, cheerful redheaded boy replied. 'Nice to know you, John,' Ben said.

He glanced at the second card, handed to him by a slim, good-looking Mexican officer. 'Ramon Guitterrez.' The young Latin flashed a bright smile. 'Yes, sir.'

'Glad to have you,' Ben said and reached for the third card.

'John Aloysius O'Neal.' He looked up at another red-head, short and freckled. 'The Irish predominate this group,' Ben chuckled.

'Don't they always, now, Inspector?' O'Neal quipped back.

'We'll see, Mr O'Neal,' Ben replied smilingly, 'we shall

see. Charles Lee Tracy. The fourth officer was the oldest of the five. He gave an air of quiet confidence and experience. 'Here, sir,' Tracy called.

'How long have you been on the roads?' Ben inquired.

'Three and a half years, Inspector.'

'I had a hunch you might have started developing boils on your butt,' Ben said. 'Good to have you here.'

'Thank you, sir,' Tracy's face lighted with a smile.

'Christopher Arnold Peale,' Ben read off the final card.

'And I've only been on the road four months, Inspector,' the blond storyteller spoke up, 'but don't hold that against me. I can drive anything that's got power. And I hear the Bomb really has it.'

Ben surveyed the man coolly. The handsome face stared back at him unflinchingly, one eyebrow raised.

'That, Mr Peale, remains to be seen. Now go get dressed.'

The five turned and moved toward the locker room. Ben glanced down at the last card and then called sharply, 'Peale.'

Peale turned on his heel and came back.

'Peale, Christopher Arnold, age twenty-three, patrolman fourth class,' Ben recited from memory.

A puzzled look swept Peale's face. 'That's right. What about it, Inspector?'

'When did you get out of the hospital?' Ben asked.

'How did you know I was in the hospital?' Peale stammered. 'I got out four days ago, but I don't remember seeing you around there.'

'I saw you before you landed in the hospital,' Ben said. 'It was my car that hauled you out of the snowbank.'

Peale's eyes widened. 'Well I'll be damned, this is a small world. I suppose I should say thank you, Inspector. But I never did know who came along. That was the worst luck I've ever had. I would have made it through that snow in good shape if it hadn't been for a damned bad wheel bearing. When it finally gave out, I'd had it. By that time the blizzard was so thick that I couldn't see a thing and there wasn't any traffic in sight. So I curled up to wait it out. I never knew it could get so cold.'

'When did you know you were losing a wheel bearing?' Ben inquired.

'Oh, about an hour or so before it finally quit,' Peale replied casually. 'I could hear it going but I was still cruising and I figured I could get into Trinidad before it died.'

'With the weather the way it was that night,' Ben said, 'the sensible thing to have done would have been to pull off at Raton and get it fixed.'

'That's a matter of judgment, Inspector,' Peale said lightly.

'I know it is, Peale,' Ben assured him stonily, 'and your judgment almost cost you your life.'

Peale shrugged.

'Go change your clothes,' Ben ordered. Peale walked back to the lockers, a bored look on his face. The older officer watched the blond move away. This one buys trouble, Ben thought. Watch this one.

▼

'Since we're crowded for space inside,' Ben said as his group of trainees stood beneath the open forward hatch of the XV-4, 'two of you will remain in the cab with me and the officer in the instruction seat while the other two will wait in the galley, or you may roam the rest of the car at will. We'll rotate in the hot seat so that each of you will have an opportunity to drive. This will go on until I feel that each of you is familiar with the basic instrumentation and operation and has demonstrated your ability to handle the vehicle under very slow speeds. After that, I will take you out one at a time as we move up the tachometer.'

He glanced at the five faces in front of him.

'O'Neal into the hot seat,' he ordered. 'Tracy and Quinton in the cab. Peale and Guitterrez in the galley. All right, in you go, galley men first.'

The five swung up into the vehicle and Ben followed them up the hatch. All morning the trainees had been walked through the Bomb, learning the layout of the vehicle and the equipment aboard. Now it was time to roll. The galley door closed as Ben slid into the left-hand seat and pulled down his work helmet. He activated the intercom system so that his voice could be heard not only by the officer in the seat beside him but by the other four in the cab and in the galley.

'I need not tell you,' he began, 'that under ordinary travel conditions you would not allow anyone to ride in the cab as Tracy and Quinton are now. There are no auxiliary cocoons in the cab. However, since we'll never be above fifty miles an hour in this phase of training, I'm breaking the rule.'

Ben closed the hatch panel and began talking to O'Neal.

'Now, O'Neal, this is your power control. . . .'

Two and a half hours later, the Bomb came to a halt back in the parking lot. Each of the trainees had had his first half hour at the controls under Ben's tutelage. He cut switches and ran the damping rods down.

'That's it in the car for today, gentlemen,' he called out. 'You report in ten minutes to Sergeant Blackwell in Engineering Classroom Seven. Immediately after that class ends, please check into the training section and pick up your copies of our training schedule. This will tell you what to expect over the next few weeks, what uniforms to wear, what extra gear you may need and what manuals we'll be using. I'll expect you all to be in the motor-pool dispatch office each morning promptly at eight.' Ben opened the hatchway. 'That's all. On your way.'

Ben tugged off his work helmet and watched the five

young men walking quickly across the parking lot to the buildings. They were talking animatedly among themselves about the Bomb.

Ben settled back in the bucket seat and fished in his coverall pocket for a cigarette. He lighted up and pulled a clipboard down from the console in front of him.

He began making notes, slowly reviewing in his mind the initial response and first-observed abilities of each of the five. When he had finished, he reread his notes and puffed thoughtfully on his cigarette. All showed high aptitudes and general competence. Guitterrez had a slight tendency to be overeager. Tracy, O'Neal and Quinton were good. At first reading, Peale indicated the highest promise. Of the five only Peale gave the impression at the end of the half hour at the controls that man and machine were in rapport. Ben stared uneasily at the clipboard. There was an easy, almost insolent blending of man and machine between Peale and the Bomb. The man had the same overconfident attitude toward the vehicle that he displayed in his relations with Ben and his fellow trainees. That bored, half-disdainful smile and condescending manner he used on his companions carried over to his handling of the Bomb.

He's good, Ben thought, but he thinks he's ten times as good as he really is.

By the end of the week each of the trainees had graduated to solo speed runs with Ben in the car. Their proficiency grew. So did Ben's sense of uneasiness. There was no reason for apprehension. Each of the five showed high capability and although Peale still had the best feel for the Bomb, the other four were almost flawless in their handling of the vehicle.

The new retro system arrived Friday morning. Ben gave his group the weekend for themselves before turning to lecture and shop classes for the coming week. The retro system was to be installed over the weekend, and the techreps and test driver Lee Hathaway slated the first test run for Monday. If all went well, Ben would join Lee in the cab for speed run and brake tests on Wednesday.

A light snow was falling as Ben walked back to his quarters. He showered and changed into dress uniform, then went to the officers' club for dinner.

The dining room was crowded, and while he waited, Ben turned into the bar. He took his drink and walked to the back of the room and sank gratefully into the soft cushions at a recessed table. The nagging sense of wrongness tugged at him as he sipped tiredly at his drink.

'Mind if I join you?' The commandant was standing beside the table, drink in hand.

'Glad for the company, sir.'

Ellington slid into the booth beside Ben.

'How's it going?' the commandant asked.

'The men are coming along just fine,' Ben replied.

'And the Bomb?'

'It runs like a dream. The retros arrived today and we'll start the hot runs Monday.'

Ellington pulled at his drink and peered at the younger man.

'Then what's wrong, Ben?' he asked quietly.

Ben shifted uncomfortably. 'Nothing, sir,' he said; 'it's going just great.'

'I've been working with people for a good many years, now,' Ellington said, 'and while I don't think I've learned a hell of a lot, one thing I do know is when something is bothering a man. You're worried about something, son. Now what is it?'

Ben let out a long pensive sigh before answering. 'I don't think I can really put my finger on it, Commandant,' he said, staring down at the wet rings on the tabletop. 'Perhaps it's a couple of things.' He paused to collect his thoughts and both men finished off their drinks. Ellington signaled to the bar man for another round.

'Maybe I do know what's really wrong,' Ben continued. 'Maybe it's because I think this whole program is wrong and that the concept of the Bomb is wrong to begin with.'

'There were some pretty high-priced minds at work on this before we started it,' Ellington said gently.

'I'm sure there were, sir,' Ben exclaimed, 'but the more I've thought about this and the more I've driven that vehicle the more certain I am that we're making a mistake.'

'How?'

Ben half-turned to face the older man. 'I know this is going to sound egotistical as hell,' he began earnestly, 'but I don't give a damn how many high-priced brains worked on that car. I've been riding the patrol now for a good many years and you said yourself that it was my experience and my record that got me this job.'

Ellington nodded.

'Then that's what I'm basing my opinion on, my experience and my record. I've covered the thruways under every imaginable condition, from 1000-density traffic in metropolitan areas to ten densities in Canada; in ice and snow and in fog and rain. You know what to expect, but what's more important, you know what you can or cannot do when the unexpected happens. You know what your car can do, how it handles in traffic and at high speed and what you have to do when there's only time to react through pure reflex.

'I tell you, sir, retros or no retros, that vehicle out there is not the answer. It's too hot, too unstable, not maneuverable enough. It will kill more people than it ever saves. Don't ask me how I know it. I just feel it.' He sank back onto the cushions, the muscles in his jaw twitching.

Ellington watched him for a long minute in silence.

'And what would you propose in its place, Inspector?' he asked finally.

'I don't know,' Ben replied tonelessly. 'Maybe

restrictions on the speed of vehicles. Maybe governors. I didn't say I had the answer. I just said that the Bomb isn't the answer.'

'You and I both know,' Ellington said quietly, 'that the traveling public is bent on genocide. That's why we don't give them a second chance. But you also know that so long as the automotive industry can produce a new and hotter model, it's going to sell it. And with the voting power that both the public and the industry have, no legislation to check speed is going to help. We can set our own speed limits. It just means that more people will be violating them and probably killing themselves and a lot of innocent people.'

'I know all that, sir,' Ben said wearily. 'I just don't think that it makes sense to send a deadlier missile flying down a crowded thruway in pursuit of a deadly missile. And that's all the Bomb is – a guided missile.'

'All right, Ben,' Ellington conceded, 'I'll let you in on a trade secret. You're not the only one with serious doubts about this vehicle. I didn't want to tell you this earlier for fear it might influence your training program. And I must tell you now, that at least for the time being, we must have the Bomb. But at the same time, there is a major project under way to develop what we know is going to be the greatest safety device in the history of powered ground travel. It may even have air applications.'

Ben turned to listen.

'What would you think of an automatic system that would reduce vehicular speed as it approached another object, no matter what the driver's wishes might be? And at any given speed?' Ellington looked at the younger officer quizzically.

'I'd say it was a miracle,' Ben replied, 'and the age of miracles is over.'

'Balls. The age of miracles has just begun,' Ellington scoffed. 'And we have a major team project under contract at Cal Tech right now that's producing just the miracle I've described.'

'How the hell is it going to work?' Ben asked.

'Essentially,' Ellington said, 'its a sensory, directional, magnetic-force field.'

Ben looked puzzled. The commandant explained.

'Don't ask me about the physics,' he said. 'I barely squeezed through quantum mechanics. But imagine a long coiled spring attached to the power controls of any vehicle. The spring – or springs – fan out from the front of the vehicle in an arc thirty degrees on either side. The faster you go, the farther the springs extend out from your car. Now visualize another car ahead, traveling slower than you. Your springs lightly touch the other vehicle but it's enough to compress the spring lightly. This shoves the power control back a notch. The closer you get, the more compression on the spring and the more pressure on the throttle until it drops down to match the speed of the car ahead. To pass, you pull right or left to a clear zone and the spring uncoils again. No clear space, no speed.

'Substitute a sensory field for the springs, coupled to a solenoid arrangement on the power control and increased by the input from another solenoid to your tachometer. The faster you go, the farther out it reaches on an exponential curve graphed to your power source. Make a final coupling to your brake locks so that when your sensory spring is fully compressed it not only cuts off power but applies your brakes. You now have a car that a dead man could drive.'

'I don't believe it,' Ben breathed.

'Believe it or not,' Ellington said dryly, 'it's already been tested under scaled-down lab conditions and it works. Now it's just a matter of coming up with a production model that can be manufactured to install on every vehicle on the road and can't cost more than fifty dollars per unit. Lick those minor factors and the roads will be bloodless.'

Ellington paused and took a long gulp of his drink.

'But those "minor" problems are at least two to three years in the solution,' he added. 'The 800- and 900-mile-an-hour car is here today. Until the sensor control is in production, we must have the Bomb. With the Bomb, we still have a prayer of overhauling the wild ones and the drunks and flagging them down before they kill someone.'

'All right,' Ben said after a moment's silence, 'I'll buy that. You haven't convinced me it's going to work, but you haven't given me a good alternative. I just pray to God that your R and D people can cut the time on the new gadget. I don't think we've got two to three years – Bomb or no Bomb.'

'I hope you're both wrong and right,' Ellington said. 'Anything else bothering you?'

'One other thing,' Ben replied, 'but in light of what you've just told me, I don't know if it's feasible, if the Bomb is only an interim enforcement vehicle.'

'What's the problem?'

'When we were coming back up track this afternoon,' Ben said, 'I remembered something that had been bugging me. We were rolling past the video tower at the upper end of the track extension when I remembered it. There are no video monitors for the red lanes. I realized the need for them, even in a standard cruiser during a blizzard last month. You haven't any notion of what patrol vehicles are in the lane ahead of you although you can monitor all of the outer lanes. Now with the Bomb and its speed, we've got to have something to tell us if we're coming up on another car in the red lane, particularly at night and under bad visibility conditions. We can't rely on eyeball contact.'

The commandant shook his head doubtfully. 'That would mean installing a new camera in every tower in the system,' he mused, 'plus installing a fifth monitor in every car. That would take a whopping appropriation and a lot of time to accomplish.'

'It probably would,' Ben agreed, 'but without it, this monster is just too damned dangerous to use.'

'I'll pass the suggestion along,' Ellington said, 'but I don't see any fast action on it. You're right, though.'

He paused thoughtfully, then looked at Ben. 'Anything else?'

Ben smiled tiredly. 'No sir. I think I've bled on you enough for one night. The prosecution rests.'

'Good,' Ellington said. 'All this conversation has whetted my appetite. Come on, I'll buy your dinner.'

▼

By noon Monday the new retro braking system had been installed and the Bomb was ready for high-speed tests. Lee Hathaway insisted that it was his job to make the first solo run. Ben's five trainees had begged for permission to cut the classroom sessions long enough to watch the first run.

After a hasty lunch, the training group piled into a cruiser and headed east along the training thruway and on down the 40-mile speed-test lane. Peale and Tracy were in the driving seats; Ben lounged in the galley with the other three officers.

Tracy as senior trainee, was in the left-hand seat of the standard unit. He eased the cruiser up to 180 and held it there, just under air-lift speed.

Peale sprawled in the co-driver's seat, annoyed at being ranked out of the driver's spot. He eyed the tachometer and snorted.

'Come on, Tracy,' he snapped, 'put this thing into high. You'd think you were afraid to drive.'

Tracy looked angrily at the slouched younger officer.

'If you like being in that cocoon so goddamned much,' he growled, 'you can go ahead and close it manually. Then I won't have to listen to you. I'll drive the way I want to,

Peale, and when you're over here you can drive as you like.'

'OK, OK,' Peale said, shrugging. 'Make like a grandmother for all I give a damn.' He slouched down farther into the seat and yawned theatrically. 'Wake me up when we get there.'

Tracy glared at the man, then turned back to the road.

Ten miles from the end of the lane, he pulled off to the right into a throng of other vehicles bearing techreps, mechanics and engineering test personnel who would watch the run and make the braking measurements.

Tracy parked the cruiser and the six men descended into the cold, overcast wintry day. A strong wind was blowing at right angles to the roadway and Ben wondered if this would affect the performance of the XV. A portable public-address system had been set up. As Ben's group walked toward a slight rise behind the parked vehicles, the horns blared. 'Five minutes to start time.'

With his trainees around him, Ben emphasized a point.

'Always remember that the jump-lift capability of this vehicle,' he said, 'is strictly an emergency procedure. Your lift requires a tremendous power surge that can be sustained for only five seconds. It takes less than a second to apply power and jump and probably not over two seconds to reapply after you've cleared your obstacle. You have twenty feet of lift against a paved surface. You could not use it on cross-country rough terrain since you'd have uneven footing that could tumble you.'

From below the speakers blared the two-minute warning.

'Lee will make this run at a max of 1200 miles an hour,' Ben told his group. 'It will take him three minutes to reach speed and in that time he will have traveled approximately fifty-four miles. The instant he hits speed

216

he will jump-lift and then come out of jump-lift in full braking retros. It's in the jump-lift attitude that the vehicle has its least braking power and its highest momentum.'

The one-minute warning sounded.

A hush fell over the crowd. The cold keening of the wind grew louder.

'He's rolling,' the horns announced.

Binoculars were swung up track for the first glimpse of the hurtling vehicle.

'Six hundred,' the speaker sounded.

A chill colder than the wind swept over Ben.

'Seven-fifty.'

Now the sound of the wind seemed to become the roar of the approaching car.

'Eleven-fifty.'

'Twelve hundred and lifting.'

'There he is,' chorused from a score of throats as glasses picked up the growing dot.

Ben watched the hurtling car drop back toward the pavement as gouts of smoke erupted from the nose retros. Now the distant sound lag came washing up the valley, still trailing sounds of the instant, but nearing the threshold of auditory pain. The blunt nose of the car appeared to turn color as plumes of smoke whipped out from the nose and curled back over the high fin. An instant later, the watchers saw it lurch momentarily. Then it was back down on the monotrack, and smoke and sparks spewed up from beneath the whipping flanges. Fifty yards before it reached a broad white band painted across the roadway, the Bomb came to a halt. Ben and his trainees sprinted down the rise toward the vehicle.

'Watch it,' someone in the jostling crowd called out, 'don't touch that nose plate. It's hotter than hell.'

Ben squeezed his way into the pack as the hatch dropped. A factory techrep scrambled up the steps and

Ben went up after him. Lee Hathaway was still in the bucket seat, his head lolling forward. Blood streamed from his nose, and his eyes were half-closed.

'Medic,' Ben yelled down the hatch, 'on the double.'

The crowd parted as a pair of Academy aid men, accompanied by a doctor, ran for the hatch. An ambulance carrier rumbled up and dropped ramp beside the Bomb.

The aid men lifted Hathaway from the seat and carried the half-conscious man to the hatch, where a dozen hands reached up to lower him to a waiting auto litter. A half minute later, the driver was on the treatment table in the ambulance with a diagnostican hovering over him.

Ben and the techrep looked down at the splatter of blood on the retracted cocoon and the floor plates.

'Thank God,' the factory man said, 'he held on long enough to stop this beast.'

It was a subdued group of trainees that piled into the cruiser a few minutes later to head back to school. Tracy turned the car over to Peale and came back to join Ben and the others in the galley.

'What do you think, Inspector?' Tracy asked. 'Does this wipe out the program?'

'No,' Ben replied, 'it just means that we've learned something new about the characteristics of the vehicle and how to handle it. Obviously, applying full retro at 1200 miles an hour exerts too high a gee pull on the crew. The braking system works, but it means that you've got to start braking sooner and less abruptly or just don't drive that fast.'

That night Ben sat beside Hathaway's bed in the school hospital. The test driver was propped up in bed, looking drawn and pale, but otherwise uninjured.

'It was a bastard,' Hathaway said. 'When I grabbed the retros it felt as though someone hit me with a sledge hammer and then put me into a drill press. I know I grayed out, and then I pulled my eyes open and found out that we were on the deck. I don't remember ever putting my feet on the track brakes, but I guess I did.'

'So we go at it differently,' Ben said. 'I'm just glad that you're all right. You scared the hell out of me when I saw you sitting in the seat with blood all over you.'

Lee smiled weakly. 'I scared the hell out of myself the minute I started down the track. Look, Ben, if you're going to let 'er out, squeeze the retro grip slowly. It's synchroed to give you gradual power. Just don't grab for your ass like I did.'

For the remainder of the week, Ben and a trio of factory drivers ran the Bomb through controlled speed tests, starting at 600 miles an hour and gradually increasing to a tops of 1000.

'It's either a case of braking sooner,' the senior techrep said at the end of the week, 'or taking longer distances to slow down. I'd say that until we've had a chance to see what the actual patrol tests are going to show in the way of need, we red-line at a thousand.'

'That makes sense,' Ben agreed. 'Even though we've got some civilian models that can hit eight and nine hundred, that doesn't mean they are going to be traveling that fast. Until I'm shown the need for speed like this thing's got, I don't intend to use it.'

The Bomb was made ready for trainee driving the following Monday, and Ben took up residence in the club bar, trying to unwind the coiled spring in his guts.

Saturday night he was paged to the visiphone.

'Darling,' Kelly's smiling face peered at him, 'I love you.'

'I love you too. So much, Baby,' Ben replied.

'I've got wonderful news, Ben,' she said delightedly. 'We're in Kansas City and we'll be in Denver Wednesday and that night I'll be down. And Ben, my darling, I'm never going to leave you again.'

'But Kelly,' he protested, 'you said you'd stay on at least until they could finish training your replacement. It's not quite a month yet, sweetheart, no matter how much I miss you and want you.'

'I know it's not a month, darling,' she replied, 'but the situation has changed.'

'How?'

'Oh, I'm so happy,' Kelly murmured, 'I could hardly wait to call you when I found out for certain. Darling, I'm going to have a baby.'

'Kelly,' Ben gasped, 'you're not kidding me?'

She shook her head laughingly. 'Positive, darling. I missed my period last week. Today I had a pregnancy test. It's definite. And Ben, my darling, I want to be near you and with you and never let you go. And I don't give a damn any more about NorCon or duty or anything except you and me, and, and, well, us. I'm resigning.'

'You're damned right you are,' Ben beamed. 'And don't you wait until Wednesday either. You resign in the morning and take a shuttle flight out here. I'm not going to have you rattling around in the back end of one of these torture boxes in your condition.'

Kelly laughed delightedly.

'Oh, Ben darling, I would never have believed that you'd start acting like a husband and father. Why, you're actually being silly. And I love you for it. But let me be the judge of my condition. Four more days aren't going to make that much difference, and Clay couldn't possibly pick up another medical tech here on such short notice. We're off-duty in Denver and that will give them time to dig someone up before Beulah is put back on the road.'

'All right,' Ben said doubtfully, 'but you be damned careful, Baby, and you tell Ferguson that if he shakes you up I'll have his head.'

▼

All day Monday and most of Tuesday were spent working the five trainees up to speed with the new retro system but without jump-lifting.

'Get a good night's sleep tonight,' Ben warned them Tuesday. 'I want your reflexes sharp as tacks tomorrow when we start jumping.'

Ben's fingers rode with each of the men as they made the first jump lifts at 800 miles an hour. 'This is about the speed you should use the lift,' he told O'Neal as they started their run. 'Remember that you haven't got the velocity that you have at a thousand or more and that you drop out faster. This means split-second reaction on your lift and power controls.'

On both O'Neal and Guitterrez, Ben overrode them on their first try. 'Still too slow,' he said. 'You'll roll up in a ball on the pavement before you catch yourself.'

Tracy's fingers and hand moved in perfect coordination when he took his turn in the seat. Ben's eyes blinked in approval inside the rigid cocoon. They turned around and came rolling back up the track extension to the training thruway. The Bomb glided past the turret-like radiodometer and relay tower near the upper end of the extension.

Back at the yard, Tracy climbed down and Peale moved into the left-hand seat.

'Now you've done this in dry-run a dozen times, Peale,' Ben told the young blond officer. 'Just do it that way for real this time and you won't have any trouble. Remember your control sequence: lift, power, off power, lift off, down power. Let's try it.'

'Finger exercises,' Peale snorted. 'Look, Inspector, my mother made me practice the piano until I was twelve years old. Anyone who can play chopsticks can operate this vehicle.'

Ben swung around in his seat and stared stonily at the younger man.

'Peale,' he said levelly, 'let's get something straight right now. I am running neither a debating society nor a popularity contest. When I tell you to do something, you damn well better do it, just the way I tell you to. And I don't appreciate your snotty remarks, either. You think you're a hot driver. I'll tell you now that there's one hell of a lot more to being a good driver *and* a good officer than the simple ability to handle a vehicle. You're not even half as good as you think you are and if I don't see some change in your attitude pretty quick, you're going to be out of this program so fast you won't even have time to pack your bag. Is that clear?'

Peale flushed angrily. 'I read you loud and clear, old man,' he muttered.

'What?' Ben barked.

'I understand, Inspector,' Peale said tightly, his hands gripping the control rests.

Ben studied the surly face for another second, then sighed and swung back in his seat.

'All right,' he said, 'let's get with it.'

Peale rolled the Bomb around and was gathering speed down the red lane almost the instant he cleared the yards. The car rolled easily down the roadway, moving quickly to the 200-mile-an-hour mark when the cocoons snapped shut and the whining air-lift impellers cut in. The car rose slightly and the full thrust of the powerful pile sent the two men back into their padded shells. There was a tight grin on Peale's face as the Bomb raced down the lane. It was traveling 700 miles an hour when it whipped past the twenty-mile marker.

'Remember, we lift at 800,' Ben cautioned.

'What are we red-lined at?' Peale demanded. The Bomb continued to gain speed.

'Never mind what we're red-lined at,' Ben snapped. 'You lift at 800.' The car shot past the 25-mile marker as the tachometer reached the 800 mark.

'Lift,' Ben commanded.

Peale kept his hand locked on the power controls and grinned tightly. 'Just a little more speed, boss,' he said, 'then I'll go. We've got plenty of room.'

'I said lift, goddamn it,' Ben roared. 'Either lift or get off the power.'

'You're the man,' Peale yelled and slammed down on the lift button. At just under 900 miles an hour, the Bomb leaped into the air.

'Jesus Christ,' Peale shouted, his fingers locked on the power grip, 'we're flying.'

Ben's fingers stabbed at the override. A snarl twisted Peale's face as he tried to finish the sequence and realized that Ben had cut him out. His feet lashed out in anger against the brake and turn pedals.

Sixty feet to the rear the tall vertical stabilizer turned at the touch of Peale's foot. The XV-4 curved to the left as Ben fought the controls. He squeezed hard on full retro as Peale looked up and screamed.

Thirty miles away the waiting trainees and scores of persons working in the motor pool stared in horror at the brilliant ball of fire rising from the valley. A half minute later they heard the rolling thunder of the explosion as the Bomb – still airborne at 800 miles an hour – smashed into the check and relay tower.

They told Kelly when Car 56 pulled into Denver.

Ellington and several of his staff members were waiting as the cruiser stopped.

Kelly stepped out, saw them and her face blanched.

'Dear God,' she whispered, 'not Ben. Please, not Ben.'

She sagged, and Clay, who had jumped out beside her, reached for her. She shook him off. 'What happened?' she demanded fiercely. 'What did you do to him?'

223

'There was an accident,' Ellington said slowly and softly. 'This morning. We don't know yet what caused it. It happened very fast, my dear. I'm terribly sorry. I'm sure they never realized what was happening.'

'Oh, I'm sure it was very fast,' Kelly cried, as tears welled up. 'Oh I'm sure it was goddamned fast. That's all you ever wanted of him. To see how fast he could go before you killed him. It's not fair. It's not fair.'

She collapsed against Clay as the full agonizing realization swept over her. Harsh sobs racked her body.

'She's right,' Ferguson said bitterly, 'it wasn't fair to kill him so that the stupid lemmings could be held back from the sea for an instant. The miserable rotten, driving lemmings.'

He spat into the dirt.

A swirl of icy wind whipped across the lot, bringing with it the distant crescendo of the thruway traffic. A pair of cruisers rumbled out to join the racing tide.